MOSES MENDELSSOHN

The Jewish Heritage Classics
SERIES EDITORS: David Patterson · Lily Edelman

Already Published

THE MISHNAH
Oral Teachings of Judaism
Selected and Translated by Eugene J. Lipman

RASHI
Commentaries on the Pentateuch
Selected and Translated by Chaim Pearl

A PORTION IN PARADISE
AND OTHER JEWISH FOLKTALES
Compiled by H. M. Nahmad

THE HOLY CITY
Jews on Jerusalem
Compiled and Edited by Avraham Holtz

REASON AND HOPE
Selections from the Jewish Writings of Hermann Cohen
Translated, Edited, and with an Introduction by Eva Jospe

THE SEPHARDIC TRADITION
Ladino and Spanish-Jewish Literature
Selected and Edited by Moshe Lazar

JUDAISM AND HUMAN RIGHTS
Edited by Milton R. Konvitz

HUNTER AND HUNTED
Human History of the Holocaust
Selected and Edited by Gerd Korman

FLAVIUS JOSEPHUS
Selected and Edited by Abraham Wasserstein

THE GOOD SOCIETY
Jewish Ethics in Action
Selected and Edited by Norman Lamm

*Published in cooperation with the Commission
on Adult Jewish Education of B'nai B'rith*

MOSES MENDELSSOHN

Selections from His Writings

Edited and translated by
EVA JOSPE

with an Introduction by
ALFRED JOSPE

The Viking Press · New York

First published in 1975 by The Viking Press, Inc.
625 Madison Avenue, New York, N.Y. 10022
Published simultaneously in Canada by
The Macmillan Company of Canada Limited

LIBRARY OF CONGRESS CATALOGING IN PUBLICATION DATA

Mendelssohn, Moses, 1729–1786.
  Moses Mendelssohn: selections from his writings.

  (The Jewish heritage classics)
  Bibliography: p.
  Includes index.
  1. Mendelssohn, Moses, 1729–1786. 2. Jews—Emancipation. 3. Ju-
daism—Apologetic works. 4. Immortality.
B2690.E5J67 1975   193   74-34046
ISBN 0-670-48993-X

Printed in U.S.A.

Thanks to the Morris Adler Publications Fund of B'nai B'rith's Commis-
sion on Adult Jewish Education for making the Jewish Heritage Classics
Series possible as a memorial to the late Rabbi Morris Adler, former
Chairman of that Commission.

Preface

The name Moses Mendelssohn sounds familiar to many American Jews, yet it is a familiarity "in name" only. The man who bore that name is hardly known, except possibly as the grandfather of the composer Felix Mendelssohn-Bartholdy. In the minds of most, Moses Mendelssohn is at best vaguely associated with the emergence of Reform Judaism or its concomitant assimilationist trends in Germany. At worst, he is thought to be responsible for the numerous conversions that depleted the ranks of German Jewry in the nineteenth century.

The contents of this volume will, I hope, correct these popular misconceptions. They should, in fact, demonstrate that Mendelssohn could not have been the "founder" or "father" of Reform Judaism (as he is occasionally referred to even in print); and they should also make it obvious that it was not because but in spite of their father's teachings that four of his six children left Judaism after his death. For these teachings prove that Mendelssohn was one of those rare human beings who find it possible to combine a nearly all-embracing intellectual liberalism with an uncompromising religious traditionalism.

The more important intent of this book, however, is to give the interested layman an insight into Mendelssohn's philosophical thinking, both Jewish and general. For although much has been written about him (pre-eminently by Alexander Altmann, whose recently published *Moses Mendelssohn: A Biographical Study* can be considered the definitive work on that subject), few of Mendelssohn's own writings or letters are available in contemporary translations. Yet these letters and writings are worth reading. Though some two hundred years have passed since they were written, many of the issues with which they deal are still relevant today. True, times and social conditions have vastly changed. But the existential questions about life and death have remained the same, as have many of the problems confronting the Jew living in two civilizations as well as in a society in transition.

Mendelssohn's answers to these questions and solutions for these problems may differ from ours. His logic may at times be faulty, his arguments farfetched, his rationality merely rationalization, his apologetics too apologetic. Still, we ought to be aware that his philosophical labors and his efforts regarding the improvement of the Jew's civic status and cultural stature were, in a very real sense, made on our behalf. Without them, we would not be what we are, and live as we do, today.

But this collection attempts to do more than give a representative sampling of Mendelssohn's philosophical work and his defense of Jews and Judaism. It hopes to transmit to the reader a feeling for the personality of the man—that appealing mixture of earnest conviction and gentle humor, highmindedness and humility, Jewish piety and humanitarian idealism—as well as an appreciation of his day-to-day concerns. For this reason, the excerpts from his writings (some translated for the first time, others translated anew) range from the mundane to the sublime. They reflect the setting in which he lived and the events to which he reacted; and they echo the crucial impact certain people, human relationships, books, and ideas had on him.

Some of the material mentioned in the Introduction reappears in the text itself. These duplications were retained in order to preserve the cogency and completeness of both components of the book, especially in view of the fact that the introduction to a work and the work itself are often read separately.

I should like to acknowledge my indebtedness to my husband, Alfred Jospe, for suggesting this project and for his participation in it, and to Dr. David Patterson and Mrs. Lily Edelman for their editorial helpfulness. Above all, I wish to thank them for sharing my husband's and my conviction that Moses Mendelssohn still has much to say to us, and for giving him, as it were, the opportunity to say it.

EVA JOSPE

Washington, D.C.
June 1974

Contents

xi

MOSES MENDELSSOHN

Introduction:

Prelude to Jewish Modernity
by ALFRED JOSPE

The most significant and creative period of Jewish life in Central Europe encompassed approximately two hundred years—from 1740 to 1940. It opened with Moses Mendelssohn, who, more than any other single individual, enabled European Jews to move from the ghetto into the mainstream of Europe culture; and it ended two hundred years later, when the Jewish presence and participation in Central European life and culture came to an end in the fiery furnaces of Hitler's holocaust, which consumed one-third of the Jewish people.

Mendelssohn, however, is important not merely for the historian of Jewish life in Europe. His significance lies in the perception and boldness of the tasks he set for himself. He wanted to end the cultural isolation of the medieval ghetto, to make the culture of the modern world accessible and acceptable to the Jews, and, at the same time, to secure their full rights of citizenship, still denied them by the state and the dominant Christian society. He wanted to bring about nothing less than the outer liberation of the Jews through civil emancipation and their inner liberation through cultural integration.

Mendelssohn was a fascinating and colorful personality, a man of unusual talents and versatility.[1] * Born on September 6, 1729, in Dessau, the capital of the German state of Anhalt, he received the traditional Jewish education of the time; yet an insatiable hunger for more knowledge soon drove him to extend his studies into other fields. Deeply grounded in Judaism's classic sources, he rapidly mastered Latin, Greek, English, French, and some Italian, partly teaching himself, partly under the tutelage of devoted friends. A child of the ghetto, small, homely, hunchbacked, with a slight stammer, he used the German language with such lucidity and elegance that he became a leading figure in German literary criticism and the philosophy of his time. A strictly orthodox Jew, proficient in the law and observing its minutiae, he shared the intellectual interests and concerns of the Christian *Aufklärer* of his time and became a close friend of Gotthold Ephraim Lessing, whose portrait of the Jew in *Nathan der Weise* (Nathan the Wise) he inspired and who called him a second Spinoza, "lacking only Spinoza's errors to be his equal." Living in Berlin merely by sufferance and not by right, he dared to criticize Frederick the Great for his French assimilationist tendencies and ineptitude in poetry. A shy and even timid person who lacked the temperament of the fighter and usually acted only under pressure or outside provocation, he fought fearlessly to win respect and recognition for Jews and Judaism. Though he did not break any new paths as a philosopher, he became one of the fashionable and influential thinkers of his time, and one of his philosophical treatises, *Phaedon,* in which he demonstrated the immortality of the soul, brought him fame throughout Europe. Though not a profound religious thinker—he actually hated theology, as he himself once remarked—he influenced Jewish religious thought for generations to come. The questions he raised continue to be among the fundamental issues confronting the modern Jew.

Mendelssohn was not the first Jew to rise to prominence in the non-Jewish world. Long before his time, individual Jews—physicians, scientists, writers, musicians—had played distinguished roles in the general European culture. Jewish diplomats and financiers enjoyed prestige and influence in the public life of England,

* Reference notes to the Introduction begin on page 44.

4

France, and Holland. In 1573 Solomon Ashkenazi was sent by Turkey to Venice to negotiate a peace treaty. Samuel Palache (?–1616) served as representative of the Sultan of Morocco in Holland. The compositions of Salomone Rossi of Mantua (1587–1628) had a dominant role in the development of the madrigal as an artistic form. Individual Jews achieved prominence in the culture of the world long before Mendelssohn's time.

But Mendelssohn was the first to make a deliberate effort not merely to acquire European culture for himself but to use his influence to bring modern culture to his fellow Jews and, speaking publicly as a Jew to the non-Jewish world, to demand respect for his people's faith and human rights. A new epoch in Jewish history begins with him. Before Mendelssohn, the Jew, by force of circumstance, had been an outsider, at best a passive observer or uninvolved spectator as far as the culture of the world was concerned. Mendelssohn was the first modern Jew to be a creative participant and formative influence in that culture. Although the emancipation of the Jews was not the achievement of any single person—it was a slow process and full of reverses—Mendelssohn became the key figure in the struggle to remove the social and cultural barriers separating the Jew from the non-Jewish world and to prepare the way toward his civic and cultural emancipation.

Mendelssohn was actually a citizen of two worlds, utterly different from one another, seemingly irreconcilable.

His Jewish world was the world of the ghetto. A word with several connations, "ghetto" most commonly signifies physical segregation, social exclusion, economic restrictions, civil disenfranchisement. The institution and its name go back to the *ghetto nuovo,* the Jewish quarter of Venice, established in 1516 to segregate and concentrate the Jewish population in a section of the city enclosed by a wall and specifically designated by law for this purpose.

This system of exclusion was in full swing between the sixteenth and eighteenth centuries. For three centuries, constituting one of the culturally and intellectually most creative periods in history, Jews were barred from participation in the progress of European civilization. Untouched by the Renaissance, excluded from the ferment of ideas which formed modernity, they were forced to live under medieval conditions until the end of the eighteenth century (and in parts of Eastern Europe until the beginning of the twentieth century). The Jew of the ghetto dwelt in this world but did not live in it. He inhabited it but was not part of it.

The story of the Jews of Berlin, which was to become the locale of Mendelssohn's life and work, illustrates what ghetto existence meant. Jews had lived in the province of Brandenburg since 1247 and in Neukölln, which was later to become a part of Berlin, since 1295. Expelled in 1446, they were readmitted in 1509, driven out once again in 1573, this time "for eternity," but readmitted in 1650, when the Great Elector legalized their residence in order to utilize their skills and connections for the promotion of trade and commerce. Twenty years later another edict brought additional Jewish settlers; and fifty of the wealthiest families of Austrian Jewry, expelled by the Austrian Empress, also received permission to settle in Berlin, provided they brought their wealth along and invested it in the country's commerce.

But the number of these "privileged" Jews was very small. The masses remained subject to medieval limitations and restrictions. They were desperately poor, restricted in their occupations, burdened with heavy and often degrading taxes. Special legislation governed their lives as a group. Their numbers were strictly controlled by the government. Their freedom of movement was restricted; many localities excluded or expelled Jews altogether. Where they were allowed to live, their rights of residence were sharply circumscribed. A few wealthy Jews were able to attain the status of *Schutzjuden* (protected Jews) with the right of domicile in the cities of Prussia. But this right was transferable only to the oldest son of the family, while all other children were merely "tolerated" and had to seek new homes as they came of age.

Special legislation reflected but, at the same time, also contributed to the contempt in which Jews were held as a matter of habit and tradition. A decree regulating the Merchants Guild in Berlin, issued in 1716 and still in force in 1802, stated that inasmuch "as the Merchants Guild is to be composed of honest and honorable persons, the following must be barred from membership: Jews, homicides, murderers, thieves, perjurers, adulterers, or any other persons afflicted with great public vices or sins." In 1780,

6

a Jewish painter who wanted to view a picture gallery in Dresden was refused admission: a Jew was not permitted to enjoy the beautiful. And in 1795, the application of a Jew for admission to the Berlin Academy of Music was rejected with the argument that it is "mathematically impossible that a Jew could be a composer." At that time the parents of Felix Mendelssohn-Bartholdy had already been born!

The term "ghetto," however, not only refers to the enforced physical, geographic, or social segregation of a group but can also be used to describe its inner world—the world Jews created for themselves within the walls that enclosed them, the world of their ideas, hopes, and aspirations. It is the world evoked by Abraham Heschel in his moving eulogy to Jewish life in Eastern Europe, *The Earth Is the Lord's*,[2] eloquently described by Mark Zborowski and Elizabeth Herzog, in *Life Is with People*,[3] lovingly brought to life by Maurice Samuel in *The World of Sholom Aleichem*,[4] masterfully delineated in Lucy Dawidowicz's *The Golden Tradition*.[5] Used in this sense, "ghetto" connotes the life style of a Jewish community that traced its origin to Abraham and Sinai, and conceived its existence as grounded in faith in God as Creator of the universe, the Source of all life and Giver of all law. It signifies a sense of purpose and destiny, enabling the Jew to draw meaning for his existence from the belief that he is a member of a people selected by God for a divine mission in the cosmic drama and that he has a message for the world, even though it continues to reject him and his message. It means a discipline of faith governing every aspect of life and seeking to sanctify every moment—eating and drinking, labor and rest, procreation and fellowship, study and education, all conceived as acts by which man hallows life in fulfillment of God's will.

But "ghetto" has still a third connotation: it also implies that the Jew, cut off from outside contact, gradually began to turn tables and make it a virtue to avoid contact with the world. Insisting on "doing his own thing," he encouraged a deliberate separation from the non-Jewish community in order to protect his own culture against corrosion by outside influences. *Hukkat hagoyim*, the imitation of Gentile customs and practices, was severely frowned upon; and, by developing a "counterculture," the Jew deliberately tried to be different in speech, in dress, in hairdo, in everyday practices. Complete isolation of Jewish life from its environment was considered not only the explicit demand of religious tradition but the indispensable condition for the preservation of Judaism's vitality and distinctiveness. Thus, the isolation of the Jew, initially imposed from without, became enforced from within as well.

As early as the thirteenth century, Asher ben Yechiel, an eminent Talmudic scholar, wrote that he could not understand how pious Jews could possibly occupy themselves with matters outside the study of the Talmud; and as late as the eighteenth century, Solomon Maimon's father told him that "he who understands the Talmud understands everything." The Jew could gain access to the culture of the world only by rebelling against the traditional repudiation of all mundane wisdom.

As a result of this self-imposed isolation, ghetto dwellers knew no modern languages. Most Jews in Berlin spoke Judeo-German, a dialect akin to the Yiddish of Eastern Europe. The standards of Jewish learning were low, the schools poor. Teachers were hired on the basis of their unblemished piety but rarely possessed any other qualifications for their calling. The study of the Talmud was the major educational aim. Fearful that knowledge of even a superficial aspect of German culture would weaken the loyalty of their flock, the rabbis discouraged the use of the German language. Indeed, to read a German book was considered a serious offense. Mendelssohn himself related the story of a Jewish boy whom he had asked to fetch a German book for him and who was caught carrying the book—not reading it! The Jewish communal authorities made short shrift of the boy: he was expelled from Berlin. (However, less than twenty years after Mendelssohn had received a prize from the Prussian Academy for a philosophical essay, the Jewish authorities were ready to honor him, notwithstanding the fact that he not only read German books but wrote them.)

This was the one world in which Mendelssohn lived and grew up. But he was also the citizen of another world, that of the literature and philosophy of his time. Its dominant trend was the desire for enlightenment.

The best definition of enlightenment was probably given by Immanuel Kant (1724–1804) when he challenged his contemporaries with the Latin exhortation *sapere aude,* "dare to use your reason":

> Enlightenment is man's release from his self-incurred tutelage.
> Tutelage is man's inability to make use of his capacity to use his
> reason without outside direction. Self-incurred is this tutelage
> when it is caused not by inability (to employ our faculty to use
> our reason) but by a lack of resolution and of courage to use
> it without outside direction. *Sapere aude!* Have the courage to
> use your own reason—that is the motto of Enlightenment.[6]

Underlying the thrust of the Enlightenment was a profound new
awareness man had of himself, a new trust in his capacity to understand himself and the world, a self-assured confidence in his ability
to perfect himself and order his affairs on earth so as to attain happiness. These notions, although expressed in numerous, often vastly
differing theories and formulations, were the matrix from which
the key themes of the Enlightenment philosophy emerged. Mendelssohn drew heavily on these themes for the developmenet of his
own views and incorporated them into his own philosophy: the
emphasis of the Enlightenment on reason rather than revelation as
the sole medium through which man can discern what he needs to
know in order to attain felicity and self-fulfillment in this world;
its notion that man is endowed with permanent, innate ideas of
what is good and true, ideas independent of all cultural changes;
its belief that all men "are to be accounted by nature as equal"
(Samuel von Pufendorf); * and its eudaemonistic orientation,
which saw the purpose of philosophy not primarily in the discovery
of truth but in laying the foundations for the achievement of
happiness by individuals and society, a state of felicity to be
brought about by the perfection of men through mutual assistance
and acts of kindness.

These ideas not only influenced Mendelssohn but also penetrated
the ghetto walls. The insistence of the Enlightenment on the use of

* German jurist, historian, and educator, 1632–1694.

reason, its rejection of dogma, its belief in progress, and its proclamation of the equality of all people, found a ready response especially among young Jews. This trend was encouraged by the fact that the number of Jews who had not only economic but social contact with the outside world increased as a wealthy upper class gradually began to emerge within German Jewry, particularly in Berlin. Despite the economic restrictions to which the Jewish masses continued to be subjected, a growing number of Jews slowly rose to positions of wealth and prominence in commerce and industry, mainly as contractors, purveyors, bankers, and court agents. Prosperity opened doors previously barred by prejudice. Social contact with Gentiles became possible and was eagerly pursued as a source of gratification and a device for social advancement. Jews of that group established attractive, often luxurious homes, spoke German instead of the Judeo-German of the masses, sent their children to German schools, frequented the theater, and became patrons of literature and the arts. Vivacious and gifted Jewish women such as Henrietta Herz and Rahel Levin presided as hostesses over "salons" that became the meeting places for Prussia's intellectual and social elite.

As the Jew moved from the ghetto into the world, he discovered that Jewish life had little of the beauty, art, and worldly sophistication that made Gentile civilization so graceful and attractive. He felt that he was the Rip Van Winkle of Europe, still clothed in the tattered rags of a life style that had long become obsolete. While he had slept in involuntary seclusion, the world had moved on, and in this world he seemed tragically out of tune with the times. His religion involved a body of beliefs that seemed contrary to reason, incompatible with the new trends of thought; and Jewish religious law demanded the practice of daily rituals and observances that were inconvenient and set him apart from his fellow men.

It was inevitable that the Jew began to question the value and meaningfulness of traditional Judaism. If the world refused to complete the process of emancipation, could it be that the fault was with the Jew himself? As long as he insisted on being different, on leading a separate existence, on maintaining certain habits that were as strange as they were inexplicable to the Gentile world, did he have the right to expect full acceptance?

10

The temptation to break with the past was great. The desire to win the approbation of the intellectually fashionable or socially admired has always produced changes in self-definition and conduct. In order to win the approval of the Gentile world and clear the way for securing equal rights, a growing number of Jews felt they had to "modernize" Judaism by discarding the ideas and life style that separated them from their environment, or even to forsake Judaism altogether, so that they could no longer be distinguished from their Gentile neighbors.

Mendelssohn attempted to bridge the two worlds by encouraging the Jews to move from the ghetto into modernity in three ways: through civic emancipation, cultural integration, and the philosophic validation of Judaism's religious tenets before the bar of reason. One or the other of these concerns kept Mendelssohn occupied throughout most of his adult life, often simultaneously.

Mendelssohn had no illusions about the complexity of the task to seek improvement in the civic status of the Jews and to assure their inalienable human rights. Here he was, one of the leading Jews of Europe, successful, respected, admired. He himself had been able to break through the barriers of prejudice and gain influence as the friend and confidant of high-ranking people. Yet he remained sharply aware of the degrading conditions under which most of his fellow Jews were still compelled to live, and he knew he was looked upon as a person to whom other Jews in need or danger could turn for help. Nor were opportunities for action missing. When the authorities of two Swiss villages denied their Jewish inhabitants the right to marry, Mendelssohn enlisted the help of Johann Casper Lavater, a Swiss clergyman with whom he had previously engaged in sharp theological controversy, in order to have the ban rescinded (1775). When hundreds of Jewish families were threatened with expulsion from Dresden in 1777, he was able to secure the withdrawal of the edict through his close friendship with a leading official of Saxony. When the Jewish community of Königsberg appealed to him that same year to refute the accusation that some Jewish prayers, especially the *Aleinu,* were anti-Christian, he presented written evidence to the contrary, as a result of which a royal order requiring the presence of a government "supervisor" in the synagogue during worship was rescinded. Upon the request of the Chief Rabbi of Berlin, Zvi Hirsch Levin, he compiled a German summary of the Jewish laws governing marriage, wills, and inheritance for use by the Royal Ministry of Justice (*Die Ritualgesetze der Juden,* 1778); and he drafted a new oath for use in the courts to replace a medieval Yiddish oath whose content and language he found degrading (1782).

Mendelssohn's direct contributions to the debate on the question of the civic status of the Jew were equally far-reaching. In 1779, the Jews of Alsace were viciously attacked in a pamphlet written by a French judge. The leaders of Alsatian Jewry requested Mendelssohn to draft an appropriate petition to the French Council of State appealing for relief from their intolerable conditions. Convinced, however, that the question of Jewish rights ought to be raised by Christians rather than by Jews, in order to receive adequate public attention, Mendelssohn persuaded Christian Wilhelm von Dohm, a young publicist and liberal spirit, to undertake the project. In response to the request, Dohm wrote *Über die bürgerliche Verbesserung der Juden* (On the Civil Improvement of the Jews, 1781), the first systematic treatise by a non-Jew advocating the emancipation of the Jews. Dealing with the position of Jews not only in Alsace but throughout Germany, Dohm declared that they possessed all the qualifications for citizenship, and recommended they be granted civic rights (*bürgerliche Rechte*) though not full citizenship rights (*Bürgerrechte*), because they were not yet ready to hold public office or engage in political affairs. However, he wanted them to retain their own communal autonomy under government supervision, including the right to discipline recalcitrant members of the Jewish community, and to maintain their own rabbinical courts for the disposal of civil cases in which both litigants were Jewish.

Though Dohm's plea had no immediate practical results, it succeeded in placing the question of Jewish rights in the center of public discussion. Others entered the debate, some supporting Dohm, others opposing him. Mendelssohn, realizing that a centuries-old tradition of prejudice could not be silenced by a single courageous voice, and that additional efforts were needed, induced another friend, the physician Marcus Herz, to prepare and publish a German translation of *Vindiciae Judaeorum,* a treatise by Manasseh ben Israel, a seventeenth-century rabbi in Amsterdam, whose defense of the Jews addressed to Oliver Cromwell in 1656 had helped persuade the Protector to readmit Jews to England.

Mendelssohn himself wrote the introduction to Herz's translation. He had become convinced that he had to add his voice to Dohm's in order to press home the attack against bigotry. But he also wanted to correct certain of Dohm's views which, though well intentioned, he found unacceptable, especially Dohm's feeling that Jews were not yet ready for the full rights of citizenship and that the Jewish community should have the authority to punish members for religious infractions or dissent. Both views were incompatible with Mendelssohn's concept of complete freedom of conscience and civic equality.

In a passionate dissent from existing conditions, Mendelssohn put the responsibility where he felt it belonged: upon the cruelty and prejudices of the world. He showed how bigotry had changed its face in every century. In the Middle Ages, the Jews had been accused of using blood, desecrating the Host, poisoning wells. In his own time, they were accused of having an aversion to manual labor, an antipathy to science and culture, a preference for trade, a preoccupation with money. "People continue to keep us away from every contact with the arts and sciences or from engaging in useful trades and occupations. They bar all roads leading to increased usefulness and then use our lack of culture to justify our continued oppression. They tie our hands and then reproach us for not using them. . . ." [7] *

Mendelssohn's plea was a moving appeal to the conscience of the world. But he knew that more than the liberation of the Jew

* See page 90.

from the restrictions of ghetto life was needed to demolish the barriers separating him from the non-Jew. The acquisition of external freedom had to be accompanied by inner renewal; release from political and social disabilities had to be associated with cultural emancipation. The world had to revise its attitude toward the Jews; but the Jews, too, had to change their attitude toward the world. Mendelssohn did not disregard or minimize the fact that the miserable condition of the Jews was not of their making. He knew that for centuries they had been kept at such a distance from the culture of the world "that one might almost despair of the possibility of improvement," [8] and that, denied access to nearly the entire range of occupations in trade, commerce, and agriculture, they had been forced into the interstices of the economic structure in their attempts to eke out a precarious living as peddlers, junk dealers,. pawnbrokers, moneylenders, and in similarly marginal occupations.

Nevertheless, Mendelssohn felt that the Jews themselves also contributed to their lowly status. Sharp and unsavory business practices, by no means unknown among them, created distrust and resentment. By rejecting all mundane knowledge and social contact with Gentiles, they helped maintain and solidify the social and cultural gap between themselves and the world. Above all, Mendelssohn was dismayed by their continuing use, as their *lingua franca,* of Judeo-German, which be considered to have become the mark of the social outcast—a sentiment shared by Lessing, who described it as the language of the "wretched rabble which roams about the fairs." Mendelssohn wanted the Jews to use proper Hebrew and proper German, not a language that made them into a caricature of what he felt Jews and Judaism really were and that contributed to the contempt in which they were held. He was convinced that the opening up of the treasures of German thought and literature to his fellow Jews would raise their cultural and spiritual level to the point where they, as a group, would receive the same welcome and acceptance he had received as an individual. In order to be able to join the mainstream of contemporary culture, they had to discard their ghetto language. The first step toward this goal was to teach them German, and the best way to teach it to them was through a German translation of the Torah, which he undertook.

Mendelssohn hoped, of course, to achieve much more with his translation. He did not want simply to publish a textbook in German for his fellow Jews; he wanted to teach them Torah. A growing number of young Jews were no longer able to read the Hebrew text in the original. But Mendelssohn found the existing translations useless: those by Jewish scholars were linguistically corrupt or inadequate, while those by Christian scholars were theologically unacceptable because of the way they read their Christian notions into the Hebrew text. Mendelssohn felt a new translation was needed to lead his people back to the sources of their inspiration, to reacquaint them with the Bible's moral vision, and to challenge them with its ethical demands in order to help elevate their moral tone and spiritual level.

In order to solicit subscriptions for his translation, he issued a prospectus called *Alim Literufah* (Healing Leaves) in 1778, referring to the need for healing the cultural ills of German Jewry. The first volume, Genesis, came off the press in 1780; the others followed rapidly. Each volume contained the German translation printed in Hebrew letters, and a commentary called *Biur* (explanation, commentary), designed to provide a better understanding of the text. The translation was entirely Mendelssohn's work, as were the Hebrew introduction and the commentaries to the first part of Genesis and the entire book of Exodus. Friends and associates contributed to the commentaries to the other books and supervised the publication of the work as a whole.

The impact of the translation was enormous. Orders were received from all over Europe. Well-known rabbis welcomed and endorsed the work, and the Chief Rabbi of Berlin expressed the hope that the translation would help put an end to German Jewry's ignorance. Several outstanding spokesmen of traditional Judaism, however, objected to the translation precisely because they were fearful that Mendelssohn's plan would succeed, and that a knowledge of German would tempt Jewish youth to pursue secular interests at the expense of their Jewish studies. Some leading rabbis issued a ban against the work, and in some communities it was burned publicly as a gesture of protest and warning. Mendelssohn was able to silence most of the opposition, especially that of its leader, Rabbi Rafael Kohn of Altona, by obtaining subscriptions for his translation from the royal house of Copenhagen, through the intervention of a friend, Councilor von Hennings of Copenhagen, making it impossible for Rabbi Kohn to take action against a book that had found the approbation of his country's rulers.

Completed in 1783, the work had a profound effect on Jewish life. The study of the Bible, long neglected, received new impetus. The translation generated new understanding of the text, while the commentary elucidated it and provided a helpful introduction to the structure and meaning of the Hebrew language.

The influence of the translation extended beyond the borders of Germany. It gave Russian and Polish Jews new insight into the literary and linguistic structure of the Bible, while the graceful Hebrew of the *Biur* contributed substantially to the renaissance of Hebrew, the language in which the Jews of Eastern Europe pursued enlightenment. Mendelssohn also encouraged a friend, Naphtali Herz Wessely, and several other writers to found a Hebrew journal, *Ha-Meassef* (The Gatherer)—the first periodical ever published by Jews—whose articles attempted to bring the best of contemporary thought and culture to its readers.

But Mendelssohn's work was not done. There remained a third dimension in his efforts to build a bridge to modernity for the Jews. For years he had battled the world to show why the Jew was entitled to a rightful place as citizen in modern society. For years he had struggled to persuade and assist his fellow Jews to prepare themselves for their entry into the modern world. But what about Judaism itself? Did it fit into the modern world? Granted that the Jew as human being had a rightful claim to the status of citizenship. But what about his religion? Was it not outmoded, an obsolete relic of medievalism that no longer had anything to say either to the Jew or to modern man? For centuries, the keystone of Jewish self-understanding had been faith in God as the Source of all life and the Giver of the Law. But was it not precisely this law that had kept the Jew apart from other people throughout the centuries? Was this faith stance still tenable or defensible? Did the Jewish way of life still have a claim on reason and emotion? Could the ancient faith of Judaism be reconciled with the demands of modernity?

This was the challenge Mendelssohn now had to confront. His Judaism had actually been challenged once before by the Swiss Calvinist preacher Johann Caspar Lavater, an admirer, who had wanted to convert him to Christianity. Lavater had translated a French book dealing with the proofs of the validity of Christianity—Charles Bonnet's *La Palingénésie philosophique, ou Idées sur l'état passé et sur l'état futur des êtres vivants* (1769)—and he dedicated the translation to Mendelssohn, challenging him in its preface either to refute Bonnet's arguments or to do "what truth and honesty demanded and what Socrates would have done had he read the book and found it irrefutable": abandon his religion and accept Christianity.

Mendelssohn, hating controversy of any kind, was reluctant to be drawn into a public dispute about the comparative merits of Judaism and Christianity. He did not want to offend Christians, yet felt he could not let this challenge to his religion and personal convictions go unanswered. He responded in a famous letter to Lavater, in which, tactfully but forcefully, he defended his loyalty to Judaism.

First, he defended his own integrity.

> I cannot see what could possibly have kept me tied to so severe and generally despised a religion if in my heart I had not been convinced of its truth. If I ever became convinced that my religion was not the true one, I would feel compelled to leave it . . . and if I were indifferent to my religion what could have prevented me from changing it in order to better myself?

He then taught Lavater a gentle lesson in how a man of reason and enlightenment ought to think and act in matters of faith.

> It is my good fortune to count among my friends many a man who is not of my faith. We love each other sincerely although both

of us suspect or assume that we differ in matters of faith. We enjoy the pleasure of each other's company and feel enriched by it. But at no time has my heart whispered to me: what a pity that this beautiful soul should be lost. Only that man will be troubled by such regrets who believes there is no salvation outside his church. It seems to me that anyone who leads man to virtue in this life cannot be damned in the next.[9]

Finally, he launched a counterattack on behalf of his Judaism. Conceding frankly that Judaism was not free from certain human additions and abuses, he was nevertheless firmly convinced of its irrefutable truth and superiority as a religion. Rebuking Lavater for his ill-considered zeal, he pointed out that Judaism was tolerant of the convictions of others. It had never sent out missionaries to make converts and, unlike Christianity, it maintained that even the unbeliever was in God's care and could attain salvation if he was a man of moral stature.

The Lavater controversy marked a significant change in the orientation of Mendelssohn's thought and work. Until then, the pursuit of his general literary, philosophical, and aesthetic interests had been at the center of his work. Though he did not give them up, after the exchange with Lavater, and as a result of it, he became involved in Jewish thought and affairs with particular intensity. His response to Lavater was the first step in his philosophic examination of Judaism.

His starting point is a theory of knowledge which, following the lead of some earlier philosophers—Locke, Shaftesbury, and especially Leibniz—distinguishes between two kinds of truth: eternal truths, *vérités de raison,* and historical or temporal truths, *vérités de fait.* Eternal truths, for instance mathematical axioms, are self-evident to reason and can be verified by the canons of logic. Historical or temporal truths are events that took place in history and require the evidence of sense experience. No person living in the twentieth century, for instance, was present when Columbus set foot on the North American continent or when George Washington crossed the Delaware. We cannot arrive at these facts by our own logic, nor do we know them from personal experience. We have to accept them on faith. But we can do so because there were eyewitnesses or similarly reliable sources who can verify the fact that those events actually did take place.

Among the eternal truths self-evident to reason and whose validity, according to these thinkers, can be established on purely intellectual grounds are the existence of a wise and providential God and the immortality of the human soul. These metaphysical truths are the essential elements of the religion of reason and constitute the themes of Mendelssohn's two major religio-philosophical works.

In *Morgenstunden* (Morning Hours, or Lectures on God's Existence, 1785), Mendelssohn seeks to demonstrate the rationality of the belief in the existence of God. His concept of God retains all elements of the Biblical view of God as the Supreme Being who possesses highest reason and wisdom and governs the world with justice and compassion. Nevertheless, Mendelssohn treats the subject not as a specific Jewish doctrine but as a principle of general metaphysics and of man's universal religion of reason. This late work, prepared for the instruction of his oldest son, Joseph, and of Alexander and Wilhelm von Humboldt, the former one of Joseph's close friends, expands views Mendelssohn had outlined earlier in an essay, *Abhandlung über die Evidenz in metaphysischen Wissenschaften* (On Evidence in the Metaphysical Sciences), for which he had received a prize from the Royal Prussian Academy of Sciences in 1763.

Mendelssohn uses several lines of argument to demonstrate the existence of God. His favorite proof is a modification of the so-called ontological argument: man finds the idea of a Supreme Being in his consciousness. This idea cannot have arisen out of man's own limited and fragmented experiences—no human being can have direct knowledge or experience of anything remotely resembling divine perfection. Therefore the idea of a Supreme Being is an *a priori* concept: along with time, space, and causality it belongs to the category of concepts that precede all experience and enable us to comprehend reality. Although these concepts "exist" in our minds, they are neither subjective nor mere illusions; they underlie and determine the character of universal experience. Now, the idea of a Supreme and absolutely Perfect Being necessarily includes the attribute of existence. If

God, by definition, is the most perfect being, He must exist; otherwise He would not be perfect; He would lack the full complement of His unconditioned possibility.

Unable to understand how anyone could not believe in God, Mendelssohn sought to strengthen his argument by still another line of reasoning. Like other thinkers of his time and before him, he saw order and beauty in the world, the rhythmic unity of the cosmos, the fact that the universe as he knew it was law-abiding. But a law-abiding universe cannot be a cosmic accident; it must have been called into being by a power other—and greater—than itself. Logic requires us to assume that everything that exists must have a cause. The world exists. Therefore it must have been caused by a power other than itself, a power that itself cannot have been caused by anything else. That power is God.

The question of the immortality of the soul is examined by Mendelssohn in two works, *On the Soul* (*Über die Seele—Abhandlung von dem Commerz zwischen Seele und Körper*), originally written in Hebrew but soon translated into German and published a year after his death, and especially in his chief philosophical work, *Phaedon* (Phaedo), published in 1767, modeled after Plato's famous dialogue of the same name. As early as 1760 Mendelssohn had expressed the wish to find the time not only to translate but to rewrite Plato's text in the light of modern psychology. He was encouraged in the decision to undertake the project by his correspondence with Thomas Abbt, a professor at the University of Frankfurt, about the destiny of man and the fate of the soul after death.

Choosing Socrates as the spokesman for his own views, Mendelssohn develops his thesis along Leibnizian lines. An infinite number of souls or "monads" constitute the inner substance of the universe. These monads—the elemental components of everything that exists—can reflect changes, but they cannot disappear, for nature never destroys any of its substances. Thus things that "perish" do not cease to exist; they are merely dissolved into their elements —the monads.

The soul must be such a simple, that is, irreducible element or substance; for inasmuch as it permeates all facets of the human personality and imposes a unifying pattern upon the diverse and

20

changing elements of the organism, the soul itself cannot be a composite that could be further dissolved or broken up into perishable elements. Consequently, it can neither be weakened by age nor be destroyed by death. It must survive the body intact; it is immortal.

> Death does not mean total annihilation, for no force in nature would suffice to destroy a thing completely. And inasmuch as no conversion from being to nonbeing is possible, such destruction would necessitate a real break. Consequently, the souls of the departed still exist.[10]

Mendelssohn is aware that this argument can be used to demonstrate only that the soul is imperishable but not that it will also retain its consciousness in a future state. That the soul will possess this consciousness and will continue to think, will, and feel emotions even after the body's disintegration is, for Mendelssohn, guaranteed by the goodness of God who has implanted in man the idea that his soul is immortal. To assume that this notion is erroneous, and that God has seen fit to create pangs of hunger in man without giving him the means to satisfy that hunger, would be incompatible with God's goodness and justice.

> I feel I cannot reject the notion of the immortality of the soul without destroying my faith in everything I have always believed to be true and good. If the soul were mortal, man's reason would be but a dream. . . . Man's lot would be the same as any animal's: to forage for food and to die. A few days after our death, it would no longer matter whether we had been a credit or discredit to our fellow creatures, or whether we had contributed to their weal or woe. . . . Robbed of his hope for immortality, man would be the most miserable creature on earth, his misery compounded by the fact that his ability to think about his condition awakens in him the fear of death and a sense of despair.*

The assumption that the body's death constitutes the end of man not only destroys man's belief in a good God; it also offends

* See page 196.

reason. For it simply makes no sense to assume that man, with his gifts and talents, his potential and actual achievements, should have been created merely to be destroyed again. Nevertheless, Mendelssohn concedes that although we can be certain on moral and rational grounds that our soul will survive our body, we must admit our factual ignorance as to the location of the soul's future abode or the nature of its future existence. We can only assume, Mendelssohn's Socrates concludes, restating a view previously expressed by Mendelssohn in a letter to Abbt, that our souls will continue in the beyond what they have already begun here on earth—to pursue the good, the beautiful, and the true, and thus come closer to that state of perfection epitomized in God. The soul's unceasing pursuit and its ever keener understanding and appropriation of truth, goodness, and beauty constitute eternal bliss.

Mendelssohn's beliefs in the existence of God and immortality, though developed as doctrines of the universal religion of reason, are basically in harmony with the views of Jewish tradition. He differs from Jewish tradition, however, in his conception of free will. Inasmuch as every act of will must have a cause or motive, it is logically impossible to conceive of human freedom as autonomous and uncaused. Therefore man's will can be free only in the sense that it is determined or aroused by a recognition of the good.

But what about the sinner? What about the many individuals who do not "take care of their souls" in this life, who succumb to the drives of the body and wallow, in the words of Socrates and later in those of the Church, in animal pleasures? What about those individuals who out of ignorance, greed, or a general lack of moral sensitivity commit crimes? What will happen to their souls? Will they be banned from God's presence and lose their share of eternal bliss? If man, as Mendelssohn claims, is not truly free, how is it possible to punish the sinner, inasmuch as he cannot be held responsible for whatever evil he does?

Mendelssohn grants that the effects of sin are everlasting. But while the principle of cause and effect governs the realm of nature, it is not operative in the realm of human volition. Here, the consequences of man's actions are not automatic or inevitable. Sin need not lead to eternal damnation; even the unrepentant sinner's soul is immortal. Retaining its capacity to think, feel, and will—the premise of Mendelssohn's theory of immortality—even the sinner's soul may yet accomplish in its future life what it failed to do on earth. As Mendelssohn writes in his reflections on his correspondence with Abbt:

> If our life really came to an end with our body's death, the vice-ridden individual (trying to gain his ignoble ends and achieve what he, with his perverted sense of values, considers happiness) would die without having seen the errors of his ways, without having learned anything. In that case, Providence would indeed be unjust.*

But this conclusion is unacceptable for a man of Mendelssohn's orientation. Since God is just and good, He must necessarily allow the sinner's soul to survive. For if the evil-doer's soul were to perish along with its body or be condemned to eternal suffering, it could never fulfill what Mendelssohn fervently believes to be the birthright of every human being, be he good or evil, wise or stupid, the possessor of a keen or blunt conscience: to exercise his innate moral faculties in order to attain man's final goal, happiness. Inasmuch as the sinner cannot become truly happy on earth while the righteous frequently suffer here on earth, only one conclusion is possible: "The soul must be immortal so that the wrongs of this life can be righted in the next."

Life in the beyond, then, is man's guarantee that justice will be done. Divine punishment and retribution are not ends in themselves but merely means of purging the sinner in order to prepare him for life in the world to come. In the final analysis, divine justice is superseded by divine goodness, which excludes no man permanently from the bliss of eternal life.

Phaedon seemed to meet a need of the time and was immediately successful. Reprinted repeatedly and translated into several languages, it was read throughout Europe. Its author was called the "Jewish Plato," and his home became a Mecca for numerous visitors.

---

* See page 165.

Yet despite the success of his general philosophical works, Mendelssohn influenced his time far more by the impact of his personality than by his contributions to German philosophy. His *Phaedon* was outdated a mere twenty years after it had appeared. Though Mendelssohn has a place in the history of philosophy, he was soon overshadowed by Kant and his successors, whose critical idealism challenged the presuppositions of the Enlightenment philosophy. Nevertheless, the influence of the "Jewish philosopher" was exceptional. The world was intrigued by this man who was a strictly observant Jew yet at the same time a leading citizen of the world of European culture. The public admired his personality, which uniquely combined a capacity to analyze issues with a keen sensitivity to human concerns, a sense of beauty, and deep-grained personal integrity.

Mendelssohn might not have raised the question whether and in what way his universal religion of reason could be harmonized with the particularism and supernaturalism of traditional Judaism, had not Lavater's challenge and critical comments by others on some of his later writings compelled him to examine the implications of his theories for Judaism. He was attacked with particular harshness for the views expressed in his preface to *Vindiciae Judaeorum*. Some critics flatly rejected his appeal for civic freedom on behalf of the Jews: Prussia was a Christian state; state and church were coextensive; Christianity was the established religion; therefore Jews were not eligible for citizenship in the Christian state. Others attacked Mendelssohn's contention that a man's religion was his personal affair and that no religious authority should be permitted to punish or banish dissenters. One of the most forceful criticisms appeared in a pamphlet published anonymously in 1782 under the title *Das Forschen nach Licht und Recht* (The Search for Light and Right: An Epistle to Moses Mendelssohn Occasioned by His Remarkable Preface to Rabbi Manasseh ben Israel's "Vindication of the Jews").[11] Its author is assumed to have been August Friedrich Cranz, a Christian writer and pamphleteer.[12] The *Forscher*'s views deserve attention as a classical example of the arguments frequently used against Jewish self-preservation and the validity of Jewish existence.

Cranz agrees with Mendelssohn's statement in the preface to *Vindiciae Judaeorum* that ecclesiastical law is injurious and that excommunication, exclusion from the religious community, cannot be exercised without serious injury to a person's civic status and well-being. He further agrees that true worship ought to be a spontaneous homage to God, founded on one's own convictions and practiced out of love for the Father of all beings. Servile awe, extorted by fear of penalties, cannot be an acceptable offering on the altar of the love of God.

But how can Mendelssohn claim that this adds up to a true picture of Judaism's position? If Mendelssohn is serious in his insistence that a man's religion should be his private concern and that religious coercion be banished, what becomes of the rabbinical statutes and laws Jews are bound to observe? What becomes of the Mosaic law and its authority derived directly from God? Is not "armed ecclesiastical law," enforcing obedience by the threat of punishment, still the firm foundation of the Jewish community and the master spring of its whole machinery? "How then, my dear Mr. Mendelssohn, can you profess attachment to the religion of your forefathers while at the same time shaking its very foundation by disavowing the ecclesiastical law given by Moses and deriving its authority from divine revelation?"

Cranz continues his attack with the classical argument of the biased: the civil disabilities to which the Jews are still subject—their exclusion from the rights of citizenship and the benefits of the social contract—"those hardships, Mr. Mendelssohn, are not the fault of the Christians. It is the religion of your fathers itself which serves as a powerful barrier that keeps your nation far removed from [the possibility of] sharing unqualifiedly the public and private benefits of society which, in a state, are enjoyed by all citizens alike." Take, for example, the "excessively strict observance of the Sabbath by the Jews. It is not the Sabbath of the nations among whom they dwell." Yet, as Cranz points out, Jews cannot hold jobs incompatible with their uncompromising Sabbath laws. And he asks, "Why not consider the Sabbath laws on the

25

same level as the biblical laws governing sacrifices? Let their observance be restricted to those who occupy the former territory of the Jews. Elsewhere, however, let it be subordinated to the social conditions of the countries in which Providence has placed the Jews since then."

Of still greater importance, in the *Forscher*'s view, is the obstacle Jewish law places in the way of the social integration of Jews and Christians. According to his understanding, Judaism declares that "all other nations are deemed unclean creatures and the people of God would be defiled by social intercourse with them. All victuals and certain drinks by the hands of a Christian are by law an abomination to a Jew. Nor does Judaism permit a matrimonial alliance between Jew and non-Jew." How then, the *Forscher* repeats, can Mendelssohn insist that religious matters in Judaism are not subject to ecclesiastical control? Indeed, if Mendelssohn has ceased to believe in divine revelation, as he appeared to have done in his exchange with Lavater, was it not incumbent upon him to abandon the traditional Jewish religion and embrace Christianity, whose fundamental verities were compatible with the religion of reason that Mendelssohn himself was advocating so persistently? [13]

Cranz's challenge posed three fundamental questions for Mendelssohn. If he indeed believed in the God of Israel who had revealed Himself at Sinai and performed miracles, how could he possibly reconcile the traditional Jewish belief in supernatural revelation with the universal religion of reason, which proclaimed that divine revelation was not needed since truth can be discovered through reflection and the use of reason? Secondly, if he believed in revelation at all, how did he find it possible to accept the Sinaitic revelation, yet to reject that of Jesus? Lastly, how could he claim that there is no religious coercion in Judaism if, as he insists, the authority of the Torah is derived from God who, having revealed His law to the Jewish people, compels their obedience by an elaborate system of rewards and punishments?

Mendelssohn realized it had become necessary for him to set forth, in a comprehensive and systematic manner, his convictions about the validity and place of Judaism in the modern world. *Jerusalem: oder über religiöse Macht und Judenthum* (Jerusalem, or On Religious Power and Judaism, 1783), his major work of Jewish interest, is his attempt to reconcile the Jewish tradition with the philosophical rationalism of his age.[14]

Jerusalem consists of two parts. The first attempts to clarify the roles of church and state and their interrelationship. It contains a powerful restatement of his convictions about the need for freedom of conscience and a fervent plea for religious tolerance. Jews cannot hope to attain full citizenship as long as the state defines itself as a "Christian" state; genuine freedom of conscience is impossible in such a setting.

Therefore, nearly one hundred years ahead of his time in Europe, Mendelssohn pleads for the separation of state and church. In broad philosophical terms he defines their respective spheres. While their aims are identical—the promotion of human welfare and happiness—their functions are different. The task of the state is to assure the well-being of its citizens. It therefore has the right to regulate their actions and override individual conviction in the interest of the whole. But although it can compel its citizens to obey the law even though they may disagree with its wisdom or fairness, it may not control or regulate their ideas or convictions; nor must it be allowed to favor one religion over another or to require its citizens to profess particular beliefs as a condition of citizenship.

Religion is something utterly different. It does not separate act from conviction in the same way the state does. In the religious realm, a person's actions must be an expression of his convictions, and convictions can neither be bought with rewards nor enforced by punishment. Religion knows no compulsion. The state governs; religion instructs and persuades. The state can exercise physical force; religion's power is love and charity. The state may punish or even expel those who are disobedient; the church seeks to influence them by instruction or at least to comfort them to the very last moment of their life. In short, there is a parallelism but no interdependence between state and church. The state must never become the tool of the church and permit itself to serve its interests or carry out its behests. In turn, religious thought and practice must be beyond the reach of the state's power of coercion.[15]

In insisting that a man's beliefs are exclusively his personal affair, Mendelssohn rejects the view of the English philosopher Thomas Hobbes, who had argued that public welfare requires that everything, even a man's personal views of right or wrong, be subject to the control of the civil authorities as the only way to stop the war of all against all. Mendelssohn comes closer to the position of John Locke, another British philosopher who influenced him, who defines the state as a society of men united for the purpose of promoting jointly their temporal, as distinguished from their spiritual, welfare. In Locke's view, the state has no business concerning itself with a person's convictions about eternal happiness and must not take note of religious differences among its citizens.

Despite the similarity of their approaches, however, there is an essential difference between Mendelssohn and Locke. Although Locke insists that no person may be compelled by external force to hold a particular belief, he grants the church the power of expulsion, inasmuch as expulsion is the sole punishment the church can administer. For Locke, toleration does not require the church to retain a disbeliever or offender.

Mendelssohn cannot accept this view, not only because excommunication inevitably leads to harmful civil consequences, but because he believes that the social contract must not be applied to matters of belief and faith. Neither state nor church may force a person to think or believe in a certain way. The church has the right and, in fact, the duty to seek to influence an individual's ideas by instruction and persuasion. But there its power ends. It must neither control his actions nor impose its beliefs upon him nor punish the disbeliever. Reason is the only judge of a man's conviction, and his actions are the only yardstick of his worth.

> Observe what men do or fail to do, and judge them by their actions. . . . Don't reward or punish them in accordance with their thoughts! Let every man who does not disturb the public welfare, who obeys the law, who acts righteously toward his fellow men, be allowed to speak as he thinks, to pray to God after his own fashion or after the fashion of his fathers, and to seek his eternal salvation where he thinks he can find it.[16]

The question remains whether Mendelssohn's critics were not right, after all, when they questioned the compatibility of these views with the teachings of Judaism. Does not the Bible proclaim an elaborate system of rewards for the faithful and punishments for the violator of its laws? Does not Judaism actually reject the very freedom of conscience which the philosopher claimed to be at its core? Does not his advocacy of these ideas imply a break with the faith of his fathers?

Mendelssohn uses the second part of *Jerusalem* to defend himself against the charge of insincerity and to counter the challenge to his Jewishness by presenting his concept and philosophy of Judaism. Following the approach of Enlightenment philosophy, he states once again that reason must be the sole foundation of truth and certitude, and that the central religious tenets—God's existence and providence and the immortality of the soul—can be demonstrated rationally.

Two conclusions must be drawn from this position.

First, if the true doctrines of religion are based on man's reason, divine revelation is no longer needed as a source of truth. For revelation cannot disclose any ideas that cannot be discovered through reflection and the use of reason.

In adopting this position, Mendelssohn rejects the approach of earlier philosophers, especially that of Moses Maimonides,* whose works had stimulated Mendelssohn's initial interest in Jewish philosophy. For Maimonides, man's knowledge of truth is derived from two sources, reason *and* revelation. Though truth is essentially rational and cannot contradict reason, it requires the support of revelation for the sake of the masses of the common people who do not know philosophy and who, unlike the true philosopher and the prophet, as Maimonides sees him, are unable to discover the truth by themselves. It must be communicated to them through revelation. Reason and revelation are parallel sources of the same truth.

Mendelssohn rejects the notion that truth can possibly be derived from two sources. It is superfluous and therefore illogical to

* See page 77.

assume that revelation can disclose a truth at which man can arrive by his own capacity to reason. No revelation or miracle can possibly convince man of the validity of anything his reason cannot understand.

But what about Judaism? If there are no eternal verities except those which can be demonstrated by reason, how can the truth and validity of the Torah and its laws be defended? Mendelssohn is aware that his rejection of revelation on philosophical grounds clashes with the classic self-image of Judaism which conceives of itself as based on the Sinaitic revelation. Yet if Judaism is revealed, it cannot, for Mendelssohn, be a religion; and if it is a religion, it cannot have been revealed.

Mendelssohn, in his second conclusion, resolves this dilemma by defining Judaism not as "revealed religion" but as "revealed law." Time and again he proclaims that the central tenets of Judaism are not specific Jewish notions but doctrines of the general religion of reason, which require no proof or act of revelation to be intelligible and acceptable to men of reason everywhere. As he puts it in *Jerusalem:*

> The voice that was heard at Sinai on the great day did not proclaim, "I am the Eternal your God, the necessary autonomous being, omnipotent and omniscient, who rewards men in a future life according to their deeds." This is the universal religion of mankind, not Judaism; and this kind of universal religion—without which man can become neither virtuous nor happy—was not and, in fact, could not have been revealed at Sinai. For who could have needed the sound of thunder and the blast of trumpets to become convinced of the validity of these eternal verities? [17]

What distinguishes the Jew from the non-Jew is not his religion, which is the common property of all men of reason, but the unique laws, statutes, and commandments disclosed at Sinai:

> Among all the laws and commandments of Moses there is none saying: thou shalt believe, or thou shalt not believe. They all say: thou shalt do or thou shalt not do.[18]

For Mendelssohn, Judaism is concerned with man's actions, not his beliefs. It does not compel him to affirm notions that defy reason; it seeks to guide and influence his daily actions.

Once again, two conclusions flow from this definition:

(1) If religion has to justify the validity of its claims before the tribunal of reason, no miracle can be used to prove the truth of any faith or doctrine that cannot be verified by reason. Mendelssohn believes in the metaphysical possibility of miracles but denies they can be used to prove anything. Inasmuch as all religions invoke miracles in support of their claims, there is no basis for trusting one claim more than another. Consequently, neither Judaism nor Christianity may have recourse to miracles to justify their claim to truth. Miracles cannot give birth to conceptions; they can at best support or confirm rational truths.

(2) For the same reason, Judaism is devoid of dogmas, a body of doctrines formally proclaimed by an ecclesiastical authority as indispensable for the attainment of salvation. Judaism addresses itself to man's will but does not attempt to control his thoughts. It requires conformity in act but grants freedom in matters of doctrine. "Man must be driven to action but may merely be stimulated to contemplation."

Mendelssohn's distinction between "religion" and "law" is crucial to the understanding of his philosophy. He cannot define Judaism as a revealed religion, for its religious affirmations are not specific Jewish notions but *vérités de raison,* principles of the general religion of reason. Judaism has nothing to add to these principles. It merely confirms them.

But that God spoke at Sinai is for Mendelssohn a *vérité de fait,* a historical event whose factuality is clearly established because it was witnessed by the entire people of Israel with incontrovertible clarity. In making this point, Mendelssohn falls back on the argument by which not only classical Jewish theology but the theologies of Christianity and Islam too seek to prove that their belief in revelation is based not on man's speculative imagination but on solid historical evidence. Islam finds proof for the Koran's divine origin in the fact that it possesses an incomparable literary beauty and perfection that could not have been produced by any human effort. Classical Christianity rests upon the agreement of the Gospels that the miracles ascribed to Jesus actually took place. And classical Jewish thought establishes the factuality of the Sinaitic event by the claim, grounded in the Biblical narrative, that God spoke face to face with the Jewish people at Sinai, that the entire people witnessed the event, and that the belief in such an event could never have persisted through the ages had not the memory of the people confirmed the actual fact of this experience. By ascribing historicity to revelation, faith—belief in revelation—is transposed into factual knowledge.

What distinguishes Mendelssohn from earlier Jewish thinkers is not that he rejects the possibility of revelation but that he defines and restricts the content of that revelation to God's disclosure of the *mitzvot,* the laws and ordinances governing the life of the Jewish people. All human beings are destined to attain felicity; but the Jew is the only one who can attain it only by observing the Sinaitic laws. No non-Jew needs the Torah; no Jew can be a Jew without it. Its purpose is not to disclose the eternal truths of the religion of reason but to strengthen them by reminding the Jew of them and stimulating him to reflect upon them. Furthermore, the commandments distinguish Jews from non-Jews and enable them to maintain their identity as a distinct group and thus to continue to serve as the carrier of the pure religion of reason.

In emphasizing that the *mitzvot* constitute Jewish particularity and are the sole content of God's revelation, Mendelssohn utilizes several sources, among them a theory previously formulated by Faustus Socinus, a sixteenth-century Christian thinker, who asserts that God can reveal only laws but not metaphysical truths and who, therefore, defines religion, objectively, as the giving of the law and, subjectively, as its observance. Mendelssohn also draws on an important distinction between the universal content of Scripture and the particularism of Jewish law made by Spinoza in his famous *Tractatus Theologico-Politicus.*[19] For Spinoza, Jewish law in ancient Palestine had a purely political character. It was the constitution of a state, and any offense against God's commandments was therefore not merely a religious transgression but a political offense punishable not as a misbelief but as a civic misdeed, as proved by the fact that the Bible offers only this-worldly rewards or punishments for obedience or disobedience of the law, but never mentions eternal bliss or immortality as one of its rewards.

This identification of state and religion came to an end with the destruction of the Temple. Punishment for "political" crimes could be applied only as long as God was also the sovereign of the Jewish state. Consequently Spinoza maintains that the applicability of Jewish law ended when the ancient Jewish state ceased to exist.

Mendelssohn views the political aspects of Jewish life merely as one element of Judaism. He makes a distinction between the Torah as the constitution of a state and the Torah as a set of rules governing the life of the individual and the community. He concedes that the political function of the laws which governed life in the ancient state was no longer applicable once the state ceased to exist. But the precepts ordering the life of the individual were never rescinded or abrogated, and Mosaic law has therefore remained valid even after its political function ended. Thus the Jewish people, by its very existence, continues to be charged with the mission unceasingly to proclaim, teach, and preach these "sound and unfalsified" concepts of God to the nations.

Mendelssohn's hope had been to demonstrate Judaism's permanent validity and enduring truth by defining it as revealed law rather than as revealed religion. He did not realize how vulnerable his definitions of both revelation and reason were.

To take revelation first: if reason is the sole criterion of truth, how can God's revelation on Sinai be "true," since it can neither be explained logically nor verified by reason? Granted that "law" is one of Judaism's vital ingredients. But Judaism is more than a system of legal precepts. The precepts themselves are grounded in a body of fundamental affirmations concerning God, the world, man, life's purpose, and the meaning of Jewish existence—affirmations that are not postulates of reason but assertions of faith.

What Mendelssohn did was simply to take the religion of reason of his time and graft upon it an emasculated Judaism consisting solely of rituals, customs, and ceremonial laws. The paradox was that he, the thinker for whom no belief was valid if it was contrary to reason, declared that Judaism's rational concepts and ideas were not specifically Jewish but principles of the general religion of reason, whereas Judaism consisted solely of elements which were not rational, which reason could neither prove nor understand, and which God disclosed to the Jews in a mysterious and nonrational act of revelation. The nonrevealed God of reason had to resort to revelation to disclose His legislation. What Mendelssohn did not succeed in showing was why man's reason is capable of discovering and demonstrating the existence of God but incapable of discerning God's plan and design for the Jew.

Nor did Mendelssohn's Enlightenment concept of reason go unchallenged, especially his contention that reason is universal and the capacity to apperceive the truth common to all men at all times and in all places. On this particular issue Mendelssohn parts ways with Lessing, his friend and mentor.[20] In an important volume, *Die Erziehung des Menschengeschlechts* (The Education of the Human Race, 1780), Lessing repudiates one of the fundamental axioms of the Enlightenment, which is also central to Mendelssohn's thought: that the truth of any "revealed" religion is to be judged by its conformity to the tenets of an abstract, hypothesized religion of "reason." According to Lessing, human self-understanding developed only gradually. Truths that may now seem obvious to reason and self-evident even to the common man were unknown or unintelligible to previous generations, which, therefore, considered them as "revelations" from God. History is characterized by growth, spiritual evolution and progress—by a movement toward greater clarity in man's comprehension of himself and of truth. Otherwise it would be impossible to explain the existence of paganism and similar primitive notions or of intellectual aberrations. If, as Mendelssohn and the Enlightenment claim, truth were accessible to all men, how explain the fact that not all men possess truth equally and that they define it differently?

Only one answer is possible for Lessing. Reason is not static but dynamic, not ever-present but in a continuous process of becoming and evolving. The truth of each religion is conditioned by its time and place in history. Therefore its insights can become outdated, superseded by later developments. Every positive (i.e., historical) religion, like every school primer, is valid only for a certain age, and the clarity with which it reflects or fails to reflect the ultimate truth depends on the stage of its intellectual development at a particular time. Each new generation possesses or can at least attain a higher understanding of religious truth than the preceding one.

This progression from an obscure to a clearer perception of fundamental truths characterizes, for Lessing, the relationship between Judaism and Christianity. The Old Testament was a primer for the Jews in the ancient Jewish commonwealth; but one of its fatal shortcomings is the absence of any meaningful concept of immortality. The Old Testament was not only succeeded but superseded by a new revelation, recorded in the New Testament, which, largely by its clear teaching of the immortality of the soul, became mankind's new and superior primer.[21]

Mendelssohn cannot make his peace with Lessing's concept of religious progress. He does not object to the idea of historical progress as such. He admits that intellectual progress takes place: science and philosophy in his day had risen far above the level attained by the Greeks. But there are two reasons for which he cannot accept the application of the idea of progress to the problem of religious truth. Lessing is wrong, first, because Mendelssohn cannot conceive that the attainment of mankind's highest goals and aspirations could be entrusted haphazardly to the vicissitudes of history; religious truth must in principle be accessible to all people at all times. But Lessing is wrong also because "progress does not apply to mankind as a collectivity but only to the individual who is destined by Providence to spend part of his eternity here on earth. Everyone goes through life in his own way . . . but that it could also have been the intention of Providence to let mankind as a whole advance steadily and toward perfection . . . is something I cannot believe." [22] Nature's goal is not the perfection of mankind but the perfection of the individual. Mankind is merely an abstraction, with no life of its own. It is a term describing a succession of individuals. Mankind does not change; only the individual does.

Mendelssohn's strange argument may have been motivated by

his conviction that the permanent validity of Judaism would be endangered if not destroyed if the Sinaitic revelation could be superseded by a later revelation proclaiming a superior degree of truth. The voice that spoke at Sinai spoke for all generations. To accept Lessing's theory would therefore mean to accept the claim that Christianity was the new truth that had come to replace an inferior and outdated Judaism.

Although one can understand and appreciate Mendelssohn's motives, his logic poses more questions than it answers. If reason is the endowment of all generations, how can Mendelssohn explain that not all people are equally reasonable or act reasonably, that error exists, that prejudices tend to obscure the truth which he claims to be man's endowment in every generation?

Mendelssohn is himself aware of this difficulty. He realizes that reason is not as ubiquitous and all-pervasive as his theory demands and that, owing to the nature of the human spirit, there are many opportunities for falsifying the eternal religious truths:

> Polytheism, anthropomorphism and religious usurpation still rule the earth. . . . As long as these troubling spirits are united against reason, the genuine theists must also provide for a kind of union among themselves if the former are not to trample everything underfoot. And wherein shall this union consist? In principles and beliefs? Then you have dogmas, symbols, formulas, reason that is fettered. Therefore, in acts, meaningful acts—i.e. in ceremonies.[23]

Precisely because reason is not ever-present and man tends to drift toward a perversion of the pure truths of reason, the laws revealed at Sinai remain necessary both as a bond of Jewish unity and to guard pure and rational theism from the adulteration of paganism and other aberrations.

But this explanation does not resolve Mendelssohn's difficulties, either. If laws are needed to guard the religion of reason from corruption, why did God provide only the Jews and not everyone else with the means to cope with this danger? If, as Mendelssohn feels, God, in His goodness, has granted reason to all men so that no group or people will be denied access to eternal bliss, should the same not apply to the revelation of the law which alone, according to Mendelssohn, will enable a people to remain faithful on the road to truth and salvation?

Mendelssohn is not aware of the paradox of his position, which compels him to subtract from reason what he grants to revelation. He sees no contradiction. The God of reason and the God of Israel are one and the same—the benevolent creator and sustainer of the world whom his reason can affirm, and the king and guardian of Israel who spoke at Sinai and ordained the laws that govern Jewish life. By obeying the commandments, the Jew in Mendelssohn worships the God in whom his reason believes. This is the only way in which Mendelssohn can harmonize his insistence on reason and man's freedom of conscience and his determination to preserve Jewish law and thus maintain his membership in the congregation of Israel. He was able to fuse in his personal life what his theory of Judaism fails to reconcile philosophically.

Mendelssohn's thinking can be understood only against the background of the causes commanding his deepest loyalties. His faith in reason was linked with a passionate concern for human equality. If knowledge of truth was indispensable to the achievement of a man's happiness, truth had to be accessible to all people without distinction of race, creed, origin, or social status. God could not arbitrarily reveal the truth merely to one segment of mankind, leaving the rest without revelation and therefore without access to happiness. A God who could deprive untold millions of felicity and immortality because of something that was not their fault would be a capricious tyrant, unworthy of worship. As he wrote in a letter to Jacob Emden:

> Are we to assume that all inhabitants of the earth, from sunrise to sunset, are condemned to perdition if they do not believe in the Torah, which has been granted solely as the inheritance of the congregation of Jacob? . . . What then are those peoples to do that are not reached by the radiant rays of the Torah? . . .

37

> Does God act like a tyrant when he deals with his creatures, destroying them and extirpating their name, even though they have done no wrong? [24]

No religion, not even Judaism, could therefore be the sole instrument through which God discloses His truth. Truth must be accessible to all men.

But it was equally impossible for Mendelssohn to surrender his deep attachment to Jewish life and his conviction that the observance of Jewish law bound him to God and united him with his people. Therefore, Mendelssohn kept insisting on the crucial importance of the law for the Jew and even proclaimed boldly that if a choice had to be made it would be better that the Jew surrender the benefits of emancipation than his loyalty to Sinai.

Jerusalem had a powerful impact. Non-Jews were impressed by Mendelssohn's persuasive analysis of the relationship between state and church and his courageous defense of man's inalienable right to freedom of thought. Mirabeau, one of the leading spirits of the French Revolution, declared that the book ought to be translated into every European language, while Kant—who was later to use Mendelssohn's definition of Judaism to derogate Judaism as "merely ceremonial law" belonging to an obsolete past—wrote Mendelssohn that he considered the little volume a masterly statement which would spur a reform from which non-Jews as well as Jews would benefit.

The impact of the work upon Mendelssohn's fellow Jews, however, was negligible. His arguments for the preservation of Jewish law, as persuasive as they seemed to him, had little influence on most of his contemporaries, who preferred the actual or presumed benefits of acceptance by the Gentile society to the burdensome task of maintaining their distinctive Jewish identity. Mendelssohn's own children were an example. Only two of them remained Jewish; the others defected after their father's death. One of the daughters, Dorothea, after leaving her first husband, the Jewish banker Simon Veit, married the famous romantic poet Friedrich Schlegel and turned Protestant, converting later to Catholicism together with her husband. Another daughter, Henriette, a teacher, became a Catholic, while Abraham Mendelssohn, father of the famous musician, Felix Mendelssohn-Bartholdy, turned Protestant. Johannes Emmanuel (originally Jonas) Veit, one of Dorothea's sons, was baptized and lived in Rome, where he became an outstanding painter of Nazarene themes.

Mendelssohn died on January 4, 1786, apparently of a heart attack. Widely regarded and memorialized as a model and embodiment of the humanist ideal, he was mourned by Jews and Gentiles alike.

In the history of philosophy, Mendelssohn occupies only a minor position. He did not create a philosophical system, nor did he become a second Spinoza, as Lessing had predicted. Already in his lifetime he was criticized severely by Johann Georg Hamann, philosopher and Protestant theologian, for the mendacity and hypocrisy with which he dared to present himself as a philosopher of the Enlightenment while remaining an orthodox Jew.[25] His general philosophical position, too, was soon challenged by the emerging systems of critical idealism by which Kant and his successors negated the presuppositions of the Enlightenment philosophy.

Nor did Mendelssohn's philosophy of Judaism have a lasting effect. Jewish thinkers who followed him soon discovered the paradoxes in his thinking and dissociated themselves from his views. Salomon Ludwig Steinheim, a physician and Jewish theologian in the early post-Mendelssohn period, who attempted to demonstrate that revelation could be defined as a philosophical concept, stated that Mendelssohn had completely misinterpreted the sacred concept of revelation, that he was "a pagan with his brain though he was a Jew with his body," and that he would gladly have joined his friend Lessing in a society where there were no longer either Christians or Jews, had it not been for the fact that he rejected apostasy for reasons of honor.[26] Peretz Smolenskin, a Hebrew writer and ardent proponent of Jewish nationalism in the nineteenth century, denounced him sharply as an advocate of assimilation and disintegration who had knowingly and maliciously led the Jewish people to the brink of self-destruction by defining Jews merely as members of a religious denomination. Long after his death, orthodox leaders continued to denounce him and his work as a destructive influence, admonishing young Jews to abstain from reading his books and not to let Mendelssohn's example seduce them into turning from their Talmudic studies to mundane matters and the study of general European culture. Moses Sofer, the founder of a famous yeshiva in Pressburg, put this injunction succinctly: *b'sifrei Ramad al tish'l'ḥu yad,* "Do not reach for the books of Moses Dessau [Ramad]."

Yet despite their limitations, Mendelssohn's thought and work possess a significance that transcends such critical partisan views. He succeeded in bridging the Jewish world and European culture in his own life and, through his work and personal example, enabled his fellow Jews to do the same. He was the first to make German the language of Jewish scholarship. His translation of the Pentateuch prepared the way for the cultural emancipation of Jews by placing the treasures of European culture within their reach. His writings and the example of his personality helped pave the road for their civic emancipation as well. As he gained the friendship and admiration of influential thinkers and statesmen, he won allies who associated themselves with his battle for human rights and created the moral and intellectual climate from which Jewish emancipation could gradually emerge.

Mendelssohn's attempt to bridge the two worlds philosophically did not and could not succeed. Judaism obviously is more than merely a system of ritual prescriptions and legal ordinances. In this respect Mendelssohn was wrong and has been rightly criticized. Nevertheless, he was wrong for the right reason. Despite the philosophical questions raised by his definition of Judaism, he comes close to the truth in his intuitive feeling that Judaism has always considered itself a way of life rather than a system of doctrines and beliefs; that there is a strong activist emphasis in Judaism; that, in the Jewish vision, man wins merit primarily by his affirmation of God through conduct, not creed; and that Judaism has manifested its historic distinctiveness not in formulations of creeds but through *Halakha*—the body of rules and laws which, according to tradition, had their origin at Sinai.

The discussion of the possibility, nature, and content of revelation in Judaism has not ended. A century and a half after Mendelssohn's death, Martin Buber, in a letter to Franz Rosenzweig, took a position diametrically opposed to Mendelssohn's:

> I do not believe that revelation is ever a formulation of law. It is only through man in his self-contradiction that revelation becomes legislation. This is the fact of man.[27]

Rosenzweig, however, came close to Mendelssohn's position when he asserted that the synagogue stands for a stern refutation of the pagan world and is the only safeguard for the completion of the work of revelation. In Israel's seclusion from the world, in its priestly way of life, it expresses the essence of revelation in an absolute form. "The synagogue is ruled by law, not by a philosophy, and not even by a dogma." [28]

Nor are some of the other issues by which Mendelssohn felt himself challenged dead or outmoded. The tension between universalism and particularism continues to agitate the minds of Jewish thinkers. Mordecai Kaplan, the founder of the Reconstructionist Movement, for instance, makes an emphatic distinction between the universal and particular elements in Judaism. For Kaplan, who takes a position similar to Mendelssohn's, truth must be universal. There cannot be one truth belonging to one group or people, and another truth belonging to a second group or people. What distinguishes one group from the other are the symbols, celebrations, festivals, rituals—the particular customs and observances, or *sancta,* as Kaplan calls them—whereby a group's insights, ideals, and historical experiences are embodied, evoked, recalled, recapitulated, and celebrated. It is these particular *sancta* that distinguish cultures and groups. While freedom as such is universal, each culture or people expresses its notions and aspirations of freedom in historically determined ways—Jews in the festival of Passover, Americans as the Fourth of July, Frenchmen as Bastille Day, Israelis as *Yom Ha'atzmaut.*

The difference between Mendelssohn and Kaplan is, of course, unbridgeable. For the former, Judaism's particular observances and *sancta* are grounded in the supernatural—God; for the latter, they are enclosed in the realm of the natural, the product of a

41

people's spirit and response to its experience. Nevertheless, both maintain that this is the only way in which the tension between particularism and universalism can be resolved in Judaism. Mendelssohn's key question persists.

Furthermore, Mendelssohn formulated a vital and continuingly important principle of public life when he proclaimed in the first part of *Jerusalem* that for the sake of human equality, there must be a separation between state and church; that a government must be neutral with regard to religious differences among its citizens; that no citizen, merely because of his religious views, has a claim to advantage over another; and that a truly free and humane society is possible only where religion remains a private matter.

To put it differently: a truly liberal society stands or falls with the distinction between state and society, based on the recognition that there is a private sphere that is protected by the law but, at the same time, impervious to the reach of the law. Religion as well as race fall within that private sphere. In Mendelssohn's words:

> Let every man who does not disturb the public welfare, who obeys the law, acts righteously toward you and his fellow men, be allowed to speak as he thinks, to pray to God after his own fashion or after that of his fathers, and to seek eternal salvation where he thinks he may find it.

Mendelssohn also is both an example and symbol of a human attitude that has significance across the centuries. A shy, reticent man, he hated controversies. He was happiest when he could settle down with his books and thoughts, talk or correspond with his friends, or play with his children. Yet this shy man, who would have loved to withdraw from ugliness and strife, stepped forward whenever there was a need to enter the arena in which the battle for human dignity and rights had to be fought. He knew that withdrawal is not a road to salvation either for the individual or for society—be it physical withdrawal into one's study, cultural or political withdrawal into a self-imposed ghetto, or the withdrawal of indifference from the battle for the redemption of man. Mendelssohn exemplified commitment to one of Judaism's crucial demands—the demand that a man validate his convictions by wholehearted participation and involvement in the social enterprise as indispensable to the fulfillment of the human spirit.

Finally, Mendelssohn's significance as a Jewish thinker lies also in the fact that, standing at the threshold of Jewish modernity in Central Europe, he was the first to recognize and define the two-fold problem that has confronted the Jew ever since the Emancipation: How can the Jew become modern man, and how can modern man be Jewish?

While Mendelssohn shared the hope for a time in which all religions and men might be united in common service to the brotherhood of mankind, he also knew that this goal, if it can be reached at all, cannot be reached on the illusory path of a homogenized society in which human distinctiveness is reduced to uniformity, that one cannot be man unless one is a particular kind of man, and that therefore the distinctiveness of the Jewish experience must be preserved.

Yet the fundamental problm of the modern Jew is that the factors and forces that once safeguarded the cohesion of the Jewish people and the continuity of the distinctive Jewish faith stance were radically changed by the movement of the Jew into the modern world. It was a movement from the ghetto setting in which Judaism was the majority culture to a Judaism that became a minority culture in its new setting of actual or presumed freedom. It was a movement from what Leo Baeck has called *Milieu-frömmigkeit* to *Individualfrömmigkeit* [29]—from life in a totally Jewish environment, in which Judaism was the matrix and context of an individual's experience, to a setting in which the non-Jewish world is the dominant milieu, in which Judaism no longer is the context of the individual's experience and self-expression, and in which the Jew must make a conscious and deliberate effort to define and justify the nature of his difference from the majority.

Hence the predicament of many modern Jews seems to be the feeling that they are confronted by an either/or proposition: either to choose Judaism at the expense of the world, or the world at the expense of Judaism. Mendelssohn tried to demonstrate that this is not a true alternative. He did not regard the Jew as limited to a choice between Judaism and the world but as able to live a meaningful and creative life as a Jew in the modern world. While Mendelssohn failed in his attempt to resolve the philosophical tension between tradition and modernity, the question he posed remains the fundamental challenge to the contemporary Jew: how the Jewish heritage, while rooted in the past and continuous with it, can be won anew by every new generation in the language of its day and in the light of its own condition.

NOTES

1. For a more detailed treatment of Mendelssohn's life and work see Herman Walter, *Moses Mendelssohn: Critic and Philosopher* (New York, 1930); Alfred Jospe, "Moses Mendelssohn," in *Great Jewish Personalities in Modern Times,* ed. Simon Noveck (Washington, 1960), pp. 11–30; and especially Alexander Altmann, *Moses Mendelssohn: A Biographical Study* (University, Ala., 1973).

2. Abraham Joshua Heschel, *The Earth Is the Lord's* (New York, 1950).

3. Mark Zborowski and Elizabeth Herzog, *Life Is with People* (New York, 1952).

4. Maurice Samuel, *The World of Sholom Aleichem* (New York, 1954).

5. *The Golden Tradition: Jewish Life and Thought in Eastern Europe,* ed. Lucy S. Dawidowicz (New York, 1967).

6. Immanuel Kant, *What Is Enlightenment?* trans. and ed. L. W. Beck (Chicago, 1955), p. 286.

7. *Moses Mendelssohns sämmtliche Werke* (Vienna, 1838), pp. 683–84.

8. Letter to August von Hennings, June 29, 1779. M. Kayserling, *Moses Mendelssohn, Sein Leben und Wirken* (Leipzig, 1862), p. 521.

9. "Letter to Johann Caspar Lavater," in *Jerusalem and Other Jewish Writings by Moses Mendelssohn,* trans. and ed. Alfred Jospe (New York, 1969), p. 113 ff.

10. *Phaedon,* Second Dialogue, Part I. (This discussion of Mendelssohn's concept of immortality and the summary of his views on free will and sin [pp. 30–31] incorporate material prepared or translated by Eva Jospe.)

11. A complete English translation of the Preface to *Vindiciae Judaeorum* can be found in *Jerusalem: A Treatise on Ecclesiastical Authority and Judaism,* trans. M. Samuels, Vol. I (London, 1838), pp. 77–116. "The Search for Light and Right," ibid., pp. 119–41; "Postscript," by Moerschel, ibid, pp. 142–45.

12. The identity of the *Forscher* continues to be the subject of scholarly discussion. Yaakov Katz identified him as Josef von Sonnenfels in "To Whom Was Mendelssohn Replying in *Jerusalem?*" (*Zion,* Vol. 29, 1964, 112–32 [Hebrew]). However, in a later study Katz concludes on

the basis of new evidence that the author probably was a certain August Friedrich Cranz, who may have written the pamphlet at the request of Sonnenfels or who may have pretended to act on Sonnenfels' behalf in order to benefit from the latter's reputation (*Zion,* Vol. 36, 1971, 116–17). Cf. Altmann, op. cit. (see Note 1), pp. 504–13.

13. In "Postscript," op. cit.
14. *Jerusalem,* op. cit. (see note 9).
15. It is important to note that Mendelssohn does not pursue his own definition to its logical conclusion. While he insists that the state may not involve itself in religious controversies or favor any particular set of doctrines, he continues to grant to the state the right to take action against atheism, epicurism, and fanaticism because they are doctrines that threaten the moral or social foundations of society. Atheism, for instance, constitutes a danger to the state precisely because "without belief in God, Providence, and a future life, happiness is a mere dream, virtue ceases to be virtue, the love of humanity becomes a mere weakness, and benevolence is little more than folly." Cf. *Jerusalem,* op. cit. pp. 37–43.
16. Ibid., p. 110.
17. Ibid., p. 69.
18. Ibid., p. 71. Cf. also Lessing's view that "the books of the Old Testament were not written to reveal a religion" but solely particular laws and prescriptions for conduct. *Wolfenbüttler Fragmente,* fourth fragment (Berlin, 1784), p. 1154 (quoted by Steinheim in *Moses Mendelssohn* [see note 24 below], pp. 10 and 24).
19. For an extended discussion of the issue, see "Mendelssohns Jerusalem und Spinozas theologisch-politischer Traktat," by Julius Guttmann, *48. Bericht der Hochschule für die Wissenschaft des Judentums* (Berlin, 1931), pp. 36–67.
20. *Jerusalem,* op. cit. p. 67. For a comprehensive presentation of Lessing's views, see Henry E. Allison, *Lessing and the Enlightenment* (Ann Arbor, Mich., 1966).
21. "Christianity was not simply a linear development from an obscure to a clearer comprehension of certain fundamental truths, such as is found in Judaism itself, but rather a qualitative leap to a new and higher perspective. The attainment of this new perspective required a new revelation, and this was provided by Christ, who became the 'first reliable, practical teacher of the immortality of the soul.'" (Lessing, *The Education of the Human Race,* quoted by Allison, op. cit. p. 155.)
22. *Jerusalem,* op. cit. p. 67.
23. *Moses Mendelssohn: Gesammelte Schriften,* ed. G. B. Mendelssohn, (Leipzig, 1843–1845), Vol. V, p. 669.
24. *Moses Mendelssohn: Gesammelte Schriften* (Jubilee edition) (Berlin), Vol. XVI, p. 178.
25. Cf. Fritz Bamberger, "Die geistige Gestalt Moses Mendelssohns,"

Schriften der Gesellschaft zur Förderung der Wissenschaft des Judentums, No. 36, Frankfurt, 1929, p. 8.

26. Salomon Ludwig Steinheim, *Moses Mendelssohn und seine Schule in ihrer Beziehung zur Aufgabe des neuen Jahrhunderts* (Hamburg, 1840), pp. 26, 37 ff. A more balanced assessment of Mendelssohn's work was made by Samuel Hirsch (1815–1889), rabbi and philosopher of Judaism: "As a philosopher, Mendelssohn was of no significance for the Jews who were not affected by either his *Morning Hours* or his *Jerusalem* and *Phaedon.* Actually, he had not meant to introduce his coreligionists to these works, for he had them originally published in German, which only a few Jews of his time were able to read. Nor did he for a moment misjudge his own place in the history of philosophy. Unless I am mistaken, it was in his Preface to *Morning Hours* that he modestly paid tribute to the star that had arisen in Königsberg [Kant], a star he could not follow. But as far as the externals of Jewish cultural history are concerned, Mendelssohn, Wessely and their school represent a turning point between the old time and the new. For it was due to Mendelssohn that Jews learned German and with it acquired German concepts and views. What Luther's translation of the Bible had achieved for the general public, Mendelssohn's translation of the Pentateuch did for the Jews. . . . As he had taught the philosophers to speak and write German, so he now taught the Jews. For he added a Hebrew commentary to his translation of the Pentateuch and in it showed the Jews the difference between a subject, object, dative, and accusative. . . ." Samuel Hirsch, *Das Judenthum, der christliche Staat und die moderne Kritik* (Leipzig, 1843), p. 112, trans. Eva Jospe.

27. Franz Rosenzweig and Martin Buber, "Revelation and Law: A Correspondence," trans. William Wolf, in *On Jewish Learning,* by Franz Rosenzweig, ed. N. N. Glatzer (New York, 1955), p. 111 (letter of June 24, 1924).

28. Alexander Altmann, "Franz Rosenzweig and Eugen Rosenstock-Huessy: An Introduction to Their 'Letters on Judaism and Christianity,'" *The Journal of Religion* (Chicago, 1944), reprinted with slight modifications in *Judaism Despite Christianity,* ed. Eugen Rosenstock-Huessy (New York, 1971), p. 38.

29. Leo Baeck, "Das Judentum," in *Die Religionen der Erde, ihr Wesen und ihre Geschichte* (Munich, 1927), pp. 401–22. Cf. also the discussion of this specific point in *The Legacy of Maurice Pekarsky,* ed. with an introduction by Alfred Jospe (Chicago, 1965), pp. 26–29.

PART ONE

Personal Reflections

Editor's Note

The terse autobiographical lines opening this section do not begin to depict the wrenching struggles that led to Moses Mendelssohn's physical and spiritual emergence from the stunting confines of the ghetto into a world of middle-class pursuits and comforts and of lifelong friendships with many of the intellectual aristocrats of his age. As a warmhearted, ever out-reaching human being, he derived great joy from these relationships. And as an almost completely self-educated man, he needed their cross-fertilizing mental stimulation. Hence, he considered most of them, and particularly his friendship with Lessing, as a testing ground for his own thinking and a clearinghouse for the wealth of ideas that threatened at times to overwhelm him in his lonely study.

The casual brevity of Mendelssohn's *curriculum vitae* is characteristic for a spirit at once humble and soaring. For it is humility that accounts for his utter lack of any sense of self-importance, even when he was already widely known as "the Jewish Socrates." And it is a soaring spirit, transcending the physical, that dismisses external events as insignificant data both in his personal life and in that of nations (history made him "yawn"), and instead searches for metaphysical meaning and inner relevancies.

Though his copious correspondence shows him as a concerned husband, father, and friend, he readily admits that his first love is a life of contemplation. Yet he can pursue this love only in odd hours, scraps of time left over from working at a trade he loathes; for as a Jew he cannot earn a living as a professional writer or philosopher. Still, the silk trade and its bookkeeping chores are already a vast improvement over the grinding poverty of Mendelssohn's childhood and youth. Sophie Becker (related to Protestant pastors belonging to his circle of friends, and an eager correspondent of his in her own right) illustrates that early penury by recounting that even at a fairly advanced age Mendelssohn regarded his having once found twenty groschen, which he used to buy a shirt, as one of the keenest pleasures of his life. Another friend recalls Mendelssohn's telling him he would never have experienced "the bliss of philosophizing" so intensely had it not been for the drudgery of bookkeeping. And it was probably due to the physical deprivations of his youth that the grown man still had such a sweet tooth he would occasionally declare, "The only thing wrong with sugar is that one cannot eat it with sugar."

Deeply rooted in the traditional sources of Judaism which sustained him throughout his life, Mendelssohn was also starved for the secular knowledge of his own time and the sophisticated wisdom of ancient Greece. Though his Jewish studies had started in early childhood and were continued under the guidance of so eminent a Talmudic scholar as Rabbi David Fraenkel (Dessau and Berlin), Mendelssohn was completely on his own as far as his secular education was concerned. He read avidly (though not methodically) any book he could get hold of, and as a young man studied with Jewish university graduates he met socially in Berlin. He gratefully accepted as tutor or mentor anyone who could teach him anything—from classical and contemporary languages to metaphysics—and soon came to represent in both his person and his writings the best of his own spiritual heritage and that of Western civilization as he knew it.

As heir and disciple of Moses as well as Plato, he was spiritually far superior to those "privileged Jews" of his era whose very wealth made them suspect to him, and to whose social life, interests, and ambitions he remained a stranger. Still, "caged birds whistle the tunes that are played to them," [1] and so Mendelssohn learned to engage in the light banter and chitchat of his well-to-do social acquaintances, even defending the wearing of wigs—and that at a time (1761) when the official act of Prussian Jewry's Emancipation (and the subsequent natural processes of acculturation and assimilation) was still more than fifty years away.

Many passages in Mendelssohn's letters, particularly those to his fiancée, highlight the fact that the world of the erstwhile ghetto-dweller from Dessau was full of paradoxes. On the one hand, he found it as difficult as any Jew of his time to secure the right of domicile in Berlin for his bride and himself, and he suffered the bitter disappointment of not being made a member of Prussia's Academy of Sciences, despite his high recommendations for that honor. On the other hand, his renown as a wise man and superior judge of human affairs spread to places on the map and strata of society he, as a Jew, was not permitted to enter, though their inhabitants sought his counsel, engaging him in lively correspondence. And it is this correspondence that became one of the most important vehicles for conveying Mendelssohn's thoughts and convictions.

1. Howard Sachar, *The Course of Modern Jewish History* (Cleveland and New York: World Publishing Co., 1958), p. 66.

AUTOBIOGRAPHICAL DATA

[A letter from Mendelssohn to Johann Jacob Spiess (1730–1814), pastor, librarian, and supervisor of the mint in Ansbach (Bavaria), who had, in his latter capacity, a medal struck in Mendelssohn's honor. Finding that, despite Mendelssohn's renown as scholar and philosopher, very little was known about his personal life, Spiess asked the author of Phaedon *for some biographical data to be printed in a numismatic publication. The following is an excerpt from Mendelssohn's reply.]*

Berlin, March 1, 1774

I cannot promise your readers that the circumstances of my life, which really are of little consequence, will prove particularly entertaining to them. My biographical data have actually always seemed so unimportant to me that I never bothered to keep a record of them. . . . The main facts I can recall offhand are approximately as follows:

I was born in the year 1729 (the twelfth of Elul, 5489, according to the Jewish calendar) in Dessau, where my father was a teacher and Torah scribe, or *sopher*. I studied Talmud under Rabbi [David] Fraenkel, who was then the chief rabbi [*Oberrabbiner*] of Dessau. Around 1743, this learned rabbi, who had gained great fame among the Jewish people because of his commentary on the Jerusalem Talmud, was called to Berlin, where I followed him that same year. There, I developed a taste for the arts and sciences as a result of my acquaintance with as well as some instruction by Mr. Aron Gumperts (who later became a doctor of medicine; he died a few years ago in Hamburg).

Eventually, I became first a tutor in the house of a rich Jew [Isaak Bernhard], later on his bookkeeper, and, finally, the manager of his silk factory, a position I am still holding. I was married in my thirty-third year and sired seven children, of whom five survive. Incidentally, I never attended a university, nor did I ever listen to an academic lecture. This [lack of formal education] constituted one of my greatest difficulties, for it meant a real struggle to get an education solely by my own effort and diligence. In fact, I overdid it, and the overzealousness with which I pursued my studies brought on a nervous weakness that renders me all but incapable of any scholarly occupation. . . .

THE DAILY GRIND
[*To Gotthold Ephraim Lessing* [1]]

Berlin, February 27, 1758

Dearest friend:

A good bookkeeper is surely a rare creature. He should be given a medal for divesting himself of his mind, wit, and all emotion, turning himself into a clod so as to keep his books in order. Or don't you agree that such a sacrifice for the sake of finances deserves to be richly rewarded?

"And what," you may ask, "happened today to give you such an idea?" Well, you cannot possibly guess that this notion occurred to me because of Mr. von Kleist's new poems.[2] I had them delivered to me at eight o'clock in the morning, planning to give some unexpected pleasure to our dear Nicolai,[3] in whose company I meant to read them. But the clamoring tradespeople around me interfered with my intentions. "What do you have there, my friend?" "And you, Madame?" "How about that young fellow over there?" "Will you excuse me? I cannot attend to you today." "But this is not one of your holidays, is it?" "No, it isn't; but I feel

1. Gotthold Ephraim Lessing (1729–1781), German poet and playwright, whose compassionate portrait of a Jew in his famous play *Nathan the Wise* had been inspired by his lifelong friend Moses Mendelssohn.
2. Heinrich von Kleist (1777–1811), German playwright and poet in the romantic-patriotic tradition.
3. Christian Friedrich Nicolai (1733–1811), author, bookseller, and co-publisher of Mendelssohn and Lessing's *Literaturbriefe* (Literary Letters) and of the *Bibliothek der schönen Wissenschaften* (Library of Belles Lettres), the latter in collaboration only with Mendelssohn.

sick. Don't let that bother you, though; just come back tomorrow."

The customers proved amenable, but my employer did not. He kept me busy till noon. Nevertheless, I managed to read a bit here and there; and this is how I noticed how hard it is to be both a bookkeeper and sensitive to poetry. I began to think of financial matters in aesthetic terms and entered into my ledgers one of those phrases used to extol the beauty of an ode. I cursed my station in life; sent the poems to our mutual friend [Nicolai], that esquire who—much to my envy!—can afford to live on his money; and felt most disgruntled.

May 1763

. . . On the whole I have, thank God, no complaints, except for that business, that dreary business! Its cares weigh me down and devour the energies of my best years. With this heavy burden on my back, I am dragging myself through life like a pack ass. And to make matters still worse, my vanity often whispers into my ear that nature probably intended me to be a show horse. What can we do, my dear friend? Nothing but assure each other of our sympathy and let it go at that. There is, however, still hope for us, if only we do not let our love for the arts and sciences grow cold. But do hurry into my arms soon, my friend. Your company alone can restore to me the fire I lost, and elevate me to a plane of thinking that is worthy of my destination. You can't imagine how stale all social contact has become for me ever since I have had to miss your companionship. . . .

INTELLECTUAL PASTIMES
[*To Gotthold Ephraim Lessing*]

February 17, 1758

Dearest friend:

I haven't written to you for quite some time because I have not done any thinking for quite some time. And neither you nor I are the kind of friends who are satisfied to entertain each other merely with assurances of friendship. Yet I really could not have written you anything but such assurances, for I must avoid all real thinking in the unhealthy air we constantly have to breathe here.

Nevertheless, my mind is engaged in playing some games. I am reading the famous essays by Abbé Trublet;[1] the man is pleasing if not too instructive. His *Pensées sur le Bonheur, sur le Plaisir, et sur les Désirs* deserve to be read. Of the most recent writers, the French are the best observers of human conduct. Depicting man's character, they occasionally discover in the deep recesses of the human heart inclinations that would elude the most meticulous philosopher. They should, however, recognize their limitations. In fact, whenever they go beyond those in an attempt to be philosophers rather than observers, one ought to keep them in check.

It appears to me that in the area of moral philosophy there is an as yet completely uncultivated field: a theory of human nature. Any general ethics merely determines that man should act in accordance with the dictates of reason—if, that is, he were capable of following these dictates in every way. But shouldn't it be possible to derive from the observations of historians, philosophers, and playwrights a generally valid theory that would show how any given character might behave in some particular case? Ancient and modern observers of the human scene, historians, and philosophers have collected much pertinent material, and all good playwrights should be equally well supplied with such data, especially when they draw their characters from life. Hence, there must be certain universal truths, a certain system, at the base of all these observations. Wouldn't it be worthwhile to find out more about them? . . .

February 27, 1758

Incidentally: the English philosophize up to a certain point, where they come to a halt. They seem too proud to read the Germans, and too complacent to plumb the depths of the soul on their own. The French philosophize with their wit: the English, with their emotions; the Germans alone are cold-blooded enough to philosophize with their intellect. . . .

1. Abbé Nicolas-Charles-Joseph Trublet, French writer of the eighteenth century.

ENGAGED TO BE MARRIED
[*To Gotthold Ephraim Lessing*]

Berlin, mid-May 1761

Dearest friend:

Let me resume our correspondence, which has been interrupted long enough. I could never have maintained so long a silence had it not been for a trip to Hamburg which enmeshed me in a thousand distractions. I attended the theater and made the acquaintance of scholars. Moreover—and this will come to you as no small surprise—I committed the folly of falling in love, in my thirtieth year! You are laughing? Never mind! Who knows what may still be in store for you? The thirtieth year could well be the most dangerous, and you, as you know, haven't reached it yet. The young woman I wish to marry [1] has no money and is neither beautiful nor learned. But (infatuated fellow that I am) I am so taken with her that I feel sure I can live happily with her. I do hope I shall not lack the means for our support, nor, if I can at all help it, the leisure to pursue my studies. I grant you still an entire year's time to compose your wedding ode for us. But then your lazy muse will have to take up her dusty lyre once again; for how could I get married unsung? . . .

[*To Fromet Gugenheim*]

Berlin, June 16, 1761

My dear little fiancée:

I should probably not use so familiar a tone with you today but should instead extend to you, chokingly and in the customary high-flown phrases, my most humble felicitations on the occasion

1. Fromet Gugenheim of Hamburg, whom Mendelssohn met in the spring of 1761 and married on June 22, 1762. They had seven children, of whom five survived.

of our formal betrothal. I find myself quite unable to do so, however. For I love you too much to stand on such solemn ceremony, and I know only too well how you yourself feel about these things. Nevertheless, there is one ceremony I must observe: I herewith send you, my dearest, a few small trifles. Will you be good enough to wear one of them on your incomparable finger as a reminder of my sincere love? There—wouldn't you say this was a compliment in the proper manner? (I rather doubt it, since it is so easy to understand.) Well, let me from now on express myself in my own way and leave the compliments to more skillful people, who, like our Rabbi Jospha Schmalkalden, know how to write in such a way that no one in the world can understand them. . . .

I am glad you have been reading Shaftesbury more than once. . . . I'll soon send you a few more useful books. Today I don't have the patience to read, for my thoughts are more in Hamburg than in Berlin. You know, I don't see any real connection between body and soul. Can't the body dwell in Berlin and the soul in Hamburg?

Don't laugh at my lovesick philosophy, my dear doctor. Believe me, all of us philosophers cut a strange figure when we are in love. Just let us consider it settled that my soul is in Hamburg. . . . Farewell, dearest Fromet, and remember always that my spirit floats around you in your room.

> *I remain,*
> *as ever your admirer and friend,*
> MOSES

Berlin, July 28, 1761

My very dearest Fromet:

Your father's letter contains a certain disclosure that pleases me very much: the good man assures me that his daughter Fromet is as beautiful as she is virtuous. Do you think I should take an honest man's word for it? Our good Mr. Abraham Gugenheim surely realizes that even philosophers like beauty. But if he'll forgive me, I think I know his Fromet better than he does. She is indeed beautiful, yet neither as beautiful as virtuous, nor even as beautiful as affectionate. I envy the felicitous way, dear Fromet, in which you express your tender love. Your little notes are full of affection and true feeling. The language of the heart is your natural language, and you display nobility of spirit rather than that cutting wit that so badly mars some people's letters. Do keep those kind and most enjoyable letters coming, my dear, my loving Fromet. It has become almost impossible for me to let a post day go by without writing to you, or to be in good spirits on such a day if it does not bring me any letters from you. And what is a man without his good spirits?

As long as we have to live apart, we must really seize every opportunity to think of and write to each other. It is no small pleasure for me to be able to imagine at any given moment that Fromet just now might be reading my letters, or writing to me; or that she is vexed because she was interrupted, or else glad because she hit upon some particularly well-turned phrase. Are you laughing, dear doctor? Or do you perhaps once again accuse me of being in love? Well then, I herewith confess my guilt. Have I not always tried to emulate you? . . .

With my fervent love,
MOSES DESSAU

Berlin, Wednesday, November 10, 1761

Dearest Fromet:

Reb Salmen Emmerich tells me you are overdoing your reading in your almost misdirected zeal. What do you want to do? Become a scholar? God forbid! To be moderately well read is becoming to a female; scholarship is not. A girl whose eyes are red from reading deserves to be ridiculed. I want you, my dearest Fromet, to take recourse to your books under two conditions only: first of all, if your heart and mind are in need of some diversion you cannot find in your social life; and secondly, if your heart needs moral support in its striving for the good. Either one of these conditions can be helped by that medicine [reading]. But too much medicine upsets the stomach. . . .

Keep well, dearest Fromet. And if your zeal must be applied to something, use it for throwing away your books. . . .

Friday, March 9, 1762 (Purim)

Dearest Fromet:

Everybody exchanges presents today, and I have nothing to give you. But I should like to tell you a little story. A disciple of the wise Socrates once said to him, "Anyone who has any contact with you, my dear Socrates, brings you a gift. Yet I have nothing to offer you but myself. Will you be kind enough not to reject me?" Whereupon the sage replied, "Do you really think so little of yourself that you must beg me to accept you? Well, then, let me offer you some counsel: try hard to become so good that your own person will be considered the best possible gift."

This is the end of my little tale. I, too, dear Fromet, shall make every effort to become so good that you may be able to say I could not possibly give you anything better than

your sincere
MOSES

ON WEALTH, FRIENDSHIP, AND SOCIABILITY
[*To Fromet Gugenheim*]

Berlin, July 7, 1761

. . . You are much too high-minded to have a true concept of a rich Berliner. When, God willing, I shall be fortunate enough to have you here with me, you will have to avoid all contact with the local wealthy people because your frame of mind and theirs are simply incompatible. Anyhow, how much company shall we seek? I shall find in you the most agreeable companion and in turn shall endeavor to have you regard me your best companion. Really—do we need other people to be happy?

Berlin, July 10, 1761

. . . You say you would have attended the wedding had I been there with you. Not at all, my dear Fromet. If I were with you, we should spend our time far more agreeably in the small circle of our friends than at a wedding. Having long been averse to this sort of public entertainment, I cannot even remember when I last attended a wedding. This may or may not be due to the fact that I feel most awkward at big parties. Suffice it to say that I have completely lost all taste for them. I am always well disposed but seldom merry and never wildly hilarious. I seek my happiness in the quiet pleasures of love and friendship; and, thank God, I have never sought those in vain. In both love and friendship, things have so far turned out exactly to my heart's desire. . . .

Berlin, August 25, 1761

. . . I have come to the conclusion that our rich people are unsuited for friendship. One's relationship to them must be no more than a close acquaintance. Friendship somehow goes with moderate circumstances. Shall I confess something to you? Well, why not? I am convinced, dear Fromet, you would not be as lovable as you are had God maintained you in your [former] rich setting. . . .

ON WIGS
[*To Fromet Gugenheim*]

Berlin, October 2, 1761

Dearest Fromet:

You are right, my dear: a man's hair is his ornament—but only if he has the time to keep it neat. For, as you know, our decadent taste insists on neatness everywhere.

Nature meant man's hair to straggle every which way down his neck, yet we want it to be stiffly arranged. If, then, our time seems too precious to us to be wasted on daily visits to a hairdresser, we simply must invent some means by which to send our hair to the wigmaker and occupy our head with more important matters at home. This is the advice, and also the personal example, I gave to our friend. One feels virtually bald with only one's own hair on the Sabbath and other holy days and barely dares to appear in decent company.

You will, I hope, approve of my oral defense of the wig's honor once I'm fortunate enough to see you in person. . . .

THE RIGHT OF DOMICILE
[*To Fromet Gugenheim*]

Berlin, Friday, March 26, 1762

Dearest Fromet:

May I, with all due respect for my esteemed fiancée, say: you are lying! I have never left you letterless, and if you want to blame someone, blame the mail carrier.

But now I have to report some news. With the help of God, we were accorded the right of domicile yesterday. From now on you are a Prussian subject like Mr. Moses Wessely,[1] which means that you must take Prussia's side in everything and, in the best Prussian manner, affirm whatever might be to our advantage. Russians, Turks, Americans—all stand at the ready to serve us, merely waiting for our signal. Our money will be worth more than the *blanko-mark;* the whole world will look for securities in Berlin; and the fame of our stock market will spread from the Schlossplatz to our house. And all of this you must now believe, for you were given the right of domicile in Berlin. . . .

IN PRAISE OF MARRIAGE
[*To Herz Homberg* [1]]

Berlin, March 15, 1784

Dearest friend:

The news has given me much pleasure that, despite your personal

---

1. A friend of Mendelssohn's with many scientific and artistic interests.
1. Herz Homberg (1749–1841), Mendelssohn's friend and his son's teacher; collaborated with Mendelssohn on his translation of the Pentateuch. An

philosophy, you too are at last following the call of nature, so that you have decided to leave the ranks of the unmarried. In the final analysis, man can find true happiness and tranquillity only in domestic life. As we approach a certain age, even the unpleasant and bothersome aspects of domesticity appear less frightening than the emptiness of an old age bereft of marital companionship. No young, lively, and outgoing person can imagine such lonely emptiness. He must accept its eventual reality on faith; for if he were to wait until he experiences it himself, it would be too late. Therefore I say, "Well done, my good Homberg. Well done, regardless of the glitter or lack of glitter of the external circumstances." You know how little my own choice was influenced by such considerations. As soon as we see a path we may—we hope—follow with honor, nature claims the right that pettiness, egotism, and vanity would deny her, insisting on that union which seems most compatible with the guileless inclinations of our heart.

LACK OF FORMAL EDUCATION
[*To Thomas Abbt* [1]]

February 16, 1765

. . . If I remember correctly, you once asked my advice in connection with a certain history you meant to write. I did not respond to your inquiry, for I was unable to give you an answer. What do I know of history? I never could get into my head anything that merely bears the designation "history"—whether natural, geological, political, or any other. And when I have to read something historical I feel like yawning, unless it is written in

educator in Prague, he later received a call to teach at Prague University, but the Emperor vetoed his appointment; see "Majesty versus Excellency," p. 72.
1. Thomas Abbt (1738–1766), a teacher of philosophy at the Universities of Frankfurt and Rinteln, and, along with Immanual Kant, a participant in the 1763 Prize Contest of the Royal Prussian Academy of Sciences. See page 20.

a particularly stimulating manner. I think history is one of those disciplines one cannot study successfully without formal instruction. . . .

. . . Tell me, my dearest friend: how do I go about acquiring even a rudimentary knowledge of history, ancient as well as more recent? Up to now, I have considered history a specifically civic rather than a generally human concern. I thought that a man without a country could not expect to benefit from a knowledge of history. I have, however, come to realize that the histories of political constitutions and of mankind are interrelated, and that it simply won't do to be completely uninformed about the former. But where do I begin? Shall I go to the original sources or should I be satisfied with those general world histories that have lately been so much in vogue? And which one of these would you advise me to read? Don't forget to let me have your reply in this matter. . . .

NO INTELLECTUAL COMPANIONSHIP
[*To Thomas Abbt*]

Berlin, March 26, 1765
. . . All day long, my dear friend, I must listen to so much idle chatter and observe as well as do so many mindless, tiresome, and stupefying things that it is no small blessing when I can talk with a rational human being at night. Probably only a very few people have any social contact with learned men in this big city of Berlin, which is bereft of all muses; and I have none. The few friends of the arts and sciences who live here do not search out each other's company, or at least no one is searching out mine. And you know how little I myself am inclined to look for other people. . . .

You are therefore the only one with whom I can discuss literary matters. And if I am not to be entirely obliterated from the book of rational beings, I shall have to write you frequently and at length. . . .

EQUANIMITY IN THE FACE OF CRITICISM

[To August von Hennings, Councilor of the Danish Legation in Berlin and an admirer and defender of Mendelssohn's Bible translation]

Strelitz, June 29, 1779

. . . Actually, the minor storm caused by my poor book [1] does not disturb me in the least. No zealot will succeed that easily in making my cold blood boil. I look upon the play of human passions as a neutral phenomenon worth observing. But if every electric spark makes one flinch and tremble, one is ill suited to be an observer.

I am, all in all, not overly sensitive—neither easily angered and upset nor moved to regret and similar disagreeable emotions. By now I am moved only by love and friendship. Yet I react even to these with such moderation that my friends frequently accuse me of being lukewarm. Still, I cannot bring myself to feel emotions I simply do not have; nor can I pretend to have them, though this seems to be required by the affectations currently in vogue. . . .

Under no circumstances shall I permit myself to react to [my attackers'] zealotry in any unseemly manner. I lost early in life, and hardly to my dismay, that youthful fire which frequently makes us overshoot our goal (with the best intentions in the world but without any sense of moderation). And now, when I am so close to the other shore, it would be folly to expose my sails to every gust of wind. . . .

1. Mendelssohn's translation of the Pentateuch, which the Rabbi of Altona banned on religious grounds. See pages 15–16.

A FATHER'S CONCERN
[*To Herz Homberg*]

Berlin, October 4, 1783

Dear Friend:

. . . You want to know how things are with my son, your pupil? I must say I am satisfied with the way he applies himself to his studies. He is making good progress, too. Most of all, his intellectual capacity increases day by day. Actually, I am not particularly interested in how much knowledge he acquires from this or that book. I am satisfied if he learns how to think, and to think not only correctly but also deeply. I regret, however, the rigidity of his character and his unyielding nature. True, these traits do not make him wicked; but they do make him unpleasant and may possibly even bode ill for his future happiness. You know him: he would rather break than bend, and has remained that way. All my efforts have, so far, been in vain. And when, despite my objections, his friends occasionally tease him, he shows enough sophistication to rationalize his shortcomings. I have almost given up hope for seeing this aspect of his character improved, unless he is fortunate enough to meet a young woman for whose sake he would discipline himself a bit more. . . .

Berlin, March 15, 1784

. . . My son Joseph has all but given up his Hebrew studies. Immediately following your tutelage, he unfortunately fell into the hands of a scholar who proved to be a hollow *baal pilpul;* [1] and as much as Joseph loves intellectual acuity and scholarly disputation, he lacks a sense for real *pilpul.* As you know, it takes a very special kind of instruction to develop a taste for this sort of mental exercise. And though both you and I underwent this

1. *Pilpul* is the method of dialectical reasoning applied to the study of the Oral Law. But the context in which the term *baal pilpul* is used here suggests something like "past master of hairsplitting."

training, [you will recall that] we agreed Joseph's mind should rather remain a little duller than be sharpened in so sterile a manner.

Well, the distaste he felt for his teacher's instruction has made him reject all Hebrew studies. He is, however, making good progress in the natural sciences. He penetrates deeply into his subject matter, and though he looks intently and searchingly at everything, he never jumps to conclusions—which such a young firebrand might well be expected to do.

We have not yet come to any decision concerning his future, and I am still not sure how best to counsel him. His talents and gifts for the natural sciences would lead one to expect him to excel in this field. As a Jew, however, he can only practice medicine, for which he has neither the liking nor the aptitude. And it is, I think, still too early to groom him for a business career. Right now, it might therefore be best to let him study whatever he wants or feels inclined to. This would, to say the least, not be detrimental to him if he were indeed to become a businessman. Or he could, if need be, do what his father had to do: muddle through, now as a scholar, now as a businessman—though this carries with it the danger that one ends up not being really either. . . .

[*To Elise Reimarus, daughter of the Deist scholar Hermann Samuel Reimarus, one of Mendelssohn's frequent correspondents*]

October 4, 1785

. . . I deeply regret that I must withdraw my son [Joseph] from his scientific studies in order to turn him into a slave of Mammon. He has no wish to enter the field of medicine; and as a Jew all that he can become is a doctor, a businessman—or a beggar. . . .

FRIENDSHIP WITH LESSING

[To Karl Gotthelf Lessing, younger brother of Gotthold Ephraim Lessing, about whose death Mendelssohn is here writing.]

February 1781

Do not let us say another word, my friend, about our loss and the grievous blow sustained by our hearts. The memory of the man we lost is too sacred to me to be profaned by any lamentations. Indeed, his memory now appears to me in a light that spreads tranquillity and a restorative serenity over everything. I no longer dwell on what I have lost by his passing. With a grateful heart I thank Providence for the blessing she bestowed upon me by introducing me so early in my youth to a man who has molded my very soul. I used to think of him as both my friend and judge before embarking upon any course of action, or before writing a single line; and I shall continue to think of him as my friend and judge whenever I shall have to undertake anything of import.

If, nevertheless, these reflections are somewhat tinged by melancholy, it is because of my regret that I did not make the most of his guidance; that I did not avidly enough seize every opportunity to learn from him; that I let slip by many an hour I could have spent talking with him. His conversation was, alas, a rich source of new ideas about the good and the beautiful, flowing from him with such effervescence and yet—much like ordinary water—for the use of all. The generosity with which he shared his insights would, on occasion, almost keep me from recognizing their great value. Moreover, he seemed to arrive at them without any effort. And once in a while he would intermingle his ideas and mine so imperceptibly that I myself could no longer tell them apart. His generosity was not of the sort practiced by some rich men who let the object of their charity know that they are giving him alms. On the contrary: he provided the spur for one's own best efforts, and thus made one deserving of his gifts.

Taking everything into consideration, my dear friend, your brother passed away at the right time. And by that I mean not merely the right time within some cosmic plan. For there, nothing really happens at the wrong time. When I say "right time" I am speaking of our own narrow sphere which measures, as it were, barely an inch. Fontenelle says of Copernicus, "He proclaimed his new [solar-centric] system, and died." Your brother's biographer will be equally justified in saying, "He wrote *Nathan the Wise,* and died." I cannot conceive of any creation of the human spirit that might be as superior to *Nathan* as this play is, at least in my opinion, to anything your brother has ever written. He could not have ascended to greater heights without entering a region utterly hidden to our mortal eyes. And this is what he has done. As for us, we are left standing here like those disciples who stare with amazement at the place from which the prophet ascended—and disappeared.

Only a few weeks before his passing I had occasion to write him that he should not be surprised if the majority of his contemporaries were unable to appreciate the value of this work of his, and that even a more refined posterity would need a long time to chew on the substance of his play and digest it fully. For he was truly more than a generation ahead of his time. . . .

[*To Professor Karl Wilhelm Rambler, a writer who was a friend of both Mendelssohn and Lessing. This excerpt is from a letter accompanying Mendelssohn's translation of the Psalms.*]

When I am at work writing, it is my wont to imagine I shall be read by a friend whom I should particularly like to please. In philosophical matters this has always been and will continue to be our mutual friend Lessing—as long, that is, as I'll be able to draw breath and strive for his approval and encouragement. For me, he will never be dead. He will be forever present in my mind, though the zeal with which he pursued the right to free inquiry has destroyed him much too soon. And I shall continue to ask myself, whenever I write a single line about a philosophical subject: would Lessing have approved?

COUNSELING IN MATTERS OF FAITH

*[To Paulus Best, a University of Cologne medical student who
had turned to Mendelssohn "in matters of conscience"]*

April 24, 1773

Sir:

I must confess that I find the contents of your letter of March 13
more than a little amazing. What in the world motivates you, re-
siding in Cologne, to turn to me of all people, questioning me in
matters of conscience? There are enough excellent men in your
own church who lack neither the wisdom nor the sincerity to show
you the way to truth and moral conduct. Moreover, there are
enough books available which deal forthrightly with these matters.
Anyone eager to learn can find much more enlightenment and
information in these writings than can be given in a letter. Nor
is there, as far as I know, any prohibition in your part of the
country against the dissemination of such books. You may, therefore, read and examine for yourself anything the sages of all nations have thought and written about these subjects.

My own contribution to the great assemblage will have to remain
most insignificant indeed. Nevertheless, since your motives are
obviously sincere, I shall answer you equally sincerely and tell
you briefly what I think about these questions. Your own thinking
as well as the reading of books that deal with these problems in
depth will then have to do the rest.

I believe that any individual must follow his own convictions,
and that he may feel wholly certain thereby not to displease his
Creator. Yet I would caution him to make the most conscientious
use of his God-given mental powers in examining the genuineness
and inner consistency of these convictions. Once we have scruti-
nized our own conscience to the best of our ability, however, we
need neither reproach ourselves nor expect to be reproached by
our Judge even if, in the end, our beliefs should turn out to be
erroneous.

We must, however, not permit mere difficulties or doubts to influence our practical conduct. As long as we do not feel completely sure in our thinking, we must, in matters of observance, hold on to the tradition in which we were raised and which was handed down to us by men worthy of our respect. We must not dare to introduce even the smallest innovation or change until we can be certain that we stand firmly on solid ground.

This is our duty with regard to our personal search for truth. With regard to others—that is, to what extent we are duty-bound to proclaim to them the truth as we see it—our obligation is narrowly limited. But I cannot discuss these limitations here, nor do they really matter in this context.

It seems certain to me, though, that one can indeed speak of eternal verities. But while I can be so completely convinced of those that I let them regulate my observances and conduct, I need not feel at all obligated to proclaim them to or impose them upon others. In fact, I may occasionally even be duty-bound not to discuss them with others at all. . . .

QUESTIONS OF CONSCIENCE

[To Sophie Becker, daughter and sister of Protestant ministers who were his friends. A few days before his death Mendelssohn replied to a Christmas Eve letter she had sent him, confiding to him her conflicting religious emotions and particularly her recent inability to pray.]

December 27, 1785

Dearest Sophie:

It has always been my motto not to forgo any of the delights I can find in philosophical speculation. No frigid "reasonableness" shall therefore keep me now from enjoying these innocent pleasures. Having added to my life a dimension of happiness it would otherwise have lacked, philosophy will simply have to continue to fulfill this function for me.

Actually, I am looking among the existing philosophical systems for the one most apt to make me both a happier and better man. A philosophy that would attempt to make me disgruntled, indifferent toward others or myself, or insensitive to the beautiful and the good is not for me.

As for the popular religious notions and practices [you mentioned in your letter]—I suppose the pleasant emotions they evoke are largely due to some fundamental truth that gave rise to these concepts and observances in the first place, though later on this truth may have become obscured by inauthentic accretions. . . . Consequently, I myself hold on to these popular notions until my own intellect is capable of replacing them or the pleasant emotions they engender with something else [that would be of superior value].

I enjoy any ritual unless it proves conducive to intolerance or discrimination against my fellow men. In fact, I derive as much pleasure as do my children from any practice or ceremony that symbolizes something true or good. Wherever possible, I try to slough off what seems hypocritical to me; but I will not give up any religious observance unless I can conceive of something better to supersede its [proven] beneficial effect.

If you, dearest Sophie, mustered enough patience to read my *Morgenstunden*,[1] you will have noticed a passage dealing with the difficult concept of a God who is both exalted above all, yet compassionately inclined toward all; and you will remember, too, that I ascribe much of the credit for recognizing this [paradoxical] truth and its significance to our Lessing. I feel these reflections of ours might be helpful to you in your present predicament. Given a heart and mind like yours, you should not find it particularly hard to comprehend their full meaning and implications, and you may derive from them genuine solace and inner reassurance.

You say the philosopher does not pray; or that at least he does not pray out loud, in words or song but, if at all, merely in silent

1. "Morning Hours," a compilation of Mendelssohn's discourses on the existence of God and similar questions, held during the morning hours when he discussed metaphysics with his son Joseph and Joseph's friends the Humboldt brothers.

meditation. Dearest Sophie: once his hour has come and he is in the mood for prayer, he will break into words and song, whether he wants to or not. Not even the simplest man, I think, sings so that God may hear and take pleasure in his melodies. We sing for our own benefit—savant and fool alike.

Did you ever read the Psalms with this in mind? I believe many of them are composed in such a way that even the most enlightened man ought to chant them with a sense of genuine edification. If it didn't betray an author's vanity, I should like to recommend to you once more my own translation.[2] Believe me, they have made many a bitter hour sweeter for me; and I prayerfully chant them as often as I feel the need. . . .

MAJESTY VERSUS EXCELLENCY
[*To Herz Homberg*]

Berlin, November 20, 1784

Dearest friend:

Exceptional men rarely do what everybody expects them to do; this is what makes them exceptional. His Majesty's decision in your affair [1] is therefore quite within the norm. And though we surely feel bad about every aspect of it, we should have felt worse had His Majesty approved of your appointment and philosophy rejected you as incompetent. As you know, I suffered a similar fate. The Academy [2] elected me to its membership, but His Royal Majesty [Frederick II (the Great) King of Prussia (1712–1786)] did not confirm this choice. Why? I never knew; I knew just as little as you now know why the Emperor does not want you as an

2. See page 104.
1. Emperor Joseph II (1740–1790) had refused to confirm Homberg's appointment to a teaching position at Prague University.
2. *Preussische Akademie der Wissenschaften* (Prussian Academy of Sciences) which, in 1763, had awarded Mendelssohn a prize for an essay on an epistemological problem. One of Mendelssohn's competitors was Immanuel Kant. See page 62.

academic instructor [*Korrepetitor*]. Religious hatred can hardly be the reason.

Yet even the mightiest and most powerful shall not make us give up! There must arise among us more and more who will excel without making much noise, who will demonstrate their accomplishments without making loud claims. Let, then, His Excellency only feel sufficiently benevolent to acknowledge our merits, and we shall yet see majesty give way to excellency.

Kindly remember me to the admirable men who have stood by you, and assure them of my most sincere respect. I shall be glad to have my son continue his scientific studies as long as he can hope to earn the approval of such men. What matter, then, if positions of honor are denied us by the high authorities, and if Joseph Mendelssohn will attain no higher station in life than Moses Mendelssohn, his father, and Herz Homberg, his teacher and friend, ever have been or will be able to attain.

EPIGRAMS

Europeans kill each other so as to gain dominion over the Ohio River, while no American has ever coveted the River Spree.[1] Yet we call Americans uncivilized. What I should like to hear now is an American teacher of morals speaking about arrogance.

Do the princes of this world really have such a quarrel with truth that a philosopher must consider himself already renowned when they do not regard him a useless creature?

O tempora, O mores! To kill people is a sure way to glory; to sire children, a way to shame!

Faith and philosophy are scorned by the great world, yet the prejudices to which they give rise are carefully perpetuated. De-

1. Berlin is situated on the banks of the Spree.

spite a general show of indifference concerning intellectual specu-lation, one still denies all comforts of life to a sizable segment of mankind simply because they refuse to share our own convictions in matters of faith or some tenet of metaphysics.

PART TWO

His People's Defender and Mentor

Editor's Note

Moses Mendelssohn's contemporary admirers, wishing to pay tribute to his spiritual and intellectual stature, said of him what had been said some six hundred years earlier of Moses ben Maimon: [1] "From Moses to Moses there was no one like Moses."

This was a fond exaggeration. Mendelssohn was neither prophet nor lawgiver, nor did he physically lead his people from slavery unto freedom. Yet he did in a very real sense contribute to paving their way from their latter-day Egypt to what must have seemed to them the promised land—Western Europe's open, or at least gradually opening, society.

Though his early ghetto experience had left him not only with a frail, misshapen body but with severe psychological inhibitions and a diffident manner, he forced himself to overcome his inbred timidity whenever his suffering brothers needed him, speaking out on their behalf with courage and dignity. And though he shrank from all public exposure (being so painfully aware of his lack of

1. Known also as Maimonides or Rambam, an acronym for Rabbi Moses ben Maimon (1135–1204); religious philosopher and codifier (as well as court physician in Egypt). Major works: *Mishneh Torah* (a codification of Jewish Law) and *Moreh Nevukhim* (Guide for the Perplexed).

sophistication that he even declined invitations from well-meaning Christians to participate in projects designed to improve the Jews' lot), he did, when the occasion arose, willingly petition any Gentile personage of whose benevolence toward Jews and whose influence in higher places he could be reasonably sure.

More significant, he performed a self-assigned, sociohistorical task: through his personal conduct, wide correspondence, and numerous publications, he served as an exemplar to Jew and Gentile alike. By conveying to them the ideals informing his own heart and mind, he guided them on their climb from the last vestiges of the Dark Ages into modernity.

In addition to his efforts to further the civil and cultural advancement of his Jewish contemporaries, he served as their teacher and arbiter in religious matters. Carefully wording his responses to inquiries about Jewish law and ritual addressed to him by institutions and individuals, he tried to do justice not only to the letter and spirit of the law, but also to the psyche of the inquirer.

Moreover, Mendelssohn rendered a special service to those of his fellow Jews who no longer understood Hebrew. He enabled them to become reacquainted with, and develop a new appreciation of, their religious heritage by providing them with a German translation of the Book of Psalms (to be followed by a translation of the Pentateuch). His translation, he hoped, would also help his "coreligionists" to improve their command of German and subsequently refine their speech and manners. The linguistic sensibilities of Mendelssohn, the writer and translator, were offended by the *Judendeutsch* [2] spoken by the majority of Germany's Jews. He pleaded with them repeatedly to abandon the mixture of German and Hebrew—which he considered a jargon garbling both languages and devoid of the beauties of either—not merely on grounds of aesthetics, but because he felt certain its continued use would be detrimental to their social progress and acculturation.

2. "Jews' German" or Judeo-German, related to the Yiddish spoken by East European Jews.

INTERCESSION ON BEHALF OF SWISS JEWS
[*To Johann Caspar Lavater* [1]]

Berlin, April 14, 1775

Revered friend of all mankind:

Never having ceased to place my fullest trust in your humanitarianism, I feel I can turn to you, my dearest friend, in a matter that concerns me personally because it involves my coreligionists —a matter, however, that must concern you, too, because it involves human beings. Specifically, it is a problem besetting the few Jews who live in Lengly and Endingen on sufferance of the Swiss government. Though I am not familiar with the particular circumstances of these people or the conditions under which they were granted the right to reside there, I can more or less imagine their sorry state of subsistence. For since I am only too well aware of the general hostility against my people, who almost everywhere are regarded as aliens on God's earth, I can picture their special situation in your country.

I am told that the Swiss authorities are about to impose still more restrictions upon these Jews. Among the oppressive measures under consideration is the prohibition to carry out the Creator's first commandment to a man, namely to be fruitful and multiply. The good people there—among whom several are known to me as men of excellent reputation, particularly their rabbi—tell me that you, revered friend of humanity, might be able to bring your influence to bear upon your fellow citizens in Zurich, and that this might substantially affect the existence and welfare of the Jews in Switzerland. Having learned of our publicly proclaimed friendship, they now ask me to be their spokesman and intercede with you on their behalf.

How I wish I could assure my brethren that their assumptions about both your influence on your fellow citizens and our friendly relationship are not mistaken. Let me implore you, revered hu-

---

1. Protestant clergyman of Zurich. See pages 17–18 and 132.

manitarian, to espouse the cause of these hard-pressed human beings by using both your reputation and power of persuasion in an attempt to retain for them at least those rights which they have enjoyed so far. Such an action would be worthy of you, hence carry its own reward. Moreover, it would also deeply obligate and elicit the undying gratitude of

your ever abiding friend and admirer
MOSES MENDELSSOHN

PETITION TO STAY THE DEPORTATION OF JEWS FROM DRESDEN

[To Geheimer Kammerrat (roughly: Privy Councilor) Baron Friedrich Wilhelm von Ferber, a high official in Dresden]

Hannover, November 19, 1777

In a state of profound distress and anxiety, yet also with a sense of childlike trust, I dare to turn imploringly to you, the great-hearted humanitarian, to ask your gracious assistance in a most grievous matter. The latest post, sir, brought me the news that many hundreds of my brethren in Dresden are threatened with deportation. Among them are quite a few who are personally known to me and of whose integrity I am convinced. True, they have lost their fortunes, so that they probably cannot pay the taxes levied against them. Yet I feel sure they have fallen upon hard times through no fault of their own, and that their present insolvency is due not to squandering or any lack of industry on their part but solely to unpropitious circumstances. Kind and benevolent father, where can those miserable wretches go with their innocent wives and children? Where can they find protection and shelter if the country where they lost their fortune expels them?

Expulsion constitutes the worst punishment for a Jew. It means not only being driven out of this or that country. It means, as it were, to be wiped off the face of God's earth. For there is no country whose borders are not barred against him by the iron-clad hand of prejudice.

80

And this harshest of punishments is to be endured by human beings not because they are guilty of some transgression but simply because they cling to their distinct religious beliefs and have the misfortune to have lost their money. How, then, can one expect integrity from an Israelite who is being penalized as severely for being poor as he would be for being fraudulent?

No, I shall not continue, for fear of inflicting too much pain upon your sympathetic heart. Moreover, I feel there is still some hope, a hope as well founded as it is comforting to me in my deep apprehension. For it is just not possible that under the reign of the best, the most charitable prince and under the administration of wise and sympathetic men such punishment could be meted out to people who have committed no crime. Nor can I believe that the guiltless and poverty-stricken—regardless of their appearance or religious beliefs and practices—will be denied the fire of a hearth, or water and shelter.

Forgive me, o most revered guardian of innocence, if this letter is not written in the proper manner. But with a heart so full and a mind so troubled, I find myself incapable of cogency or composure. Nonetheless, I am fully aware of the great respect and high regard

> owed you
> by your
> etc.

RELUCTANCE TO PARTICIPATE IN CIVIC AFFAIRS AND POLITICAL PROJECTS

[*To Isaak Iselin (1728–1762), a Swiss representative of the philosophy of Enlightenment. Iselin had invited Mendelssohn to become a member of the* Patriotische Gesellschaft (*Patriotic Society), whose goal was the promotion of man's happiness through the perfection of society at large.*]

Berlin, May 30, 1762

. . . Frankly, my most esteemed friend, I am afraid you greatly overrate my talents. You seem to consider me competent to col-

81

laborate with you in a field of endeavor that you, in conjunction with the Patriotic Society, intend to cultivate. I, however, have every reason to mistrust my abilities in this particular area. The influence of a man's origin, upbringing, and entire way of life on his mental outlook becomes nowhere more evident than in this noble subdivision of philosophy. The fortunate citizen of a republic looks upon human society from a much higher vantage point than the subject in a monarchy. Yet even such a subject occupies a position in civil life superior by far to that assigned to me. True, under the rule of a Frederick,[1] freedom of thought flourishes almost as beautifully as in a republic. Yet you know how little accustomed my coreligionists are to any participation in the pursuit of civil liberties. The life of civil oppression to which we have been condemned by an invidious, long-festering prejudice paralyzes the wings of our spirit with its dead weight, rendering us incapable of even attempting the high-soaring flight of those who were born free. I know myself well enough to realize my own weakness in this respect, and I have too high a regard for the Patriotic Society not to admit my shortcomings.

Moreover, my daily routine leaves me but a few hours' leisure to study my favorite subject, omnipresent at our schools here: metaphysics. And to avoid intellectual dryness, my mind indulges in frequent excursions along the graceful pathways of belles-lettres, which actually have a closer connection with speculative philosophy than is generally assumed. But inasmuch as belles-lettres exert only a very indirect influence on the body politic, I almost despair of my ability ever to make a useful contribution to its affairs. . . .[2]

[From Mendelssohn's Preface to the German translation of Vindiciae Judaeorum. *See page 13.]*

. . . I am too far removed from the Cabinets of the great [rulers] and everything that might exert any influence upon them to be able to participate to even a small degree in this grand under-

1. Frederick II (the Great), King of Prussia (1712–1786).
2. After some additional correspondence Mendelssohn did, however, accept (in a letter dated August 27, 1762) Iselin's invitation.

82

taking.[3] I live in a state whose ruler, one of the wisest ever, has made the arts and sciences flourish and has so widely expanded man's freedom of thought (which is grounded in his reason) that the effect of this expansion extends to the lowliest of the state's inhabitants. Under this ruler's glorious scepter I have found both the motivation and opportunity to educate myself, to think about my brethren's and my own destiny, and to engage to the best of my ability in reflections concerning the nature of man, fate, and Providence. Still, I have never had any social contact with the great. Having always lived in obscurity, I never felt the drive or inclination to participate in the affairs of this busy world. My entire social life has always been restricted to the circle of a few close friends who pursue paths similar to my own. And now I am still standing in my distant, dark corner, waiting with childlike longing for whatever decision an all-wise and all-good Providence will make in all these matters.

[To "a man of high standing" who, shrouded in secrecy, had sent an anonymous and no longer extant letter to Mendelssohn with a plan for a Jewish state]

Berlin, January 26, 1770

I must confess that I know no more about the political constitutions of governments than what I have been able to learn in my day-to-day dealings with people whose station in life is not much above my own. How, then, can I judge the merits of a project which is predicated on a profound understanding of [political] statistics?

Taken as a whole, your idea indicates a grand design; it must have originated in a mind conscious of its own prowess. The author's zeal for tolerance, his abhorrence of a hierarchical system, his views on religion and ethics prove that he is used to formulating

3. Gotthold Ephraim Lessing and War Councilor Christian Wilhelm von Dohm (see pages 12 and 85) were, in their respective ways, engaged in working for the civil improvement of the Jews and their eventual emancipation.

concepts of both wisdom and magnitude. And the very confidence with which he speaks of so bold an undertaking instills in me an uncommonly high regard for his character.

Whatever intellectual boldness I myself may possess extends, however, to matters of philosophical speculation alone. For my experience in practical matters has always been confined to so narrow a sphere that I never learned to cope with really large issues, or look beyond ordinary problems. And who can stand taller than he is?

My people's character, as I see it, therefore constitutes the greatest obstacle in carrying out your project. We have not been sufficiently prepared to undertake anything of such magnitude. The oppression under which we have lived for so many centuries has drained our spirit of all its vigor. And while this is something for which we are not to blame, we cannot deny that our natural desire for freedom is by now totally inert. It has been transformed into a monkish virtue which manifests itself in praying and passive suffering rather than in action. Moreover, I cannot even expect my widely dispersed people to have that spirit of unity without which any plan for their future, no matter how well thought through, must founder.

There is still another aspect to be considered: it seems to me that such a venture would require vast sums of money. Yet I know that my people's wealth consists more in credit extended than in actual capital. I therefore doubt their ability to raise such sums, no matter how much their desire for freedom or how little their love of the glittering metal may hold sway over them.

But apart from all these difficulties, I should think such a project could be realized only if all the great European powers were engaged in a war so that each of them would be preoccupied with its own affairs. In the present quiet situation, a single jealous government (and there would be more than one) could frustrate your plans. My concerns in this respect would seem more than justified by the unfortunate experiences of the Crusades.

I therefore return herewith the papers entrusted to me, along with my solemn promise of eternal silence [with regard to their contents]. And I also promise to suppress my desire (which is only natural and might, under different circumstances, even be considered praiseworthy) to make the acquaintance of a person who commands my sincere respect.

NOT EVEN A SINGLE STEP

[At Mendelssohn's suggestion, Christian Wilhelm von Dohm (1751–1820), a high official in the Berlin War Office, had written a memorandum in 1781, called "On the Civil Improvement of the Jews," an essay of great importance for the eventual emancipation of the Jews. However, Johann David Michaelis (1717–1791) of Göttingen, a theologian and cofounder of German historico-critical Bible exegesis, gave the work a negative review. The following is an excerpt from Mendelssohn's reply.]

Our hoped-for return to Palestine, a concept so troublesome to Mr. M. [Michaelis], has no bearing whatever on our attitude to the government. This has been proved by experience, at all times and in all places where Jews have enjoyed a measure of tolerance. It is simply man's nature to love the land where he fares well. Even the religious dreamer, whose pronouncements would seem to express different emotions, saves his religious enthusiasm for ecclesiastical occasions with their prescribed ceremonial prayers, but otherwise does not give the matter any thought. Moreover, our Talmudic sages had the foresight to emphasize again and again the prohibition to return to Palestine on our own. They made it unmistakably clear that we must not take even a single step preparatory to a return to Palestine, and a subsequent restoration of our nation there, unless and until the great miracles and extraordinary signs promised us in Scripture were to occur. And they substantiated that prohibition by citing the somewhat mystical yet truly captivating verses of the Song of Songs (2:7; 3:5):

> *I adjure you, O daughters of Jerusalem,*
> *By the gazelles, and by the hinds of the field,*
> *That ye awaken not, nor stir up love,*
> *Until it please.*

Therefore all attempts by such project-makers as Langallerie [1] and his likes to get at the purse of rich Jews have so far utterly failed, despite their own claims to the contrary.

A MODEL SOCIETY IN GERMANY?

[To Baron von Monster, a member of the German nobility, who lived in Rathenow, Brandenburg, and who had written to Mendelssohn on February 15, 1785, asking his advice concerning a "city state" which Monster meant to establish on a tract of land on the banks of a German river. The settlement, to consist of an equal number of Jewish and Christian families, was to represent a model society, with full civil rights for all. The project, however, was to be kept strictly confidential.]

Berlin, February 21, 1775

Your Highness:

I am most obliged to your Excellency for the trust you place in me. To be truly worthy of your confidence I must, however, ask your permission to entrust your grandiose idea to a group of enlightened friends whose knowledge of worldly affairs I trust more than my own, and for whose discretion I can vouch. I much enjoyed reading your plans; yet there remain in my mind many unanswered questions, a fact I ascribe exclusively to my inexperience in matters of this kind.

I am at a loss to explain, for example, (1) why Your Excellency insists on keeping the project secret; what could you possibly have to fear by making it public? (2) how the system of civil liberty you wish to establish could be maintained by that handful of people without outside support or connection; (3) why you insist on a predetermined number of Christians and Jews; and, (4) why you feel you must enter into certain contracts with them.

1. In 1717, Langallerie (1656–1717) had proposed a plan for the establishment of a Jewish state, and apparently had tried to solicit funds for such a venture.

If I were to counsel you according to my own understanding of your project, I should certainly advise you to go ahead. You ought to make your plans public, however, and announce the conditions under which you would be prepared to admit to your small state—as a citizen entitled to share equally in all public benefits—any man of good standing, regardless of his beliefs or lack of them.

I assume that you have secured the approval of the king and his realm, and that you can guarantee that you have nothing to fear from any neighboring government. If so, enough persons would surely be found who would fling themselves into your arms and gladly accept all your conditions. I should think the required number of people would soon enough arrive from Holland alone. They could then either be settled in such a way that the city you envisage would develop gradually and naturally, or they might combine their efforts and immediately start building such a city, though I cannot quite see why your Excellency insists so absolutely on the latter course of action.

Should you, however, wish to save yourself the trouble of answering these and similar questions, I would again ask your permission to discuss the matter with my friends. Your Excellency need not fear that this might prove in any way disadvantageous. On the contrary, it might well result in better advice and produce more valuable assistance than can be offered by

your obedient servant
MOSES MENDELSSOHN

SUITABILITY OF JEWS FOR MILITARY SERVICE
[From Mendelssohn's reply to Michaelis's negative review of Dohm's "On the Civil Emancipation of the Jews." See page 85.]

I rather doubt the validity of Mr. Michaelis's statement that we are unsuited for military service. If he meant to say religion as such should sanction wars of aggression, I should like him to name that wretched religious system which would actually do so. Certainly not Christianity. Moreover, are Quakers and Mennonites not tolerated, and tolerated with rights and privileges greater by far than our own?

Instead of speaking of "Christians" and "Jews," Mr. Michaelis constantly uses the terms "Germans" and "Jews." He apparently does not regard the difference between us as limited to matters of religious conviction alone. Instead, he wants us to be considered aliens who have to accept whatever living conditions the landowners deign to grant us. But this is precisely the first question: would the landowners not be better off to admit as citizens those they now merely tolerate, rather than draw—and at great cost—additional aliens into their country? And I should also like to see another question discussed: how long, for how many millennia, must this situation of landowner on the one hand and alien on the other continue to exist? Would it not be best for mankind and civilization if this distinction were gradually to be forgotten?

I also think public law should not have to make special allowances for personal convictions. Prescribing whatever is best for the common weal, it should undauntedly pursue its own path. Actually, it is up to the individual to deal with any problem that might arise from a collision of his personal convictions with public law.

Any man called to the defense of his country should hasten to comply. In such cases, people usually know quite well how to modify or adjust their convictions so as to make them compatible with their civic duty. To call a possible conflict between the two to their attention is quite unnecessary. This problem will have taken care of itself within a few centuries, or be forgotten. By this method, Christians, regardless of their original teacher's doctrine, became world-conquerors, oppressors, and slave traders. And by this method Jews, too, can be made suitable for military service.

UNJUST REPROACHES

[Rabbi Manasseh ben Israel (c. 1604–1657) of Amsterdam corresponded with Oliver Cromwell and then went to England in an attempt to gain the Jews' readmission into that country. To substantiate his arguments, he wrote Vindiciae Judaeorum *(Vindication of the Jews), which represents a refutation of the British clergy's objection to such a readmission. The following is from Mendelssohn's Preface to the German translation of Manasseh's work.]*

It is strange to observe what different garb prejudice puts on throughout the ages in order to oppress us, and to raise objections to our admission as citizens [to any given country]. At a time when superstition was rampant, we were accused of wantonly desecrating holy places; of piercing crucifixes and making them bleed; of feasting our eyes on children we had first circumcised by stealth and then torn apart; of using the blood of Christians for our Passover celebrations; of poisoning public wells, etc. We were declared guilty of heresy and obduracy and were said to practice occult arts and black magic. For all that, we were tortured, robbed of our fortunes, driven into exile, and even put to death.

Now that times have changed, these calumnies no longer have the desired effect. Now we are being reproached for our superstition and backwardness, our lack of moral sensitivity, discriminating taste, and refinement. We are judged incapable of pursuing the arts and sciences or plying a useful trade. Above all, we are rejected as unsuited to serve in the army or hold government offices, owing to our imputedly uncontrollable penchant for cheating, usury, and lawlessness. These more recent charges have now taken the place of those earlier and cruder accusations as justification for our exclusion from the ranks of useful citizens and our expulsion from the womb of the state.

Formerly, every conceivable effort was made and all sorts of measures were taken to make us not into useful citizens but into Christians. But the fact that we were too stiff-necked and obdurate to let ourselves be converted was reason enough to regard us as superfluous ballast on this earth, and to attribute to us, depraved monsters that we are, any abomination that might expose us to the hatred and contempt of all mankind.

Now that this zeal to convert us has abated, we are being treated with utter superciliousness. People continue to keep us away from every contact with the arts and sciences or from engaging in useful trades and occupations. They bar all roads leading to increased usefulness and then use our lack of culture to justify our continued oppression. They tie our hands and then reproach us for not using them.

PRODUCERS AND CONSUMERS
[From Mendelssohns' Preface to the German translation of Vindiciae Judaeorum]

Several recent publications repeat the assertion that Jews are unproductive [members of society]: being neither farmers nor artisans nor craftsmen, they do not assist nature in bringing forth her own products, nor do they transform these products into something else. They merely transfer the country's raw and finished products from one place to another, and thus are mere consumers who must become a burden to the producers. In fact, even an author known for his keen and usually discerning mind [Jean-Jacques Rousseau (1712–1778)] has lately complained loudly that the producer has to take care of too many middlemen, hence feed too many good-for-nothing mouths. Common sense, he argues, should tell us that the cost of natural as well as man-made products rises in proportion to the number of middlemen who, though contributing nothing to the production of these goods, wish to reap the benefit of their consumption. He therefore offers some well-meaning advice to all governments, admonishing them either not to tolerate Jews in their territories at all or else to permit them to cultivate the land and learn craftsmen's skills.

The author's arguments may be well intended, but they are weak and by no means as convincing or irrefutable as he seems to think. What, actually, does he mean when he speaks of producers and consumers? If only the man who helps to create something that can be touched and seen, or the man who improves such an object by manual labor is to be called a producer, then the most significant if not largest segment of the population consists of mere consumers. According to this principle, neither the teaching nor the military professions could be said to produce anything at all, with the possible exception of the books written by members of the former.

By the same token, one would also have to discount all distributors of food, be they merchants, freight carriers, or any others employed in transporting goods by land or water. In the final analysis, this would leave mostly farm laborers and journeymen in the class of so-called producers, for it is the rare landowner or master of a trade who still works with his own hands. Except for this respectable but small group, the state would then be comprised largely of people who neither cultivate the land themselves nor improve its natural products by the work of their own hands. Most of the population would be nothing but consumers; and among them—worse yet!—would be all those useless mouths the producers would be forced to feed.

All this strikes us as nonsensical; and insofar as our conclusion is correct the fault must lie with the author's presupposition. And this is precisely it. For to produce is not just to make, but also to do. Not only the individual working with his hands deserves to be called a producer but also the man doing anything that directly or indirectly contributes to the welfare or happiness of his fellow man. In fact, the less you see the extremities of such a person in motion, the more he might deserve to be called a producer!

Many a merchant engaged at his desk in speculation or planning in his easy chair some new project is actually more productive than the laborer or draftsman, though those may be making a bigger noise. The soldier, too, is a producer, creating the preconditions for the country's calm and security. So is the scholar; though he seldom creates anything of material value, his work produces something that is of at least equal worth: good counsel, information, and pleasurable diversion. Only a fit of ill humor could have caused a wise man such as Rousseau to express the notion that a biscuit-baker in Paris is more productive than the Academy of Sciences. The well-being of both the state and the individual is contingent on a variety of material and nonmaterial things, physical and spiritual goods. And whoever contributes to the production or enhancement of these goods in any way, directly or indirectly, cannot be called merely a consumer; far from being a parasite, he has worked for the bread he eats.

ARE ANY MEMBERS OF SOCIETY EXPENDABLE?
[From Mendelssohn's Preface to the German translation of Vindiciae Judaeorum]

All in all, how can one speak of people who are of no use to the state, of no practical value to a country! This kind of language seems to me unworthy of a statesman. True, men can be more or less useful [to society]; being engaged in this or that occupation, they can make a greater or lesser contribution to their fellow man's or their own happiness. But no state can without considerable damage regard as expendable even its lowliest and seemingly most useless inhabitant; and no wise government will consider a beggar a burden, or a cripple as wholly useless.

AN OUTCRY AGAINST DEFAMATION

[The following letter from Mendelssohn to "a Jewish friend"
of his was quoted by Lessing in his reply of September 1754
to Michaelis's critique of Lessing's play The Jews.]

Sir:

I am enclosing issue number 70 of the *Göttingen Literary Gazette*. Read the Berlin article. Those learned gazetteers review chapter four of Lessing's writings, which you and I have so often enjoyed reading. And would you believe what they find wrong with the comedy *Die Juden?* [1] Its main character, who, as they put it, is much too noble and generous. The pleasure that the beauty of such a character gives us, they say, is vitiated by its improbability, so that all we are left with in the end is the wish for the actual existence of such an individual.

These remarks make me blush with shame. I am unable to express fully the emotions they invoke in me. What humiliation for our oppressed people! What utter derision! True, the ordinary Christian has always considered us nature's excrement and a sore on the body politic. But I should have expected a fairer judgment from educated men, if not that absolute truthfulness for the lack of which we are habitually berated. How mistaken have I been to assume that any Christian writer might have as much truthfulness himself as he demands of others! Honestly, how can a person with any sense of decency have the cheek to declare it unlikely that an entire people could produce even one single honorable man? A people, moreover, from whose midst—in the words of the author of *Die Juden*—arose all the prophets and the greatest of kings. If the reviewer's cruel judgment be justified, shame on humanity! But if it be unjustified, shame on him!

1. *The Jews,* written in 1749, was, as Howard Sachar points out in *The Course of Modern Jewish History* (p. 46), "the first creative literary effort in modern times—by a Christian—to portray a Jew in sympathetic terms, as a cultured individual of refined and elevated sensibilities."

Is it not enough that we must suffer the Christians' bitter hatred in so many cruel ways? Must one also slander to justify the injustice with which we are treated?

Let them continue to oppress us, to impose restrictions upon our existence in the midst of a free and fortunate citizenry, to expose us still more to the world's mockery and contempt—so long as no one attempts to gainsay our virtue, that singular consolation of hard-pressed souls, that sole sanctuary of the forsaken. . . .

Can this review, this cruel condemnation of our very soul, really have flowed from the pen of a theologian? These people think they promote the cause of Christianity by pronouncing all non-Christians murderers and thieves. I am far from holding a low opinion of the Christian religion. Yet I feel strongly that those who disregard all principles of humaneness in order to establish its truth are actually furnishing the most convincing proof against that truth. . . .

If you think about it, it would seem that certain virtues are more common among Jews than among most Christians. Consider the enormous revulsion Jews feel against murder. There is not one single incident showing that a Jew (with the exception of professional thieves [sic!]) ever committed a murder. And yet, how easily might the mere use of some profanity incite an otherwise decent Christian to take his fellow man's life! But it is the Jews who are said to be mean. Well, if meanness spares human blood, it is a virtue indeed!

Look what compassion Jews show to all people, and what generosity to the poor of both nations [Christians and Jews]. Yet most Christians' treatment of their poor deserves to be called harsh. Actually, the Jews let their virtues carry them almost too far. Their compassion makes them overly sensitive to the point of injudiciousness. And their generosity borders on extravagance. Still, if only those who tend to overdo things would overdo them in the right direction!

I could add much about their diligence, their admirable temperance, the sanctity of their marriages. But their social virtues alone suffice to prove the *Göttingen News* wrong. And I can only pity anyone who is able to read such a sweeping indictment without horror.

94

PHILANTHROPY: AN EXTRAORDINARY THING?

*[From an undated reply to a letter from Joachim Heinrich
Campe (1746–1818), director of the Philanthropin, a school
in Dessau for the sons of the rich as well as for the training of
teachers. This institution had been founded in 1774 by Johann
Bernard Basedow (1723–1790), an educator who, influenced
by Jean-Jacques Rousseau, introduced educational reforms
into the German school system. Basedow headed the
Philanthropin until 1778, when its direction was taken over
by Campe. At that time the school announced its willingness
to admit both Jewish pupils and teachers. When none applied,
Campe wrote to Mendelssohn, expressing with some irritation
his sense of frustration about the Jews' apparent lack of
appreciation for his institution's liberalism. Moreover, he
pointed out that the Philanthropin's benefactor, the Prince
of Dessau, would surely consider it an affront if the Jewish
community were not to recognize "his benevolence and noble
intent" and act upon it.]*

Assuming that everything is really the way you see it in your
somewhat timid endeavor for that good cause, and assuming (or
even taking for granted the fact) that not a single adherent of my
faith will avail himself of the Philanthropin's offer—so that many
an adherent of your faith will feel justified in breaking into guffaws
of derision—what are we to conclude? That you have every
reason to regret the step you have taken? Certainly not. Instead,
we must conclude that up to now neither Christians nor Jews
have enjoyed a truly "philanthropizing" [*philanthropinische*] education, and that mankind therefore needs so much the more an
institution dedicated to this idea.

You raise the question how the Prince, my most gracious
sovereign, will react to all this. To judge by my own impression
of his character, he will think it unlikely that the wiser among the
Jews are also the richest. Thus, he will continue to take a paternal

interest in those who are assuredly not rich but might possibly become wise by their exposure to that humanitarian movement. I consider it inconceivable that our ruler should henceforth regard the Philanthropin with less than [his customary] benevolence.

But, dear friend, was the step taken by the Philanthropin for my brethren's benefit really all that extraordinary and bold? Is it not inherent in the very concept of a philanthropical institution to welcome any individual as a human being worthy of an education, whether or not his father is circumcised? And have the founders and directors of this institution really been so utterly daring by declaring themselves in agreement with its basic orientation? Do they really fear they might have harmed if not destroyed the cause of philanthropically oriented education by their frank acknowledgment of its humanitarian principles? I must confess I fail to bring this more than Melanchthonian [1] pusillanimity in accord with your own and Basedow's principles.

I, for my part, consider the offer of the Philanthropin's directors worthy but in no way extraordinary. The admittance of Jewish pupils and students is a common occurrence at all German elementary and secondary schools. And as for those minor, merely pedantic discriminatory practices with regard to academic promotions and contests which are still in effect at some universities, no one takes them sufficiently seriously to have them formally abolished.

Your intention of accepting non-Christians as teachers is surely no more amazing than are the facts that the Royal Prussian Academy of Sciences elected a Jew to its membership; [2] that the Society of Amateur Nature Explorers here counts among its members first-rate scholars, Privy Councilors of the Treasury, and Jews; that Mendes d'Acosta [3] served as the Society's secretary in London a few years ago; and that even during the darkest periods [in Jewish history] chairs of Oriental languages, medicine, or astronomy were not infrequently held by the circumcised. At the

1. Philip Melanchthon (1497–1560), German humanist, reformer, and educator, who took a mediating position between Luther's and Calvin's theological views.
2. See page 72.
3. Emanuel Mendes d'Acosta (1704–1791), Jewish nature explorer.

beginning of this century, the Elector Palatine appointed Spinoza as a teacher of philosophy at his academy, fearing no damage to its reputation.

Consequently, I cannot see the slightest reason why your public declaration should prove detrimental to you in any way, or make anyone scorn you. What rational being can think that Basedow and you could be so ridiculously intolerant as to keep a skilled book-keeper from instructing your pupils in the art of bookkeeping merely because he feels he cannot accept the New Testament?

WISDOM'S HIGHEST GOAL
[*To Geheimer Kammerrat Friedrich Wilhelm von Ferber* [1]]

September 22, 1777

. . . With the noble use your Honor is making of your time and energy, you surely have scant reason to envy any mortal who can do no more than reflect upon the best use man might make of his time and energy. To do good is, doubtless, the pinnacle of wisdom. All philosophical speculation should lead to it. True, to reach that height one must have passed through the speculative stage. Yet if man stops there, he only half achieves the ultimate purpose of his existence; hence, he must be content with his lot to represent but a road sign and milestone on life's pilgrimage to happiness. Blessed is he upon whom Providence bestowed the will as well as the power to spread morality and brotherly love among men by his works and deeds, thereby counteracting all prejudice wherever it stands in the way of man's pursuit of happiness. He has a higher vocation than the man who can merely engage in contemplation and wishful thinking. . . .

1. See page 80.

RESTRICTIONS AND FRUSTRATIONS

*[To Brother Maurus Winkopp, a Benedectine who considered
Mendelssohn his father confessor]*

July 28, 1780

Your dear, cordial letter of April 24 has been lying here, right
before my eyes, ever since I received it. I have read it more than
three times, and have thought about it often. Yet it is only today,
almost the last day of July, that I pick a lovely morning hour to
answer your warm note. Shall I, indeed can I, make excuses?
Actually, all the things that usually serve as valid explanations in
such a situation really have come together in my case: illness,
travels, domestic distractions, and inescapable frustrations. All
these excuses, however, have been used and abused so often they
have lost all credibility. But what really begins to trouble me now
is the thought that my long silence may possibly have caused you
many an uneasy hour. You may have been afraid that your letter
fell into the wrong hands, or you may—oh, forgive me, dearest
Winkopp, if this should indeed be the case. Do forgive me. Your
trust has not been wasted on someone unworthy of it, though it
has probably been given to one who neglected to imagine what a
youthful, open soul must feel when its offering of frankness seems
to meet with cold indifference. Do forgive me, and tell me soon
that you now feel reassured, and that you continue to love me
despite my negligence.

How utterly different the relations like-minded men can establish
with one another are from those imposed on human beings by
their class, religion, sociopolitical conditions, habits, prejudices,
pride, or vanity! In a place where I cannot set foot without desecrating it (in the eyes of its inhabitants) lives a man who is my
brother in spirit. And here I am, in this so-called tolerant land,
leading a life so restricted, so narrowly circumscribed by real intolerance that I must, for the sake of my children, let a silk factory

imprison me all day long, much in the way in which you let yourself be confined by a monastery. Moreover, I may not dedicate myself to the muses as devoutly as I should like because my superior will not permit it.

Once in a while, I take an evening stroll with my wife and family. "Papa," one of my children asks innocently, "what is that fellow over there yelling after us? And why do these people throw stones at us? What have we done to them?" "Yes, Papa dear," another speaks up, "they always follow us in the street and call us names. They cry 'Jews, Jews!' Do they think it bad to be a Jew? Why else would they keep away from us?" Alas! Averting my eyes, I sigh to myself: "Man, oh, man, is this what you have finally accomplished?"

A PLEA FOR INTRAMURAL TOLERANCE

[In this excerpt from his Preface to Manasseh ben Israel's Vindiciae Judaeorum, *Mendelssohn admonishes the rabbis and elders of the Jewish communities to remain tolerant of their fellow Jews and not to abuse any privileges the state might grant them if they were finally given that measure of religious autonomy the Church already possessed—the right to expel dissidents.]*

You, my brethren, who have so long chafed under the oppressive yoke of intolerance, probably now feel you might derive a measure of satisfaction were you but given the power to press an equally heavy yoke upon your own subservient brothers. Revenge seeks an object, and, if it cannot find it anywhere else, will feed on its own flesh. In all likelihood, you were also misled by what you have always seen around you. For until recently, the nations of the earth seemed to harbor the delusion that religion can uphold its tenets only with an iron-clad fist; that the doctrines of salvation can be spread only by persecution and pronouncements of bans; and that a true concept of God—who is love itself, as all of us proclaim—can be taught only by methods of hate. You may have permitted yourselves to accept these false notions and thus have come to regard the right to persecute as the most desirable privilege your persecutors could grant you.

Give thanks to the God of your fathers, give thanks to that God who Himself is love and mercy, that this delusion seems to be on the wane. Nations are becoming more tolerant of each other. They are beginning to show you, too, a glimpse of that care and concern which, with the help of Him who guides the human heart, may grow into genuine brotherly love. Oh, my brethren, follow the example of love just as you used to follow that of hatred. Strive to emulate the virtues of the nations whose vices you used to feel compelled to imitate. If you wish to be shown concern, tolerance, and forebearance by others, show concern, tolerance, and forebearance to each other. Love—and you will be loved!

Berlin, March 19, 1782

ON TAKING AN OATH

[A circular, published in 1783 and directed to all government agencies and courts of justice, contained the following admonition—prepared "with the help of a Jewish scholar famous for his knowledge and integrity," namely, Moses Mendelssohn—to all Jews required to take a public oath.]

Any devout Israelite involved in a legal dispute is obligated to confess the truth to the authorities, be they Jewish or Christian, and, if requested, swear to that truth. An oath requested by the Christian authorities is therefore, in accordance with the teachings of our rabbis, not to be regarded as unlawful or coercive. Anyone deceiving the Christian authorities by swearing falsely, or by making mental reservations while swearing, thus profanes the name of God and commits perjury.

Perjury is the most heinous crime of which man can be guilty. The moral universe rests on righteousness, truth, and peace, as our rabbis say. Thus, unrighteousness and lies are highly punish-

100

able offenses in themselves, having a shattering effect on the moral universe. And in the case of perjury the offense is compounded by the sacrilege of calling on the God of truth to witness an untruth, or by [the pretense of] asking the God of righteousness to punish unrighteousness. To commit perjury is to abuse the name of the Most Holy by a shameful act. And it is for fear of such an abuse that the whole world trembled when the God of our fathers let the words be heard on Mount Sinai: "Thou shalt not take the name of the Lord thy God in vain" [Exodus 20:7].

While any other criminal can escape God's punishment by repentance and a change of his ways, the perjurer, even though he repent earnestly, cannot hope for forgiveness without making adequate amends. It is explicitly stated, "Thou shalt not abuse the name of the Eternal, your God, for an untruth" and "the Eternal, your God, shall not leave unpunished him who abuses His name for an untruth." [1]

In any other instance where a crime is committed, the punishment is meted out solely to the sinner, those who share his guilt, or those who could have prevented the evil deed. But where perjury is concerned, the criminal's entire family must suffer; in fact, the whole country where he lives suffers from the divine punishment following his crime. The perpetrator of any other crime is frequently forgiven because of the mercy of our long-suffering God. But a perjurer is punished immediately and without delay. As the prophet says, "I cause it [the curse] to go forth, saith the Lord of hosts, and it shall enter into the house of the thief, and into the house of him that sweareth falsely by My name; and it shall abide in the midst of his house, and shall consume it with the timber thereof, and the stones thereof" [Zechariah 4:12].

1. Exodus 20:7. The Jewish Publication Society's version is ". . . for the Lord will not hold him guiltless that taketh His name in vain."

ON BURIALS

[*A Response to a Question from the Jewish Community in Schwerin*]

Berlin, May 1772

I acknowledge the receipt of your kind letter of last month in which you tell me your sovereign ordered you to keep all dead bodies for three days before burying them. You seem to be worried and vexed by this edict and feel that your sovereign wants to force you to abandon the religion of your fathers, break a Mosaic law, or disregard a rabbinic injunction.

I confess I am at a loss to see why you feel so strongly about this issue, and why you intend to raise such objections to it. Though I realize that your rabbi is a Talmudic scholar in his own right and that he has sufficient contact with other scholars to arrive at a decision in this matter, I do not hesitate to give you my personal opinion. You may reprimand me if I am wrong. But, contrary to your own apprehensions, I do not think that compliance with the order of your authorities would constitute even the slightest violation of Jewish law.

True, our sages assert that any man who keeps a dead body overnight violates a negative law (a law asking that we refrain from doing something). These teachers of ours, however, do permit the keeping of bodies overnight if this is being done in honor of the deceased; if more time is needed to secure a coffin and shrouds, or hire wailing women to accompany the bier (an Oriental custom so alien to the spirit of Judaism it was abolished long ago); or if the deceased's relatives cannot be informed immediately, or the word cannot be spread quickly enough in great cities (see *Yoreh Deah* 357).[1] But if the keeping of bodies over-

---

1. *Yoreh Deah:* one of four parts of the *Shulḥan Arukh,* the standard code of Jewish law and practice, compiled by Joseph Karo and first published in 1565.

night was then permitted for such negligible reasons, how can one now insist on an immediate burial unless even the remotest chance of a reawakening or restoration to life has been ruled out completely?

If, nonetheless, our teachers omitted from their list of reasons for which it was permitted to delay a burial the need to take every precaution to avoid a fatal mistake, we need not be surprised. At that time, the danger of burying someone alive simply did not exist. All deceased were kept in subterranean vaults or caverns; there, they were watched over for three days, in order to see whether they might by chance still be alive and give signs of coming awake. As Tractate *Semakhot* [2] explicitly states, "Though the dead were being watched for three days at the burial site, this was not considered by anyone an imitation of Amorite customs.[3]

Our teachers approved of the body's speedy removal from the family's dwelling because there was not the slightest danger that any sign of life might go undetected under the given circumstances. But we, whose present customs permit no such close observation of our deceased, should indeed delay their burial. For how could we ever justify our negligence if we were to realize too late (and such incidents do occur, and have been recorded) that what we judged to be a dead body was merely an inert one?

The most experienced physicians are unanimously agreed that there is no conclusive symptom by which to determine whether death has really occurred. A man can sink into so deep a coma that there is neither a [discernible] pulse nor any breathing, so that those around him think him dead though he is still alive. To make sure there really is no life left in a body, one must therefore wait until it begins to decompose. That our teachers agreed with the physicians becomes clear not merely from the above quotation or from the fact that they report actual cases where a seemingly dead person who had been taken to the vaults did revive later on, but also from other Talmudic passages.

2. Hebrew for "joys," euphemistic title of a small tractate, *Evel Rabbati,* that deals with the laws of mourning.
3. The Amorites were early Semitic inhabitants of Palestine. The rabbis of the Talmudic period, calling all idolators Amorites, referred to any superstitions or evil practices as "the ways of the Amorites."

I am sending you the enclosed draft of a plan which you may wish to submit to your sovereign. He will most probably be satisfied with it, so that subsequently all mortals may feel at peace about the way in which they will be gathered unto their fathers. If, however, your sovereign should insist on having his order carried out, you can do nothing better than follow our ancestors' example by building on your burial ground a vault where, according to ancient custom, the dead can be washed, and then watched over for three days before being buried.

I consider this, rather than the rejection of sensible regulations, the duty of any religious community. In fact, our rabbis should make this clear to their congregations and should lend them their support in this matter.

But I realize that you will not follow my advice anyhow, for habit is a powerful thing. And who knows whether my suggestion will not even make me a heretic in your eyes! Be that as it may, though; my conscience is clear. . . .

TRANSLATING THE PSALMS

[The following is an excerpt from Mendelssohn's preface to his translation of the Psalms (published in Berlin in 1783, with a second revised edition in 1788), which he dedicated to his Christian friend of many years, the poet Karl Wilhelm Ramler (1725–1798). Several German Bible editions, for instance those published in Prague and Vienna, included this translation, which, in 1841, was also transposed into Hungarian.]

I herewith offer to my reader the fruit of more than ten years' labor, a labor that has enhanced many an hour and made many a sorrow less bitter for me.[1] I did not translate the Psalms in their numerical sequence; instead, I chose one I particularly liked, another that seemed especially in tune with the mood of a given moment, a third because I was impressed with its beauty or chal-

1. See page 72.

lenged by its difficulty. Despite my preoccupation with a variety of incongruous matters, the psalm of my choice would then continually be on my mind, and I would ponder its contents until I felt as familiar as I could ever hope to be with its spirit and its author's intent. After that, it was but a minor effort to write it all down [in German].

Now I am asking you, dear reader, to peruse this work the way I wrote it. Select a psalm that harmonizes with your mood, and forget for a while everything translators, exegetes, and paraphrasers have said about it. Let the way it reads be your criterion for judging my translation. . . .

Later on, as you compare this translation with others, you will find many passages where I deviate widely from all my predecessors. Rest assured, however, that I never did so without exercising my critical judgment. In any given instance, I had to be convinced —to say the least—that my wording made the spirit of the original come more alive; that it came closer to the real meaning of the text; or that it was stylistically preferable.

I am so little enamored of innovations that I actually kept more closely to Dr. Luther's [2] language than to that of later translators. It seems to me that Luther not only translated correctly but that he transposed the text into the most felicitous German. I therefore did not hesitate to make use of certain Hebraisms he incorporated into the vernacular, though they may not sound like idiomatic German. But since their continual use not only has made them part of our language but has imparted to them a sense of religious devotion, a translator would lose much were he to disregard them completely.

As I said before, I think I can justify every one of the passages that deviate from earlier translations. Should I, however, have strayed from the text itself, the mistake would be due not to any deliberate choice on my part but to a lack of insight. But I do not wish to prejudice my case, and therefore offer the psalms as they are, without further critical comment.

2. Martin Luther (1483–1546), leader of the German Reformation, whose translation of the Bible into German is still widely used today.

AGAINST BASTARDIZATION OF LANGUAGES

[*To Ernst Ferdinand Klein (1743–1810), who at the time was Assistant Councilor of Law in Breslau and who later became a famous jurist and law reformer. Asked by the Prussian government to draft a new formulation for the oath required of all Jews at certain court procedures, Klein had turned to Mendelssohn for advice.*]

August 29, 1782

. . . I should, however, not at all like to see a legal authorization of the Jewish German dialect [*Judendeutsch*],[1] nor a mixture of Hebrew and German as suggested by Mr Fraenkel.[2] I am afraid this jargon has contributed more than a little to the uncivilized bearing of the common man. In contrast, it seems to me that the recent usage of pure German among my brethren promises to have a most salutary effect on them.

It would vex me greatly, therefore, if even the law of the land were to promote, so to speak, the abuse of either language. It would be much better if Mr Fraenkel tried to put the entire admonition into pure Hebrew so that it could be read in either pure German or pure Hebrew, or possibly in both, whichever might be best under the circumstances. Anything at all rather than a mishmash of languages!

1. See page 78.
2. Rabbi Joseph Jonas Fraenkel (1721–1793), of Breslau.

PART THREE

A Seeker of Truth

Editor's Note

Mendelssohn's letter-exchange with Lavater and other Christian correspondents (with some notable exceptions, particularly Lessing) clearly shows his painful awareness of the precariousness of his own social position. Though recognized in the literary and intellectual circles of his time as a richly gifted, well-read, and philosophically respectable thinker and widely revered for his sagacity and kindness, he remained "the Jew." As such, he was a potential troublemaker, a religious reprobate, or a likely source of social embarrassment.

Yet despite the evidently necessary circumspection and gingerly cautious style that characterize much of his writing, particularly his published correspondence, Mendelssohn stands out as a man of firm convictions and of a moral courage that is nothing short of amazing for a Jew of his time and place. And though he had to take great care not to offend the fundamentalists in either the Christian or Jewish camps, his reflections on both Christianity and Judaism convey his sense of integrity and his determination to remain an independent thinker.

Mendelssohn's definition of Judaism as "revealed legislation" (as juxtaposed to Christianity as "revealed religion") constitutes

109

an original though debatable idea. He sees Judaism also as that "natural religion" or "religion of reason" whose commandments, statutes, and "straightforward rules" are binding for any Jew (but only for a Jew). The observance of these laws, however, requires no act of faith, for they are grounded in and fully congruent with reason.

It is incompatible with the Jewish notion of an all-good, kind God to assert (as Christianity does) that man's happiness in this life and his salvation in the next depend on his affirmation of a revealed faith. Moral convictions and ethical conduct follow naturally from rational insights, at which all men of good will and searching mind can arrive, without the aid of supernatural acts or miraculous deeds. In matters of religious observance, however, the Jew has no choice: he must walk on that road to salvation mapped out for him by God's revelation of a body of specific laws. We do not know, Mendelssohn admits, why God chose to reveal his law only to the Jews. All we know is that he apparently "deemed it wise to bestow on this particular people some particular grace."

Mendelssohn considers Judaism superior to Christianity because it does not ask man to abdicate his reasoning power. He therefore would not convert on grounds of conviction—a surprise to those of his Christian acquaintances who took it for granted that so enlightened a Jew would sooner or later leave the "obscurantist" parochialism of his misguided fathers' religion. And since he finds sham conversions for reasons of expediency utterly repugnant, he rejects with dignity any attempt, subtle or otherwise, to become "unified" with his Christian brothers. Yet he does not share the attitude of a majority of his fellow Jews who—for understandable historical reasons—fear or even hate Jesus and all he stands for. Mendelssohn asks only that he himself be granted the same right he asks for all men: the right to seek enlightenment and a reasoned conviction wherever they can be found and to undertake the search with open eyes.

110

REVEALED RELIGION VERSUS
REVEALED LEGISLATION

[*An excerpt from* Jerusalem, or On Religious Power in Judaism, *a work in which Mendelssohn, attempting to reconcile
the "eternal truths" of Judaism and the rational insights of
contemporary philosophy, deals with questions of revelation
and religious legislation*]

It is true: I recognize no eternal verities but those that can be
grasped by man's reason, and demonstrated as well as validated
by his intellect. But Mr. Moerschel's [1] notion of Judaism is wrong
if he thinks I could not have made such a statement without depart-
ing from the religion of my fathers. On the contrary, I think I am
expressing a view that is as essential to the Jewish religion as it is
characteristic of the distinction between Judaism and Christianity.

To sum it up briefly: I believe Judaism does not know the concept of revealed religion in the sense in which Christians understand this term. The Israelites have a divine legislation: laws, commandments, injunctions, and rules of conduct—instructions they
received so they would know what God wants them to do in order
to attain temporal and eternal happiness.

In a miraculous and supranatural manner, Moses revealed to
them these teachings and precepts; but he never handed down to
them dogmas, doctrines about man's salvation, or general principles
of reason. These the eternal God reveals to us, as to anybody else,
at all times through nature or in any other manner [*Sache*] but
never through the spoken or written word.

1. David Ernst Moerschel, an army chaplain in Berlin who had written a
postscript to the pamphlet *The Search for Light and Right;* its author, the
Christian writer and pamphleteer August Friedrich Cranz, challenged the
theological "truth" or validity of Judaism. Mendelssohn's essay *Jerusalem*
represents his response to this challenge. See *Jerusalem and Other Jewish
Writings by Moses Mendelssohn,* transl. and ed. by Alfred Jospe (New
York: Schocken, 1969).

REVELATION, SALVATION, REDEMPTION
[*The following reflections are part of Mendelssohn's* Gegenbetrachtungen über Bonnets Palingenesie (*Bonnet's Palingenesis: A Counterinquiry*). *See pages 17 and 132.*]

To prove that revelation is necessary [for mankind's salvation] is, I have always felt, a most dangerous undertaking.[1] For all these proofs are predicated on the assumption that man's need for revelation is more universal than the contents of revelation itself. But why would the majority of men be able to exist without any true revelation if this lack were to spell depravity and misery for all mankind? And why would the two Indies, for instance, have to wait until it pleases the Europeans to send them some missionaries with a message without which they cannot live virtuously or happily—a message, moreover, the Indians in their present state of knowledge would find unintelligible as well as inapplicable to their particular circumstances? . . . All we have to do to find out the best possible way of carrying out certain divine plans is to see how God in His perfect wisdom has already carried them out. And we can be sure He has chosen the means most suitable to attain His own ends.

And what are the means by which the Supreme Being guides the greater part of mankind to these ends? They are wondrous indeed, and as such wholly compatible with the wondrousness of God Himself.

As soon as they have developed any societal forms at all, even the most primitive and uncivilized peoples hold certain beliefs or moral convictions regarding those truths of natural religion which seem indispensable to man's happiness. Initially, these beliefs were grounded in crass prejudices. Those who first perceived the existence of some significant truth may, so to speak, have sensed it within themselves without being able to communicate it to others. As they began to contemplate nature in general and human nature in particular, they probably encountered all kinds of problems

1. See page 122.

which they could solve only by a belief in a higher, all-good power:
in Providence and the immortality and future rewards of the soul.

We are inclined to accept as true anything that presents us with
a natural solution to a variety of problems. Contemplating the interrelatedness of these problems, we may well arrive at a moral
certainty. Looking at each problem individually, we may occasionally even feel a demonstrable certainty. But when man first grap-
ples with all these questions, he can hardly discern any probable
answer; and though he may have certain insights, they are as yet
so vague that he would be greatly embarrassed if he had to give a
cogent account of them.

How then can he communicate these thoughts to an uncivilized
people that is not yet able to grasp philosophical concepts? Experience shows that in most civilizations such concepts grow out of
a people's early, erroneous beliefs. In fact, it is superstition that
convinces the common man of many a significant truth indispensable to society's welfare. . . .

As a people becomes increasingly civilized and enlightened, reasoned judgment takes the place of early misconceptions. The free-
thinker who demolishes some false belief that had previously served
to buttress a practical truth commits a vile act. Yet this vile act may
quite frequently create an opportunity to replace the shaky support
superstition occasionally lends to truth with a more durable one.
And once a people is sufficiently enlightened, all truths that are
indispensable to mankind's salvation can be based on rational
insights.

Does this mean that revelation is unnecessary? It does indeed
—for those people who have never experienced such an event.
The Supreme Being would most assuredly have revealed Himself
to them had they been incapable of realizing the purpose of their
existence without such revelation. He granted a revelation to the
Israelites not because men, as men, could otherwise not attain
salvation, but because He deemed it wise to bestow on this particular people some particular grace. All other nations on earth,
Judaism teaches, can and actually should live by their natural
lights and thereby attain salvation. It is this particular people alone
to whom the Creator, for very definite reasons, revealed some

special laws by which they are meant to live, be governed, and attain salvation.

Since then, to be sure, this people has no longer been permitted to seek salvation by any other road than the one delineated for them by God. And since then, this people has had to suffer patiently and in submission to the divine will whatever humiliation, oppression, derision, and persecution it encounters along this road, from which it must not swerve by even a single step. This burden, however is not to be shouldered by anyone not born under Mosaic law. Anyone not charged by God with these difficult [religious] duties should live in accord with the law of nature, secure in the knowledge that man, as man, is innately capable of comprehending and fulfilling the demands of virtue, hence of attaining salvation.

While the Israelite does not claim to be the only creature God selected for salvation, he feels he is the only one for whom there is no other way to attain this state. And it is true that he hopes for a special [namely eternal] reward for obeying this divine command, for he assumes that otherwise God would not have favored him with this special revelation.

Now, if the Nazarenes, for their part, would simply contend that God revealed the doctrine of immortality to them, too, by an act of special grace and in an extraordinary manner, we could all be satisfied. But [they go further than that and] they surely go too far when they pronounce this revelation as absolutely indispensable [to man's salvation]. To do so virtually means to criticize God's rule over the rest of mankind. For what should we think of this rule if God had really granted the exclusive means for attaining salvation to one people only, though salvation is the goal of every man's existence? . . .

Wherever the Supreme Being made use of supranatural means to attain a certain end, we can be entirely sure that He, in His wisdom, deemed all natural means less suitable. But I for one am too aware of my [judgmental] limitations to assert a priori that there is only one way by which God in His supreme wisdom can carry out His designs.

114

JUDAISM AND CHRISTIANITY

[To Karl-Wilhelm, Hereditary Prince of Braunschweig-Wolfenbuettel (1735–1806). This letter (exact date unknown) is a reply to a complimentary comment the Prince had sent to Mendelssohn on January 2, 1770, after having read his Phaedon *(see pp. 186 ff.). Much impressed with Mendelssohn's wisdom and humanitarianism, the Prince wanted to know (a) why the philosopher accepted as historically authentic and as intellectually convincing and valid certain testimonies in the Old but not in the New Testament; and (b) why he rejected that testimonial evidence recorded in the Old Testament (hence accepted as divine inspiration even according to Mosaic teachings) which serves as the basis for the Christian faith.]*

. . . First question: "What rationale has a philosopher who regards the Mosaic laws as binding to acknowledge the validity of certain historical testimonies given in the Old Testament while denying that of similar accounts in the New Testament?"

Your Highness, I cannot place my confidence in any testimony which, as I see it, contradicts an established, irrefutable truth. According to the New Testament (or at least to its interpretation in the official textbooks) I must, at the peril of losing my eternal salvation, believe in (1) the trinity of the divine Being; (2) the incarnation of a Deity; (3) the Passion of one person of this Deity after he has divested himself of his divine majesty; (4) the satisfaction and gratification of the Deity's first person subsequent to the suffering and death of the now reduced [to merely human status] second person. In addition, I must believe in numerous other doctrines similar to or derived from these four.

Now, I neither can force any thinking person to accept my own judgment as his guideline in these matters, nor do I wish to do so. How indeed could a lowly creature like myself be that presumptuous? But I cannot accept as truth anything not convincing to

115

me. And I must confess I regard the above-mentioned doctrines as running diametrically counter to the fundamental principles of cognitive thinking. Thus, I feel compelled to reject these articles of faith, which I cannot bring into accord with anything my own reason and much thought have taught me about the nature and attributes of the Deity.

If I were to find such doctrines in the Old Testament, I would have to reject its credibility too. And even if some miracle-worker were to awaken before my very eyes all those who have been dead and buried for centuries, so as to prove the validity of certain docrines, I could merely say, "True, this miracle-worker has brought the dead back to life—yet I cannot accept his teachings."

I find in the Old Testament, however, nothing resembling these doctrines, nor anything else that seems to me to contradict reason. Hence, I feel confident I can accept both the historicity and credibility we unanimously ascribe to these writings, and on good grounds. The distinction I make between the books of the Old and New Testaments is simply this: the former are in harmony with my philosophical views, or at least do not contradict them; but the latter ask of me a faith I cannot profess.

I know that some illustrious men, cherishing truth as well as Christianity, privately regard all these doctrines (which seem obnoxious to any sound mind) as merely human addenda. These scholars hold that the founder of Christianity was a man just like the rest of us. But they think of him as God's emissary and prophet—somewhat like, if not greater than, the founder of the Jewish religion—who received God's unmediated call to restore the sacred standing of the old, the natural religion; to instruct men in their duties and teach them how to attain salvation; and to substantiate those teachings by performing supranatural acts.

In addition, I should like to address the following requests to those reformers of the dominant religion:

1) They must not base their system . . . on the hypothesis that Judaism and, even more so, natural religion are inadequate means to ensure man's salvation. Since all men must have been destined by their Creator to attain eternal bliss, no particular religion can have an exclusive claim to truth. This thesis, I dare to submit, might serve as a criterion of truth in all religious matters. A revela-

tion claiming to show man the only way to salvation cannot be true, for it is not in harmony with the intent of the all-merciful Creator.

Having revised some basic tenets of their religion, these teachers [the illustrious men mentioned before] actually no longer have the least justification in asserting its exclusiveness. For if the founder of Christianity merely felt called upon, or intended, to restore natural religion and assure men of their eternal salvation, it would follow that I can reach this state simply by living in accordance with the principles of natural religion, and by wholeheartedly accepting the doctrine of man's immortal soul. But my salvation cannot possibly be contingent on my professed belief that a certain human teacher was once given the divine mandate to verify this doctrine by performing miracles.

2) This purified system will, I hope, have no room for the notion of man's eternal punishment in hell. For when the doctrine of divine justice mentions satisfaction and gratification, it does not mean that God metes out punishment for His own gratification. It means, instead, that He punishes or chastises the sinner for his own good. In the divine economy, any sinner's punishment is rescinded as soon as it is no longer needed as a remedial means to put him on the road to eternal salvation.

3) It seems inconceivable to me that an all-just Being in His divine kingdom could permit an innocent man to take upon himself, even voluntarily, the guilt of another. This point, too, is in need of some obvious revisions.

4) The concept of original sin [1] is as foreign to sound reason as it is to the Old Testament. Adam sinned and died. His children sin and die. But that does not mean that Adam's sin caused his descendants to be [spiritually] dead to all that is good, or to fall [irredeemably] into the clutches of Satan.

5) As for Satan and evil spirits, I should like to be free to believe whatever my own reason deems acceptable. The Old Testament says about this subject no more than is rationally explicable.

6) The founder of Christianity never stated explicitly that he meant to abolish the Mosaic Law or exempt Jews from it. [2] At least

1. See page 124.
2. See page 122.

I have found no such assertion in any of the Gospels. In fact, the apostles and disciples wondered for a long time after his death whether pagans had to accept the Mosaic Law and undergo circumcision once they converted [to the new religion]. Eventually, it was decided not to put too great a burden on them. But nowhere in the New Testament can I discover any cogent reason why Jews, even those who embrace Christianity, should be exempt from the Law of Moses. On the contrary, the apostle himself circumcised Timothy. One ought to see, therefore, why I personally find it impossible to dispense with the Mosaic Law in my own life.

If, in addition to the previously discussed revisions of the principal religious tenets, these suggestions were to be accepted along with their corollaries, and if the New Testament were to be interpreted and explained along the same lines, one would arrive at a religion Christians and Jews could equally affirm. Given this premise, the adherents of Judaism could gladly admit that a prophet and emissary of God once felt called upon not to abolish the Mosaic Law but to address to all mankind his sermons about the sacred teachings of virtue and its reward in the life to come. And the followers of Jesus, on the other hand, would then have to be interested solely in the affirmation and dissemination of these teachings, a mission once given to the founder of their religion.

If the divine origin of this mission were to be acknowledged, so much the better. But whether it be acknowledged, doubted, or even rejected makes no difference as far as the validity of this religion is concerned. I cannot repeat this often enough: what is of utmost importance is not the historical truth of a [religious] mission but the logical truth of a [religious] precept.

Second question: "On what grounds does a thinking Jew reject those attestations to the truth of the Christian faith already recounted in the Old Testament, and thus accepted as divine inspiration even according to the teachings of Moses?"

I have read them, those Old Testament passages in which the truth of this faith is said to be grounded—I have read them all more than once, with close attention and within their context. How unutterably grim mankind's fate would be were its eternal salvation to depend on certain explanations of obscure passages in a book written in a foreign and by now dead tongue, in times immemorial and for a people in Asia! I think I understand the language of the original text as well as any latter-day Hebraist, for it is, as it were, my second native tongue. Yet it would seem to me that these passages contain not even the slightest hint of a proof [by which to substantiate New Testament events and claims].

Could I possibly be blinded by my own bias? I hardly think so. Instead, I consider it rather obvious that the explanations of a good many of these passages by certain theologians are either simply wrong or highly contrived and arbitrary. But I feel reassured when I notice that the more recent exegetes, expounding the Bible with discriminating taste and sophistication, have already seen fit to discard many an interpretation once considered definitive.

As for myself, I take the liberty of regarding these exegetical disputes as a learned pastime that also occasionally affords me a certain pleasure. But (and may God have mercy upon my soul!) I cannot possibly discover the ground for my eternal salvation by interpreting the meaning of Daniel's puzzling dreams or by reading such meaning into a prophet's sublime poetry. The intent of these writings is to awaken man's heart, not to instruct his mind. . . .

God in His great goodness, looking into our hearts, knows how sincerely I am searching for truth and how firmly I am resolved never knowingly to offend a soul. . . . I feel nothing but contempt for the petty minds of those freethinkers who take a malicious delight in disturbing the serenity of innocence; and I feel nothing but pity for the zealot who, misguided by his own conscience, achieves the same result. I therefore make bold to ask your Highness to destroy this letter. I should like to make sure that it will never fall into the hands of someone who might either make the wrong use of it or, if he were a cleric, feel compelled to enter into a dispute about it.

Our common Father, judging us by the decisions of our conscience, cannot condemn a heart that fervently loves Him, even if ignorance (but never evil intent) may cause it to go astray. . . .

ON JESUS
[To Johann Caspar Lavater]

January 15, 1771

. . . It is an ingrained prejudice or rather a misconception of your fellow Christians to assume that all Jews incessantly blaspheme Christianity and its founder. . . .

Many of my brethren whom I have the pleasure of knowing personally have enough wisdom and moderation to use neither blasphemy nor contumely [with reference to Jesus]. And I also know many who will follow me even further and acknowledge the guilelessness and moral integrity of Christianity's founder. It must, however, be explicitly stated that this acknowledgment of ours is based only on the reports of Christian witnesses (for, I repeat, we have no Jewish sources on which to rely), and that it is predicated on certain assumptions, namely: (1) that Jesus never considered himself coequal with the Father; (2) that he never claimed to be a person of the godhead; (3) that he therefore never arrogated unto himself the divine prerogative of being worshiped; and (4) that he never intended to abolish the religion of his fathers, though there were evidently many instances when he seemed to suggest the opposite.

These assumptions are of the utmost importance. For if they turned out to be invalid, that is, if some of his [Jesus'] ambiguous utterances—which indeed do seem to contradict our interpretation—had to be taken literally after all, our judgment concerning the moral integrity of his intentions would have to be completely reversed. . . .

120

ON FAITH AND REASON
AND THE ABROGATION OF MOSAIC LAW
[*To Elkan Herz, a wealthy merchant friend*]

Berlin, July 22, 1771 (11th of Av, 5531)

. . . Christians in general and theologians in particular easily accuse others of deism, because their own revealed religion superimposes on natural religion a very great deal that goes beyond and against reason. We, however, can praise God for having given us the teaching of truth. We have no dogmas that go beyond or against reason, nor do we add anything but commandments, statutes, and straightforward rules to natural religion. Our religious principles and tenets are grounded in reason, and therefore not in any conflict with it. Rather than contradict the findings of rational investigation, they are fully congruent with them. This actually constitutes the pre-eminence of our religion, our true and divine religion, over all other confessions of faith. . . .

[*From* Bonnet's Palingenesis: A Counterinquiry. *See note on p. 112.*]

I live under what is probably the world's most powerful and enlightened government. Its people claim to possess reliable evidence that God assured their forefathers in the most compelling way and under extraordinary circumstances that theirs would be eternal salvation. The wisest men, worthy of our veneration, speak of this matter with such firm conviction that I for one cannot possibly doubt their sincerity. And their persuasiveness as well as the manner in which they use philosophical arguments to undergird their religious doctrine make it appear natural that they should have brought the most rational of men completely over to their side. Insofar as their creed comprises the [moral] certainty that mankind can anticipate salvation in the life to come, it is in full accord with rational thought and divinely revealed teachings. And

121

I cannot see why I should not, to that extent, accept a doctrine so salutary, beneficial, and auspicious for mankind.

I also see, however, that the teachers of this faith do not, as some of them would seem to do, promise eternal salvation to all mankind. Instead, they give such an assurance only to those who accept their [so-called] historical evidence, while threatening the rest [of us] with eternal damnation. We are to believe not merely that all men will be saved. We must believe, too, that only the founder of their religion can give us such a guarantee. Otherwise, eternal damnation rather than eternal bliss will await us.

This idea is repugnant. Given such restrictions, this faith cannot truly promote mankind's welfare: instead, it must prove burdensome to man's reason. And it is this sacred reason which firmly convinces me that God has intended man to attain salvation by leading a life of virtue. . . .[1]

The wise, just, and all-good God we worship is so full of compassion He cannot possibly have created even the lowliest worm for a life of eternal misery. Out of compassion for the limitations of the human mind, this merciful God may conceivably have chosen to assure His creatures—in a special way as well as through a special emissary—of the eternal salvation awaiting them. But how could He have made this salvation contingent on their acknowledgment of His emissary's divine authorization?

And yet, these reflections alone would not be sufficient to make me reject the Christian doctrine of salvation. Among its adherents are, I know, teachers of a more humanitarian bent. They either do not see at all such harsh demands in their religious writings, or else are willing at least to qualify them to such a degree that it becomes quite evident they do not consider the kingdom of heaven their exclusive prerogative.

But I am also told that the founder of Christianity abrogated the laws of Moses. Those laws which God Himself has validated? How can that be? The founder, moreover, does not even proclaim, in the name of God and in so many words, that he really does intend to abolish part of the Law—or, if so, which part. Are we therefore to infer whatever we may wish from vague pronouncements or inconclusive acts? Or are we to let these divinely sanctified laws

1. See page 114.

pass muster before us so as to decide which to reject, qualify, change, or keep? Is such a procedure really congruent with the wisdom of God?

This God who had His laws proclaimed, publicly and under many extraordinary circumstances, to an entire people by a special emissary—this God should now abolish these very laws, and not even publicly or by an explicit proclamation but, as it were, in silence? Inconceivable! [2]

The more I come to know this religion (which is so highly recommended to me), the more my reason shrinks from it. True, mankind's eternal salvation is the final goal of this religion, as it is of all others. But under what conditions am I being offered this state of bliss! What shackles for my reason! If these doctrines are not true, God has not sent Jesus of Nazareth. And if I do not believe them, He has not sent him for my sake. . . .

The Christians' religion turns out to be quite different from its projected image. It does not merely offer mankind a guarantee for its eventual salvation but concomitantly attempts a complete transformation of our notions regarding God, His attributes, omnipotence, justice, wisdom, and rule of the world. But all these concepts, along with the assurance of eternal bliss, comprise a coherently interconnected whole. If, therefore, I cannot accept the principles of this faith, I can also ascribe no veracity to its founder. What, then, can I be expected to think of his divine mission? . . .

In accordance with my previously stated view [3] that I must reject any doctrine that contradicts all sound reason and thus my own rational judgment, I cannot regard the founder of Christianity as a divine emissary, sent to proclaim these [completely changed] teachings. I cannot in the least believe his assurances of our future happiness; for inasmuch as I feel compelled to reject [what is considered] the truth of his teachings, I must necessarily also deny that its source is divine. And as to the objection that he has validated his mission by miracles: what can miracles prove? . . . I consider it unnecessary to examine in depth all testimonies [with regard to miracles] and their credibility, to count them and compare or weigh one with or against the other. For though all evi-

2. See page 118.
3. See page 116.

dence be against me, it would merely follow that I should from now on hold even the most reliable evidence suspect—and such a state of mind and heart I would not wish upon any enemy of mine.

ORIGINAL SIN
[*From* Bonnet's Palingenesis: A Counterinquiry]

We believe that man was created in the image of God; yet he was meant to be a human being and thus prone to sin. We do not know the concept of original sin, however.[1] Adam and Eve sinned because they were human; they died because they had sinned. And this is the way of all their descendants: they sin and they die.

But they die a mere physical death. And death of the soul is inconceivable to me. True, Maimonides [2] asserts in his tractate on repentance that the soul of the godless will be destroyed, and he rightfully regards this as the harshest possible punishment. But I myself agree with the son of Naḥman,[3] who contradicts this assertion in his tractate on retributive justice, denying the destruction of the soul and the everlastingness of punishment.

The fact that these theologians hold divergent opinions (and on so crucial a point at that!) does not mean, however, that they denounce each other as heretics. Nothing of the sort! In fact, when some zealots attacked Maimonides as a heretic after his death, urging that his writings be burned, Naḥmanides defended him most emphatically.

Not God's own infinity [and infallibility] but man's [finiteness and] fallibility serve as divine criteria for meting out the sinner's punishment. We have no concept of an offended majesty asking to be avenged; nor do we speak of a retributive justice that must

1. See page 117.
2. See footnote, p. 77.
3. Moses ben Naḥman (also Naḥmanides or Ramban, 1194–1270); outstanding Spanish Talmudist, Kabbalist, and Bible commentator, and the first great rabbi to declare the resettlement of Palestine (where he spent his last years) by Jews a Biblical precept.

124

be done—as punishment for the guilty, or for some innocent willing to take upon himself another's guilt. To our way of thinking, it seems unjust to spare the guilty, and more unjust still to let the innocent suffer. Even if the innocent, full of good will, should offer himself in another's stead, God in His ultimate wisdom could not approve of such a scheme. Nor could such voluntary suffering satisfy the divine sense of justice; for God's justice and His all-wise lovingkindness are one.

God does punish us if the evil of punishment is the only means to eradicate the evil of sin; but in this case it is the sinner himself who must suffer, not someone in his stead. Yet as soon as the evil of punishment is expendable, that is, as soon as the evil of sin can be controlled by some other means, it is entirely in keeping with God's attributes to show mercy to the sinner. Nor is God's justice diminished by such an act. For divine justice (I cannot repeat this point often enough) means wisdom and kindness; and when wisdom does not object to kindness, justice itself will be satisfied.

We do not recognize any intermediary who is to make peace between God and man. If it is in keeping with [divine] wisdom to show clemency to sinful man, no intermediary need plead for this act of mercy.

ON CEREMONIAL LAW
[*From* Bonnet's Palingenesis: A Counterinquiry]

As for the laws of Moses—we believe that they are absolutely binding on us as long as God Himself does not revoke them with the same kind of solemn and public declaration with which He once gave them to us.[1] You say we no longer know the purpose of some of them? Very well. But wherever did the Legislator declare them to be valid only as long as we are aware of their purpose? And in the absence of such a declaration, what mortal dares to delimit their validity? Man may change the laws of man in accordance with changing times and conditions. But the laws of God must

1. See pages 122–123.

remain unalterable until one can be absolutely sure that He Himself proclaims their modification.

Will these laws ever be changed by God? Here, our scholars' opinions are divided. Some regard them as absolutely immutable, making this view an article of faith. Others, however, do not think it improbable that—at the time of some future, miraculous restoration of the Jewish nation—the most sublime Lawgiver might decide on a second public legislative act. In that case, many of our present ceremonial laws might undergo one or another change. My own thinking about these matters is this:

As I have already said several times, all our rabbis hold the Mosaic laws to be binding only on the Jewish people. All other nations are to keep the law of nature and the religion of the patriarchs.[2] But since most peoples have by now abolished—much to the detriment of truth—the simpleness of this original religion, harboring instead misconceptions of God and His rule, the numerous Jewish ceremonial laws and ceremonies may have the incidental purpose (among other intents we do not always fully comprehend) of visibly distinguishing this nation from all others by reminding us unceasingly of those sacred truths none of us should ever forget.

Most religious customs make this explanation quite obvious; its proof can be found, in so many words, in Holy Scriptures. Our customs and ceremonies serve to remind us that God is the One who has created the world, ruling it with wisdom. And they are to impress upon us the fact that this One God is the absolute Lord over all nature; that He liberated the Jewish people, by extraordinary acts, from Egyptian oppression; that He gave them laws, et cetera. This is the intent and purpose of our customs, which must necessarily appear to be superfluous, burdensome, and ridiculous to anyone lacking an insight into their true nature.

Now, all Old Testament prophets agree (and reason fondly en-

2. Mendelssohn refers here not to the three patriarchs Abraham, Isaac and Jacob but to Noah and the seven injunctions given to him. The so-called Noahian Laws, derived from the early chapters of Genesis and binding on Jew and Gentile alike, prohibit blasphemy, idolatry, sexual immorality, murder, robbery, social injustice, and the eating of a portion of a living animal.

126

tertains the hope) that religions will not indefinitely be at variance; that at some time there will be one shepherd tending one flock; that the knowledge of the One true God will cover the entire earth as the waters cover the sea [Isaiah 11:9]. At such a time, God in His wisdom may well deem it no longer necessary to separate us from other peoples by special ceremonial laws. Instead, He may, through a second public manifestation, introduce some [other] external practices by which the hearts of all men would be joined in worship of their Creator, in mutual love and charity. This notion is so blissful man's soul would like to dwell on it serenely, imagining the happiness that could be mankind's after so salutary a revolution. But what anxiety seizes us as we awaken from this dream and see how miserable men are being made by their present divisiveness!

ON THE MESSIAH
[*To Johann Casper Lavater*]

Berlin, January, 15, 1771

. . . I cannot quite agree with what you say about the Messiah I am supposed to expect. A *messiah spiritualis* is, as far as I know, the redeemer through whom we hope to be saved. But I do not expect such a Messiah, for I hope to be saved by my God alone, without any mediator. The Messiah described in your essay is, in my opinion, a *messiah terrestris,* whom I also do not expect to be *universi terrarum orbis rex, omniumque gentium supremus et legislator et judex.*[1] In mankind's present condition, such a state [of affairs] would mean man's undoing. It would, in fact, be the end of both man's freedom and all his noble endeavors to develop and cultivate his innate gifts and thus come closer to salvation. Only if man were to divest himself of his very nature would such a Messianic reign serve the best interests of mankind.

1. "The king of the entire universe and the supreme lawgiver and judge of all nations."

ON MIRACLES

[From "A Postscript" to Mendelssohn's exchange with Lavater. See pages 17 and 132.]

Berlin, April 6, 1770

According to the teachings of my religion, miracles neither constitute a criterion of truth nor can they furnish us with the moral certainty that a given prophet really did have a divine mission. In our view, it was the public revelation of the Law alone that provided us with such an assurance. For here the emissary needed no accreditation, since all the people heard with their own ears the divine mandate given to him. Here, there was no need to confirm certain truths and precepts by miraculous acts and wondrous deeds. Instead, it was evident to the people that this prophet had indeed been appointed God's emissary: every one of them had heard him being summoned. As it is written: "And the Lord said unto Moses: 'Lo, I come unto thee in a thick cloud, that the people may hear when I speak with thee, and may also believe thee forever'" [Exodus 19:9]. Also: "And he said: 'Certainly I will be with thee: when thou hast brought forth the people out of Egypt, ye shall serve God upon this mountain'" [Exodus 3:12]. Hence, our belief in revelation is authenticated not by miracles but by the giving of the Law.

The admonition in Deuteronomy 18:15 to obey a miracle-working [1] prophet is, according to our rabbis, nothing but a positive commandment.[2] As such, it reflects the will of the Lawgiver rather than any verifying power inherent in miracles. By way of analogy,

1. This adjective does not appear in the Hebrew original. The Jewish Publication Society translation of the verse reads, "A prophet will the Lord thy God raise unto thee, from the midst of thee, of thy brethren, like unto me; unto him ye shall hearken."
2. According to Jewish tradition, the Law of Moses consists of 613 *mitzvot*, which are subdivided into 248 positive and 365 negative commandments. The former represent precepts ("thou shalt . . ."); the latter, prohibitions: ("thou shalt not . . .").

we might cite another positive commandment that asks us to base legal decisions on the testimony of two witnesses,[3] though this testimony is thereby not regarded as absolutely conclusive evidence. In one word, our rabbis hold that the belief in miracles is grounded in the [supranaturally revealed] Law alone, on the premise that this Law represents an incontrovertible truth. . . .

Moreover, I find passages in the Old and even in the New Testament which indicate that it is quite possible for seducers of the people or false prophets to perform miracles. How else, for instance, should we interpret the phenomenon of the Egyptian magicians? The Old Testament even mentions certain instances where the people not only should not listen to prophets and dreamers of dreams (though these may show them signs and perform miracles) but should actually put such imposters to death (Deuteronomy 13:2). And the New Testament states explicitly, among other passages, "For false Christs and false prophets will arise and show great signs and wonders, so as to lead astray, if possible, even the elect" (Matthew 24:24).

Whether these miracles are manifestations of some sort of magic or occult powers or whether they represent merely an abuse of some special faculty given to certain individuals for a higher purpose is not for me to say. Yet I feel that our Scriptures make it eminently and irrefutably clear that the performance of miracles must not be considered infallible proof of a divine mission. I therefore think I am entirely justified in asserting that any argument against the beliefs of my fellow Jews proves nothing at all as long as it is based on the "infallible evidence" of miracles. We simply do not acknowledge any such infallibility. And I feel equally justified in asserting that this kind of argument would enable us to defend any religion's claim to truth. For I know of no religion lacking in accounts of miracles; and I certainly must grant every man the right to affirm the credibility of his forefathers.

Any revelational event is perpetuated through tradition and [historical] monuments; on that we are agreed. But according to the principles of my religion, it is not the performance of miracles

3. "At the mouth of two witnesses, or three witnesses, shall he that is to die be put to death; at the mouth of one witness he shall not be put to death" (Deuteronomy 17:6).

alone but a public act of legislation that constitutes the source of this tradition.

[*From* Bonnet's Palingenesis: A Counterinquiry]

A sense of disbelief we cannot easily shake off seizes us when we are faced with accounts of miracles that are supposed to have happened without the grandiose accompaniment or public manifestations [surrounding the revelation at Mount Sinai]. We know that men mislead others as easily as they are misled by them. We know how enthralled they are by prejudice, superstition, and fanaticism. We know how often a man's character is so complex a mixture of reason, fanaticism, superstition, deceptiveness, cunning, and simplemindedness that to distinguish among them all proves difficult to even the most perspicacious observer. We know, too, how often man's evil intent engenders some good, and his good intent some evil. Comparing, then, one account with the other and setting testimony over against testimony, we feel engulfed by a sea of doubts—and withold our judgment.

I do, however, observe the following rule: as long as the account of a miracle does not have a manifestly inauthentic ring and the thesis it is meant to confirm is not merely acceptable but also congruent with the substance of the divinely revealed Law, I am quite inclined to accept it without further question. And if such a thesis is actually conducive to the promotion of good among men, I do not even mind being called too credulous. If, though, this thesis is not in accord with my God-given reason or with Scriptures, I shall revert to my disbelief and continue to disregard such miracles.

MAKING ONE'S OWN RELIGIOUS DECISIONS

[*The antirationalist philosopher Friedrich Heinrich Jacobi (1743–1819) had accused Lessing of having been a Spinozist and, by implication, not merely a pantheist but an atheist. Mendelssohn, deeply upset, defended his late friend and restated his own religious views in a pamphlet written shortly before his death and addressed to "Lessing's Friends." These paragraphs are excerpted from it.*]

I for my part persist in my Jewish heterodoxy. I doubt that it is given to any mortal to speak with angelic purity; but I would not rely even on an archangel's authority with respect to these eternal truths on which the doctrine of man's salvation is based. I must, therefore, either stand on my own feet or fall. In actuality, I am merely returning to the faith of my fathers, which, true to the original meaning of this term, represents not a belief in doctrines or theories but a trust and confidence in [the goodness of] God's attributes. I place my full and unreserved trust in God, who, in His omnipotence, *could* endow man with the faculty to discover for himself, independent of the dictum of authority, those truths that constitute the basis for human salvation. And I feel a child's confidence in Him who, in His lovingkindness, *would* endow man with this faculty.

Fortified by this unfaltering faith, I seek enlightenment, and through it [a reasoned] conviction, wherever I may find them. And —praised be my Creator's saving grace and goodness!—I think I have found both. Moreover, I am sure than any man can find them if only he undertakes his search with open eyes instead of shielding them from all rays of light.

REJECTION OF CONVERSION

[*To Johann Caspar Lavater, who thought a Jew of Mendelssohn's philosophical stature, universalist views, and tolerant outlook should leave the narrow confines of Judaism. He therefore dedicated his translation of* La Palingénésie philosophique, ou Idées sur l'état passé et sur l'état futur des êtres vivants *by the French philosopher and psychologist Charles Bonnet (1720–1793)—a work in which that author tries to demonstrate "the historical truth" of Christianity—to Mendelssohn, asking him to act with the moral integrity of a Socrates and either refute Bonnet's arguments publicly or else convert, also publicly, to Christianity. See page 17.*]

Berlin, December 12, 1769

. . . My hesitation to enter into religious disputes has never been due to fear or lack of conviction. If I may say so, it was not just yesterday that I started studying my religion, having recognized early in life my obligation to examine [the rationale for] my views and actions. And the fact that ever since I have devoted whatever leisure I had to the study of both philosophy and the humanities has been due solely to my desire to be well prepared to undertake such an evaluation of my position. I surely had no other motives for my studies. For a man in my circumstances cannot possibly expect the slightest material advantage from the kind of knowledge I have been acquiring. I have always been only too well aware that these intellectual pursuits would never equip me for making my merry way in this world. But would they make me happy? Ah, dear sir! The civil conditions under which my co-religionists and I must live keep us so effectively from any free exercise of our mental capacities that it cannot add much to our contentment to learn what human rights are really all about. But this is a subject I had better avoid. Those who are aware of our plight and have a human heart will sense more about all this than I can express.

If my decision after all these years of study had not been absolutely in favor of my religion, I should have considered it necessary to proclaim this fact publicly. I do not see why I should continue to feel bound to so overly demanding, so universally despised a religion unless my very heart remained convinced of its truth. If, moreover, my investigations had made me realize that the religion of my fathers was false, I should surely have felt compelled to leave it. For were I secretly inclined toward another faith, I would be a base reprobate to hide this innermost conviction instead of owning up to the truth. But what could possibly induce me to behave in so base a manner? As I said before, were I ever to experience a change of heart concerning my religion, only one course of action would be open to me, a course determined by prudence, love of truth, and my own sense of integrity.

If only I were indifferent to both religions, ridiculing and deriding all forms of revelation, it would be easy to listen to the counsel of expediency while silencing the voice of conscience. What could hold me back? Fear of my fellow Jews? They are not powerful enough to constitute a threat. Obduracy? Inertia? A clinging to familiar notions? Having spent much of my life evaluating religious claims, I should by now be considered above sacrificing the fruits of my labor to such human weakness.

As you can see, the outcome of my investigations confirmed my sincere belief in the rightness of my religion. Otherwise, I would have made a public declaration to the contrary. But since my studies served to corroborate the validity of my religious heritage, I was able to continue quietly on my own path, without any need to justify my beliefs before the world.

I cannot deny, however, that I have discovered certain wholly human additions and abuses which, alas, badly tarnish my religion's original luster. But where is the man who, looking for truth, has found his religion completely free of human pronouncements detrimental to that truth? All of us must recognize that noxious effluvium of hypocrisy and superstition—all of us who, in our search for truth, wish we could wipe out such poisonous accretions without doing any damage to all that is authentic and good in our religion.

And it is this good, my religion's essential truth and validity,

133

of which I am as firmly and irrefutably convinced as you or Mr. Bonnet must be of your own faith. Hence I herewith swear before the God of truth who has created and sustains both you and me— that God in whose name you challenged me publicly and in writing —that I shall continue to adhere to my religious principles as long as my very soul does not undergo a complete transformation. . . .

Nevertheless, it would never have occurred to me to enter into a dispute about Judaism even if every textbook of polemics had tried to demolish it, every scholastic exercise to disprove it. Anyone even slightly familiar with rabbinics—including those half-educated people who derive their information from trashy pamphlets no sensible Jew would read or even know about—could have made the most ludicrous statements about Judaism without eliciting so much as a single critical comment from me. For I meant to change the world's despicable image of the Jew not by writing disputatious essays but by leading an exemplary life. Moreover, my religion and philosophy as well as my station in life make it mandatory that I avoid all religious controversy and deal in my published writings only with those insights or fundamental issues that are of equal significance to all religions.

According to the principles of my faith, I must not seek to convert anyone not born a Jew. The zeal for making proselytes runs diametrically counter to the spirit of Judaism—assertions to the contrary by certain people notwithstanding. Our rabbis teach us unequivocally that the written and oral Law that constitutes our revealed religion is binding for our people alone. "Moses commanded us a law, an inheritance of the congregation of Jacob" [Deuteronomy 33:4]. All other nations of the earth, we hold, were enjoined by God to adhere to the law of nature and the religion of the patriarchs.[1] All who live in accordance with the laws of this religion—that is, the laws of nature as well as of reason—are called "the righteous among the nations," [2] and theirs, too, will be eternal bliss. . . .

1. See page 126.
2. "The righteous among all nations will have a share in the world to come" (*Tosefta Sanhedrin* XIII.2). Maimonides, in his digest of rabbinic law, declared, "The pious of the Gentiles will have a share in the world to come" (*Hilkhot Teshuvah* III.5).

134

Our rabbis are not only far from feeling any compulsion to proselytize but make a point of enjoining us to dissuade with the most serious arguments anyone asking to be converted. We are to tell any would-be convert how unnecessarily heavy a burden this decision would put on him; for while in his present state he is required to observe merely the Noaḥian laws [3] in order to be saved, he would have to observe all the strict laws of Judaism—or become subject to the Divine punishment awaiting those who break them —were he to embrace the religion of the Israelites. In addition, we are to confront him with a description of the misery, oppression, and contempt that are our people's present lot so as to prevent him from rashly taking a step he might later regret.

It should be evident, then, that my fathers' faith does not ask to be propagated. We are not being urged to send missionaries to the two Indies or to Greenland so as to preach the precepts of our religion to those distant peoples. If we take these precepts seriously, we actually should envy the inhabitants of Greenland; for, alas, as far as we can tell from all available reports, they apparently find it easier than we to live in accordance with natural law. Anyone not born a Jew, I repeat, need not observe our religious laws. Their observance is incumbent upon us alone, a fact that cannot possibly offend our neighbors. But even if they should think our views absurd, there would still be no need for disputatiousness. We act in accordance with our convictions and need not be concerned when those whom we ourselves consider exempt from any observation of our laws doubt their validity. Whether the people who deride us for keeping our laws and customs are acting in a manner that can be called righteous, conciliatory, or humane is, however, a question best left to their own conscience. Inasmuch as we have no intention of winning others over to our side, any quarrel is surely futile. . . .

If there were among my contemporaries a Confucius or Solon, I could love and admire these great men and yet, true to the principles of my religion, not feel the ridiculous urge to convert them. To convert them? For whatever purpose? Inasmuch as they would not be members of "the congregation of Jacob," [4] they would not

3. See page 126.
4. See page 134.

be obligated to observe our religious laws. And on our central religious teachings we could, I feel sure, readily agree. As for your question whether I think a Confucius or Solon could partake of eternal bliss: I believe that no one who shows men the path to virtue in this life can possibly be damned in the life to come. What is more, I can say this without fear of having to justify my convictions before an illustrious board of inquiry, as that upright man Marmontel was forced to do at the Sorbonne.[5]

It is my good fortune to count among my friends many an excellent man not of my faith. We love each other sincerely, though we must assume or can be virtually certain that we harbor completely divergent views in religious matters. I not only enjoy their company but feel a better man for it. Yet my heart has never secretly whispered to me, "What a shame that so beautiful a soul should be lost," though such sentiments seem to trouble those who are convinced that salvation cannot be found outside their church.

To be sure, any man has a natural duty to propagate knowledge and promote virtue among his fellow men in an attempt to eradicate, to the best of his ability, their prejudices and errors. Hence some people seem to think it incumbent upon them to argue publicly against any religious theories they consider wrong. But since not all misconceptions we encounter in our fellow men are equally harmful, they need not all be dealt with in the same manner.

Certain views, however, prove wholly detrimental to mankind's welfare. Their harmful effect on all ethical conduct is so obvious they cannot be expected to yield even some incidental good. These must, therefore, be immediately fought by all men concerned with mankind's welfare. Here, the most direct line of attack is doubtlessly the best. Actually, it would be irresponsible to employ delaying tactics or choose circuitous routes in discharging one's duty. To this harmful category belong, on the one hand, that fanaticism, hatred of one's neighbor and the hatred-spawned desire to persecute him (all of which are but manifestations of prejudice) and, on the other hand, that irresponsible conduct, sybaritic opulence, and amoral atheism which bespeak man's waywardness.

5. Jean François Marmontel (1723–99), French writer and contributor to the *Encyclopédie,* whose political novella *Bélisaire* was censored by the Sorbonne.

Disturbing both his own and his neighbor's peace and serenity, they stunt man's moral development and thus inhibit his striving for truth and goodness.

Yet some of my fellow men's convictions, though erroneous in my eyes, belong to a category of higher theoretical principles so far removed from life's practical concerns that their harmful effects are not immediately felt. But because of their very nature, these principles assume great significance in the eyes of those who not merely adhere to them but actually build their moral and societal systems on them. To argue publicly about such fundamental convictions just because we consider them misconceptions would be like tearing up the ground on which a building stands in order to make sure its structure is sound. Anyone interested more in mankind's welfare than in his own public image will refrain from making his personal thoughts about such matters public. In fact, he will avoid an outright attack on another's religious beliefs and proceed with the greatest caution, so as not to cause the overthrowing of an ethical principle—suspect though it may seem to him—before his fellow men are ready to replace it with the one he himself regards as true.

For these reasons, I may feel compelled to remain silent even when confronted with what I consider to be preconceived notions concerning other people, or false judgments concerning other religions, as long as they do not constitute a direct threat to natural religion or natural law. Such notions or beliefs may actually, though only incidentally, be conducive to promoting man's welfare. To be sure, our actions, if wrongly motivated, hardly deserve to be called moral; and it would be far better and safer to base the promotion of the good on truth—wherever it is recognized—than on error and prejudice. But as long as this truth is not yet recognized or widely enough accepted to have as great an impact upon the masses as their long-standing prejudices, these prejudices must be almost sacred to anyone who cherishes virtue.

Such cautious reserve is especially called for where a people, though harboring beliefs we regard as mistaken, possesses admirable moral and intellectual qualities and can count among its ranks a good many great men who deserve to be called benefactors of mankind. Rather than disregard the eminent achievements of such a people by attacking them for what we think their all too human error, we should show them all due respect and spare them embarrassment.

These considerations, then, reflecting insights gained from my religion and philosophy alike, motivate me to avoid carefully all religious disputations. And if you add to all this my place in society at large, my reticence must surely seem justified to you. For I am a member of an oppressed people that finds itself compelled to appeal to the authorities' good will for protection and shelter. These they are not given everywhere, and nowhere without limitations. But as long as they find even some degree of toleration and protection, my fellow Jews gladly do without many liberties other human beings simply take for granted. And since many countries deny them the right of domicile altogether, my people are more than ready to appreciate the benevolence of any nation that will admit them under bearable conditions. As you know, Zurich, your own city, will not even permit this circumcised friend of yours to visit you.

My coreligionists are quite aware of the debt of gratitude they owe to any government that includes them in its humanitarian considerations by permitting them to worship the Almighty unmolested, in the way their fathers did. In the country of my residence, they actually enjoy a considerable degree of religious freedom. Should they not refrain, then, from attacking their protectors on a point that is of particular sensitivity to any man of integrity? . . .

I have read your translation of Bonnet's treatise with close attention. After everything I have said so far, it should no longer be an open question whether his arguments have convinced me. . . . He can have written only for a public that already shares his convictions and wishes to read only whatever confirms its own beliefs. And as long as an author and his readers agree on their conclusions, they will quickly agree on their premises as well.

But I am more than amazed that you, sir, should consider this essay sufficiently convincing to a man who, true to his [religious] principles, must hold completely opposite views. You cannot possibly have put yourself into the place of someone who, rather than sharing the author's convictions from the very outset, is trying to find them substantiated in his work. But if you did attempt to put yourself into my frame of mind and still believe, as you apparently do, that even Socrates would find Mr. Bonnet's proofs irrefutable, I can merely conclude that one of us must be a noteworthy example of the strong influence bias and upbringing exert on all men, even those who are sincerely searching for truth.

[*From Mendelssohn's "Postscript" to the foregoing correspondence*]

During the few hours my business affairs leave me for recreation, I would prefer to forget all divisiveness and enmity that ever have set one man against another. To that end, I try to eradicate from my mind any sense of animosity I may have felt during my working day. In these happy hours I like to give myself over to a feeling of release and serenity, a mood I have not yet learned to combine with the aggressive stance of a religious disputant. I simply was not born an athlete—in either the moral or the physical sense of the word. . . .

For many years I have tried to maintain a certain middle position between dogmatist and skeptic. In matters of fundamental religious or ethical convictions, I am a dogmatist. That is to say, I have made my decision and firmly stand on the ground where, I believe, I can find the greatest measure of truth. But when it comes to judging my neighbor, I am a skeptic. That is to say, I have my doubts; for I greatly distrust my ability to convince any man of the truth of my own convictions, the more so since I grant him the same right I claim for myself—the right of free religious choice. It can therefore only please me that Mr. Lavater is content to conclude our public exchange herewith.

Actually, why should we let the public witness such a disputation? It is unbecoming to both Mr. Lavater and myself to entertain an idle readership by a public spectacle that would merely be perplexing to those not firm in their beliefs and would provide malicious pleasure for those who scoff at truth and goodness.

The truths both of us affirm and accept are not yet so widely disseminated that a public discussion of the points still dividing us could be of much use. What a happy place this world would be if

139

only all men were to accept and act upon the sacred truths that are the common possession of the best among Christians and Jews! May the Lord of hosts hasten the coming of those happy days when no man will do evil or hurt his fellow man. Then the whole world will be as full of knowledge of God as the sea is of the waters that cover the deep [Isaiah 11:9]. These are the days of which it is said that no man will need to teach his friend, nor one brother the other. For all of them, small and great alike, will know the Lord [Jeremiah 31:34].

[From an undated letter to Lavater]

The playlet is over, the curtain has come down; now let us embrace each other in our thoughts. Does it matter that you are a Christian preacher whereas I am a Jew? If we were to return to the sheep and the silkworm whatever they have lent us, both of us would be nothing but men.

[It is interesting to note, though, what the author had to say about the entire Lavater exchange in private. The following is taken from a letter he wrote about a year later to Elkan Herz.]

November 16, 1770

You ask me why I entered into the [Lavater] dispute. I only wish I had entered it more vigorously. Otherwise I feel, thank God, no regrets so far. Anyone with any brains at all must surely realize that this was an insipid exchange. I wish to God for another such opportunity so that I could do the same thing all over again.

Some people think they must accept everything and remain silent; I do not. When I consider what it takes to make people acknowledge the sacredness of our faith, I simply cannot understand why certain coreligionists of ours are always yelling that I should, for Heaven's sake, stop writing about these things.

God knows I did not like to disengage myself from this dispute. It was a matter of submitting my will to that of others. If I had had my own way, my reply would have been wholly different.

140

[*From* Bonnet's Palingenesis: A Counterinquiry]

Certain valorous authors decry the abjection with which the persecuted Jews of an earlier day permitted themselves to be slaughtered like cattle, without offering the least resistance. I can answer this accusation only with the following questions:

Does not a man demonstrate courage who would rather suffer the most disgraceful death than mouth a few words that could place him alongside his persecutor? Is a man contemptible for letting himself be torn apart by the hands of a raving maniac rather than betraying his own conscience?

The fiery courage of anyone defending human rights and resisting all who would deny them is admirable indeed. But can sound judgment really call cowardice that invincible spirit—often housed in a body too weak to fend off physical aggression—which looks unflinchingly into the eyes of death, a death that could be prevented by an act of hypocrisy?

Such inhumane scenes, the Almighty be thanked, have become a thing of the past, at least in most of civilized Europe. As men begin to understand that the God of love cannot have meant them to practice their religion by becoming executioners of their fellow men, the spirit of bloody persecution seems gradually to be disappearing from this continent. But does this also mean the disappearance of that spirit of civil persecution which, though permitting the weaker [members of society] to stay alive, denies them all benefits by which a humanitarian government could enhance the quality of human life?

Oh, my fellow men who are children of another faith! Can't you understand that life has but little value if it lacks those rights and privileges only society can grant? And that undeserved derision and contempt frequently seem more bitter than death itself? Yet both derision and contempt follow every footstep of those professing the Jewish faith. Deprived of all civil recognition and kept on the lowest rung of civilized society, we cannot develop the talents or faculties with which kind nature may have endowed us—and endowed us just as richly as all her other children; nor can we make use of those gifts for our own good or that of our fellow men. Wherever others are shown the most loving tolerance, we benefit the least. Wherever the arts and sciences flourish, we are kept in a state of barbarism. While the enlargement of the population of certain states is sought, we are subjected to special restrictions keeping us from increasing our numbers. Everything possible is done to make us into useless citizens, only to have it held against us that we are not sufficiently useful. Anyone capable of moving his tongue or pen is free to heap scorn on a people made despicable by every possible means.

Steadfastly and patiently we bear all this debasement, though we could be well off if only we found it possible to pretend. Instead, our misery is compounded by the fact that we are permitted only the most narrowly circumscribed means of making a living, and that we must pay numerous levies and taxes simply because we are Jews. And to that must be added the threat of banishment, which is not yet unusual in several states, as well as various other offenses against us in which even the most civilized countries still indulge.

What, then, is it that keeps us from muttering a false confession that would make us and our descendants indistinguishable from those who now scoff at us? Nothing but our love for the religion of our fathers, a faith our hearts consider true and our lips will not deny. Were it not for this faith, we could easily avail ourselves of the means by which to overcome all our misery, so that our existence, at least outwardly, might assume an aspect of affluence and well-being. One does not even ask us genuinely to accept a doctrine we cannot believe. All we are being asked to do is to mouth some words and forget our conscience. We clearly recognize those means, so enticingly offered us from all sides, for what they are. But our love for our fathers' religion is stronger than any misery we may have to suffer, is stronger even than death.

AGAINST A FALSE UNION OF FAITHS
[*From* Jerusalem; *see page 111.*]

If you, my brothers, are interested in man's genuine happiness, let us not pretend to find uniformity in a realm where multiformity is the obvious plan and goal of Providence. No man thinks and feels exactly like his fellow man. Why, then, should we use false-hoods in dealing with one another, and in our discussion of the most crucial issues of our life hide behind masks that render un-recognizable the distinct features given us (surely for some pur-pose) by God? Would we not thereby be taking it upon ourselves to counteract Providence and frustrate, if at all possible, creation's very purpose? Are we not deliberately attempting to nullify our vocation in this life and our destiny in the life to come?

Rulers of the earth, if an unimportant coinhabitant may raise his voice in the hope of reaching your ear, he would say, "Do not trust those who would glibly counsel you to set out on so harmful a course. For if you were to listen to them, our most precious jewel, our freedom of thought, would be lost. Remember for the sake of both your and our happiness that a unification of faiths [1] does not bespeak true tolerance but its very opposite. . . .

Do make man's conduct your concern, and judge his actions by his compliance with wise laws; but grant us that freedom of thought and speech which was given to us as our inalienable right by the Father of all. . . .

Make at least a start in preparing a path for our [as we hope] more fortunate descendants, so that they may reach that high level of culture and universal human tolerance for which reason still yearns in vain. Do not reward or punish adherence to any doctrine, and do not entice or bribe any man to embrace a religious faith. Allow any individual to speak his mind, to pray to God in his own

1. Such a "unification of faiths" was suggested by several of Mendelssohn's Christian contemporaries and was rejected by him as a euphemism to cover up an attempt to convert Jews.

way or that of his fathers, and to look for his eternal salvation wherever he hopes to find it—provided he does not disturb the public peace or break any public law, and provided, too, that his relationship to you and to his fellow citizens is above reproach. And let no one in your territories act as a talebearer or judge of what might go on in another's heart and mind. No one dare arrogate unto himself a right belonging to the Omniscient alone.

If we are to render unto Caesar what is Caesar's, you yourselves should render unto God what is God's. Love truth! Love peace!

[*To Herz Homberg* [1]]

March 1, 1784

. . . I am far from reacting as favorably as you to the mood of tolerance so prevalent in all our newspapers. As long as the proponents of a unification system continue to lurk in the background, this falsely glittering, tinseled tolerance seems to me more dangerous than open persecution. Unless I am mistaken, the devious notion that kindness and tolerance rather than harshness and persecution constitute the best means to achieve conversion has already been mentioned in Montesquieu's *Lettres persanes*.[2] And it is my impression that our time is dominated by this principle rather than by wisdom and brotherly love. If so, it would be so much the more urgent for the handful of people who wish as little to convert others as to be converted by others to consolidate, united by a firm bond. And what should constitute this unifying bond? This leads me to point out once again the need for observing the ceremonial law, unless we wish to see mere hypotheses turned into law, or books turned into symbols. . . .

1. See page 61.
2. Charles de Secondat, Baron de la Brède et de Montesquieu (1689–1755), French political philosopher. In his *Lettres persanes,* he ridicules the evils of his day, dealing satirically with religious tolerance, political corruption, justice, and the rights of man.

AGAINST CHRISTIAN MISSIONARY ZEAL
[To the Reverend O. J. B. Hesse, a Protestant minister who had published critical remarks about Mendelssohn's letter to Lavater]

. . . Had your comments reached me a few weeks earlier, I should probably have found it impossible to refrain from responding to at least some of them. I am amazed, for instance, that one is still willing to accept as valid an argument that uses the fact of our civil oppression as evidence for the erroneousness of our religion.

In addition to running counter to all philosophical procedure, this kind of logic contradicts the very spirit of the Gospels, or so it would seem to me. Did not Jesus and the apostles tell us emphatically that we must not apply any conclusions drawn from [conditions as they are in] the temporal [world] to [those that might prevail in the realm of] the eternal?

Moreover, is it not true that we could enjoy all privileges and advantages of civic life if we were only willing to engage in certain pretenses, as did our brethren in Spain and Portugal? Did they not flourish, as many of their descendants still do today, and live in prosperity, civil recognition, and political honor? And while those among us who really did convert to Islam certainly have made no change for the better with regard to their religion, they just as certainly have experienced a vast improvement in their living conditions. Whether they are feigned or true Moslems, the road to the highest public offices is open to them.

Or, to look at it differently: does not a sizable and far from disreputable segment even of the Christian population live in a state of civil oppression here, and of religious oppression there? How long have some of the noble spirits among them had to suffer under the yoke of superstition and hypocrisy till it pleased Providence to grant them happier times? Yet even in these happier times—how do you yourself feel about the religion that is the most powerful and prevalent in all Europe? How much, do you think, would the dominion of truth gain if the missionaries (Jesuits and Herrenhuter [1] alike) were to succeed in turning all nonbelievers into the kind of men they themselves are?

No, I cannot accept this method of using the unfathomable ways of Providence to prove her final intent. And the peculiar thing is that everything possible is being done from the Christian side in an effort to keep this kind of argumentation from growing obsolete. The more painstakingly we are kept oppressed, the more triumphantly are we proved [morally and religiously] wrong.

RELIGIOUS TOLERANCE
[*To J. H. Obereit, a Swiss physician and philosopher*]

March 13, 1770

. . . You ask me which of all the world's religions I consider the most likely to inculcate the most perfect conduct toward God and man—hence make such conduct really possible.

I should think it would be that religion which is the most tolerant, permitting us to embrace all mankind with equal love. Nothing makes us as narrowminded as a religion that excludes certain men on principle. Though it may not incite us to bloody persecutions, it is apt to produce in us a certain lack of lovingness and a pride in what we regard as our singular worth in the eyes of God, thus putting a wrong slant on even our best inclinations. . . .

1. Originally known as Unitas Fratrum, the Herrenhuter sect was founded in Bohemia by Johannes Hus, and seceded from the Catholic Church in 1467. Almost three hundred years later, its adherents were given asylum, a somewhat different religious orientation, and a new name by the Saxonian Count L. N. von Zinzendorf, whose missionary work in America in the middle of the eighteenth century led to the organization of the Moravian Brethren.

May 23, 1782

. . . Let every man live in accordance with his beliefs and convictions, and love his neighbor as he loves himself. To worship God and do good unto man are the purpose and goal of our existence; they represent our destiny in this life and our hope for the next. All else is insignificant. Suit yourself, my brother, as long as you contrive to love God as well as peace. . . .

[*To Gotthold Ephraim Lessing* (*discussing Freemasonry*)]

November 1777

. . . I am convinced that anything one group of men keeps secret from another is rarely worth serious investigation. . . .

THE COMMON BOND OF THE JEWS:
RELIGIOUS OBSERVANCE, NOT ARTICLES OF FAITH
[*To Herz Homberg*]

. . . You and I do not agree on the need for ritual laws. Even if they had lost their significance as a kind of script or symbolical language, they would still be needed as a unifying bond [for our people]. And this bond, I feel, will have to be preserved in the plan of Providence so long as polytheism, anthropomorphism, and religious usurpation still hold sway over our world. So long as these vexatious offenders of reason are banded together, all genuine theists must also unite in some manner, lest the others trample us underfoot. But what should constitute this unifying bond? Religious principles and beliefs? This would mean articles of faith, symbols, formulas—or a shackling of our reason. Instead, we must be unified by our religious observances [*Handlungen*], and meaningful observances at that. Hence, [religious] ceremonies must serve as our bond.

147

Actually, all our endeavors should have but one goal: to do away with the habitual misuse of those ceremonies and to infuse them with a genuine and authentic meaning. In this way, the [original, symbolic] script, blurred beyond recognition by hypocrisy and clerical ruse, might once again become legible and intelligible.

We should, however, obstinately resist that Jesuistic cunning which asks us with a show of great affability to join ranks with the other side—only to get hold of us. They approach us with stealthy gait, seemingly taking the first step but actually not moving at all. This resembles the "unification system" [1] of wolves which, in their great desire to be "united" with some sheep or lambs, try their best to turn them into wolves' flesh. . . .

[To Abraham Wolf, a Jewish mathematician who lived for some time in Mendelssohn's house and served Lessing as prototype for the Dervish in his Nathan the Wise]

July 11, 1782

. . . Neither modern nor ancient Judaism has any real symbols of faith. Very few principles or doctrines have been laid down for us. Maimonides [2] enumerates thirteen; Albo,[3] however, limits their number to merely three without being considered a heretic by anyone.

What has been prescribed for us are laws, customs, rules of conduct, and ritual observances [*Handlungen*]. We are free, however, with regard to doctrines. Wherever there is a difference of opinion among the rabbis, any Jew, be he uneducated or learned, may agree with one or another. For "these as well as those are words of the living God," as the rabbis wisely say in such instances.

Nevertheless, many who do not understand the meaning of this saying ridicule or else misinterpret it as a denial of the *principium contradictionis*. But Christians apparently now do realize how much human blood might have been spared had they always acted according to this adage. Judaism means conformity

1. See page 143.
2. See page 77.
3. Joseph Albo (1380–1445), Jewish theologian. His three articles of faith: the existence of God, divine revelation, retributive divine justice.

with regard to ritual observance [*Handlungen*], and freedom where religious doctrine is concerned, except for a few basic principles on which all our teachers are agreed, and without which the Jewish religion simply could not go on existing.

THE *ALEINU*

[*A defense of the* Aleinu *prayer, which the supervisor of the synagogue services in Königsberg. Professor G. J. Krypke, had denounced (in 1777) to the government, reporting that it contained attacks on Christianity*]

The *Aleinu* is one of our people's most ancient prayers. While it was originally meant to be used solely on Rosh Hashanah as a solemn introduction to rendering homage to the supreme Lawgiver and Judge of the world, its sublime significance led to its adoption as our daily concluding prayer. There are many arguments that prove irrefutably that several of the *Aleinu*'s passages refer only to pagans and their idolatrous practices and not, as some enemies and defamers of the Jewish people falsely assert, to Christians worshiping the same King of kings we adore, the Holy One, blessed be He. Nor is it true that this prayer contains any veiled kabbalistic allusions to the Christian Messiah. I shall, however, limit myself to enumerating here the most important arguments against these allegations.

Several of our people's scholars think this prayer originated at the time of Joshua, the son of Nun, some holding it was composed by this saintly man himself. . . . Though other writers have their doubts about this, one thing at least is certain: the *Aleinu* must already have been in existence at the time of the Second Temple. For it is a known fact that no changes have been made in any of the main Jewish prayers, the *tefillot shemonai esrai,* since the period of the Great Sanhedrin, the time of the Second Temple.

Now, the New Year Day's proclamation of adoration, which was to be preceded by the *Aleinu,* certainly constitutes one of the most important and most solemn Jewish prayers. And one may

149

rest assured that it was introduced at the very latest by the men of the Great Sanhedrin, that is, at the time of the Second Temple. The prayer's contents makes this assumption likely, for it deals exclusively with the eradication of idolatry and the establishment of a universal belief in the One, true, omnipotent God. It makes not the least mention of either the nation's liberation or the rebuilding of the Temple, which would hardly be the case had it been composed after the Temple's destruction.

Furthermore, the author of the *Aleinu* makes a distinction between his own nation, the nations of other lands, and the generations of the earth. This shows clearly that at that time the people must still have been living in its own country. In my opinion, it therefore makes no sense whatever to look for a secret allusion to Christians and their Messiah in this prayer. Its authors obviously lived during the period preceding that of Jesus the Nazarene—a time when paganism was widespread and idolatry, for the eradication of which the *Aleinu* asks, was still the dominant religion everywhere outside of Judea.

Nor should it be assumed that this prayer was changed later on, or that some secret allusions were added. For as previously pointed out, it has always been a matter of conscience for the Jew not to let the slightest change slip into any of his main prayers. The *Aleinu* in particular was so highly regarded by Jewish scholars that they not only counted and wrote down its every word and syllable but also made absolutely sure that not one of them was changed. Moreover, this prayer is cited without the least alteration even by writers living under Moslem rule.

Jews in Asia as well as Africa recite the *Aleinu* in the identical terms used by us here, though their environment is devoid of any manifestations of Christianity to which they might wish secretly to allude. I am therefore more than a little amazed that Professor Krypke should have accepted on faith—that is, without any investigation whatever—the word of the ex-Jew Peter[1] (see

1. Peter, a converted Jew who, around 1400, instigated the jailing of Lippmann-Mühlhausen (fl. c. 1400) and other Jewish authors by accusing them of having insulted Christianity in their writings.

Nitzaḥon Number 348),[2] when he quotes that "the term *varek* (something empty) must be understood to mean Jesus Christ because, according to the Kabbala, the words *varek* and *Yeshu* have the same numerical value." How can this teacher of the Hebrew language fail to take into consideration the fact that the prophet Isaiah, who surely cannot be accused of any such allusions, uses the term *hevel varek* in order to describe something in which one places a vain trust, an empty hope? "For Egypt helpeth in vain, and to no purpose" (Isaiah 30:7).

The author of the *Aleinu* undoubtedly had this passage in mind, as Rabbi David Abudraham [3] justifiably assumes, when he used a similar term to describe the heathens' vain and futile trust in their idols. And this is precisely why it seems likely to me that the author lived after the prophet Isaiah's time and not, as some will have it, at the time of Joshua. . . .

2. *Sepher ha-Nitzaḥon* (Book of Triumph), a polemical work by Yomtov Lippmann-Mühlhausen.
3. David ben Joseph Abudraham, fourteenth-century Spanish commentator on Hebrew liturgical customs and practices.

PART FOUR

Ultimate Questions

Editor's Note

Though Mendelssohn did not create a new philosophical system, he was a genuine philosopher in the literal meaning of the term: he loved wisdom, was versed in and devoted to philosophy, and met all vicissitudes of life with equanimity. The wisdom he loved was more than mere erudition. In fact, he was not interested in knowledge for its own sake, which, in his view, led all too often to an empty display of intellectual showmanship. He regarded knowledge—pre-eminently philosophy, which he frequently referred to as "world-wisdom"—not as an end in itself but as the best possible means by which to attain a true understanding of the world and of man's nature and destiny. And he generously shared his hard-won human insights, the results of his "philosophizing," with any other "seeker of truth" he encountered.

Mendelssohn felt that nothing exists without reason, no matter for how fleeting a moment. And nothing ever ceases to exist without having achieved something tangible. In all nature, living things progress from a lower to a higher stage of development, approaching, if only to some small degree, their fullest potential. This advance toward perfection constitutes the very purpose of life. It is, however, a progress made exclusively by the individual plant, animal, or human being, not by any given species or mankind as a whole. Any living thing reaches greater perfection simply by being, that is, by utilizing its physical endowment, and improving it in the process.

But man, who has been given a mind in addition to his physical endowment, must make the maximum use of his intellectual faculties to enhance his stature as a human being. Since to know more is conducive to becoming a better, more moral person, man must strive ever to increase his knowledge and understanding. Moral improvement is the way to advance toward life's true objective: happiness on earth and salvation in the beyond.

Happiness on earth, though, is not to be found in a self-centered life. To become happy is to make happy—to contribute, in whatever form, to the well-being of others. And salvation in the beyond means neither redemption from sin by an act of atonement, nor escape from eternal damnation by an act of faith. Salvation or "eternal bliss" is, in Mendelssohn's conception, a state of near-perfection in which the soul, contemplating the world's inner harmony and the place assigned to man within the cosmic plan, reaches that comprehension of truth, of beauty, and of God's intent for his creatures which constitutes man's final goal.

WHAT IS MAN'S DESTINY?
[*Excerpts from letters to Thomas Abbt*]

Our all-wise Benefactor has sent us here so that we might steadily exercise and thereby improve our faculties. That this represents His will is evidenced not merely by the very nature of our drives, desires, and passions but also by the character of our pleasures, displeasures, and tastes and even by our wilfulness and sense of self-importance. The uneducated man senses the force of all these impulses, though he may not be able to articulate his emotions. The educated man tries to control his inclinations rationally, and is happiest when he can make his own will correspond closely to the real purpose of his natural drives, the purpose intended by God.

But does our Benefactor's plan for us extend beyond our destiny here on earth? Since no substance is ever destroyed, it continues throughout its existence to serve its [divinely] intended purpose.

Is there, then, some inner connection linking our future to our present state? There is indeed, and it is as perfect as the order of all God's designs, or as the syllogism of a logical demonstration in which the conclusion follows from all preceding premises.

The blossom torn off by the north wind, the seed that will not take root and sprout—they are blown away and disintegrate. Yet their components, reorganized, assume another form, fulfilling, in their new shape, the divine intent. Would they be able to do so had they not first been either blossom or seed? Just as in a logical demonstration one argument must proceed from the other to arrive at a correct conclusion, so God, too, proceeds in the most direct manner toward the realization of the goals He has set for man.

There [in the beyond] too, O man, there too you will serve mankind. But you could never do so had you not first exercised your faculties here on earth, just as you could never become a man had your basic constitution not already rudimentarily existed in your father's blood.

The divine order of things is characterized by unity of purpose. All intermediate ends are at once means, all means ends. Do not think of our life here as merely preparatory, or of our future life as an end in itself. Both are means, and both are ends. God's plan extends into all eternity, and the transformation of all substances continues indefinitely.

Questions and answers.

1) What is man's destiny?—To serve, in congruence with his rational insights, his divinely intended purpose; perpetually to become more perfect, and to attain eternal bliss through that state of perfection.

2) But how shall those thousands incapable of rational investigation determine the nature of God's intent for them?—They carry out their assignment by their existence alone, without intellectual

speculation. Do the heavenly bodies not move according to a plan unknown to them? The Eternal One did not make even the stilling of a creature's hunger contingent upon its reasoning power, let alone the fulfilling of His intent for us.

3) And what about the death of infants?—No baby dies without having developed at least some rudimentary skill, if only that ability to feel [some sensations] which starts in his mother's womb. And what amazing changes, now that I think of it, take place within such a tiny seminal being until, in its next developmental stage, it learns to react to hunger, warmth, or wetness! Can you doubt that these early achievements already constitute a certain actualization of whatever plan the Creator has for this child? As it undergoes a reorganization of its components, even the seed that never comes to fruition progresses from an earlier to a later stage of development; and that stage represents that seed's fulfillment of its divinely intended purpose.

4) Still, why is it that thousands upon thousands of potentialities are never actualized, not even to the modest degree possible here on earth?—What do you mean by the term "possible" in this context? Possible by, or possible without neglecting schemes that are by far more significant? Do you dare give an answer? As to the question of why such a vast potential [human as well as any other] always remains unrealized: because much of it can serve God's over-all plan in this or that form, without having to go through all possible stages.

5) But why would this hold true in some instances and not in others?—For the same reason for which it cannot be denied that the different parts of a watch [though unlike in design and function] all serve a single purpose. This wheel turns fast, that one slowly; and a third moves almost imperceptibly. Since all of them serve a common purpose, why do they not turn at an equal speed? Here you have it: a common purpose. And it is precisely because of its singleness of purpose that the plan [whether God's or the watchmaker's] requires all those multifariously functioning parts.

Each tool in God's workshop serves its own purpose. This purpose could not be served equally well by any other implement;

nor is the performance of any one tool exactly the same as that of another.

THE DEATH OF A CHILD
[*To Thomas Abbt*]

Berlin, May 1, 1764

Some recent events in my domestic life have so shattered me that I did not even feel like writing to my friends, though this is normally my favorite occupation. Death has knocked at my door, robbing me of an innocent child that lived among us for only eleven months, though these, thank God, were happy and full of promise.

My friend, these eleven months of innocent living were not in vain. In this short time, the little girl's mind developed amazingly. She progressed from a tiny creature that merely cried and slept into a small rational being. Much in the way in which young blades of grass push through the hard soil in spring, she began to show the first signs of distinct emotions. She indicated compassion, hatred, love, and admiration, she understood what was said to her, and tried to make herself understood.

You may well ridicule my naïveté and look upon my rationalizations as weakness—the weakness of a man seeking consolation and unable to find it anywhere except in his imagination. Perhaps a sense of self-preservation compels me (without indulging my foibles too blatantly) to adopt any doctrine conducive to my peace of mind.

Yet I cannot believe that God has put us here on earth like, say, some foam upon a wave. Indeed, I must embrace the opposite view simply because it seems less absurd, and promises me more comfort. . . .

GOD'S CREATURES: WHAT IS THEIR PURPOSE?
[*To Thomas Abbt*]

Berlin, March 26, 1765

. . . The well-known dictum that in God's creation all means are ends and all (intermediary) ends merely means may yield more insights than we have thus far assumed. If Maupertuis,[1] for instance, asks: "Is the fly so wonderfully built for the sole purpose of being devoured by the rapacious spider in a single instant?" I should like to reply: "The works of God do not provide us with ready answers or definite statements of purpose." The primary purpose of this flying machine's artful construction is evidently the mere existence of this small insect. But why? For the simple reason that those things that look like flies may be alive and have sensations. And if you continue with your nearsighted "but why?" you might as well turn all creation into a desert. That proud yet poverty-stricken thing, man, asks of anything that seems of no use to him personally: "What is it for?"

The fly's existence may well serve some secondary purpose. In fact, this is the way it must be, unless my conception of the interrelatedness of ends and means in nature is totally wrong. Flies probably clean the air; or they may possibly announce an impending change of weather by stinging us; in addition, they also provide nourishment for spiders. Moreover, God probably has definite intentions with regard to every single fly. But who can fathom those?

Similarly, natural science asks: "Why is there such an infinite number of tiny organisms and cells in the seeds of animals and plants, if only a single one will come to fruition while all the others perish?" My reply is: "The small animals and plants are proportionately as important in nature as the large ones, and one cannot

1. Pierre Louis Moreau de Maupertuis (1698–1759), French mathematician and astronomer who, invited by Frederick the Great, headed the new Academy of Sciences in Berlin from 1741 to 1756.

160

say that the former exist merely to give rise to the latter. True, semen and seed have an inherent disposition to become grown animals and plants. But who says they must undergo this transformation in every instance? And why does one deny any purpose to their existence merely because they have not developed fully or grown to their full size? Though the majority of them do lose their ability to grow, they grace creation even in their infinitesimal smallness. Still, even those reduced to infinitesimally small organisms stop neither living nor fulfilling God's intent. And if their inner organization had not been exactly the way it is, they would in all likelihood have been unable to fulfill this intent.

But what exactly is this intent? Here, I believe it is time to touch one's finger to one's lips and seal them. Despite all our searching inquiries, this wise "I do not know" remains our last resort. This, however, does not at all mean a negation of those things we do know.

With this, I am coming closer, I think, to the meaning of your question. For it may be similar with man and his life on earth, if, that is, one can clearly define those specific characteristics that make us rational beings. Since we exist, we may deduce with some certainty that the world would have been less complete without human beings. And what is our purpose, what are we to do down here? All of us must do not only what we have to do but in fact what we can never fail to do—namely, develop our mental faculties, though some will necessarily do so to a higher degree than others.

In what way does man's destiny differ from that of other beings? Only in the way in which we make use of our specific gifts on earth to achieve that degree of perfection given us [as our potential goal].

Why are only so few men aware of the purpose of their existence? Because man can fulfill his purpose even when he is unaware of it. Few men ever realize the purpose of their hunger, and those who do may have the poorest appetite. Man, you say, does not know why he is here. Oh, but he does know it rather well, if only because he sees, feels, compares, incessantly exercises his ability to think. And he does all this with great gusto. The only thing is that he lacks such abstract notions as "purpose," "existence," "means," et cetera, so that he is unable to sum up logically his incessant emotions and acts. I for one do not even see why you insist that this is particularly necessary.

Some people die before reaching that level of development possible here on earth. This is true enough when you consider mankind's total potential. But if we look upon it [a prematurely ended life] as a partial potential, seeing the single individual as determined and circumscribed by certain conditions, we may well arrive at a different judgment. For then we should see that each person reaches that level of development he could and should have reached in the given circumstances and context.

This would also hold true for the seminal cell that was never conceived and therefore neither could nor should have developed at this time. But this does not mean that its innate dispositon, even its rudimentary development or potential, is completely lost. For, as I said before, except for their general main purpose, God's works do not demonstrate His intent so unequivocally, so obviously, that one would be justified in saying that every means is lost merely because we do not see the end to which it might be leading.

. . . THAT JUSTICE BE DONE
[*To Thomas Abbt*]

Berlin, July 20, 1764

. . . You ask about my compatriots' future destiny. But which compatriots? Those who live in Dessau or those who dwell in Jerusalem? Once you answer this question, I might reply, in the words of Molière's Pancrace, *"Je m'en lave les mains. Je n'en sais rien. Il en sera ce qu'il en pourra. Selon les aventures."* [1]

As long as my [philosophical] system remains undisturbed, I shall do likewise. Pompadour, Brühl, the Jesuits, inquisitors, pirates, tyrants, poison-mixers, or traitors—does it really matter?

1. Roughly: "I wash my hands of this. I know nothing about it. What will be, will be. These are the chances one has to take." From *Le Mariage Forcé.*

With a German metaphysician's cold detachment I pull my thread-bare coat tightly around me and say, quoting Pangloss,[2] "This is the best of all possible worlds."

I can merely repeat a statement to which I have already frequently resorted: it may not be necessary that my own eyes see justice done. Yet it is absolutely necessary that justice be done eventually so that (and this I regard as most important) the souls of the godless do not remain forever as maimed as they all too often are at the moment of death.

To tell the truth, I think very little of a justice that is merely retributive. The purpose of all chastisement is correction. And in the case of divine judgment, this can only mean the moral improvement of the chastised subject. Such improvement cannot forever fail to materialize. It will take place at some time to come. And from this you may infer what I think about our destiny. . . .

MAN: THE ULTIMATE END IN THE COSMIC PLAN
[*To Thomas Abbt*]

. . . You ask me what I think concerning my destiny as a man: first of all, I must worship [God] and perform good deeds. Then, I must strive for happiness. I realize that by the same token by which God Himself cannot be happy without acts of kindness and goodness, His lowliest creature cannot be entirely unhappy as long as he can do some good. True, I cannot determine with any degree of certainty the part I was assigned in all of creation, nor can I know how far I and my kind have progressed within the cosmic plan.

But this much I do know: I am a member of a group of beings who must and can worship God and perform good deeds, beings who represent not merely means to higher ends within the cosmic plan but ends in themselves—and ultimate ends at that. Thus, my heart and mind can be filled with the sweet consolation that I shall one day exist in a different state, one of enhanced ability to wor-

2. A character in Voltaire's satirical work *Candide* who constantly cites, and by implication ridicules, Leibniz's famous saying.

ship and do good. I shall then see in a clearer light the great truth that goodness toward others constitutes happiness, and that the more happiness I can create the happier I shall become. And I can create happiness in this world by trying to promote order and harmony, gladness and enjoyment, wisdom and virtue.

This expectation of mine (surely neither deception nor delusion!) is fully commensurate with the nature of things—my own nature as well as that of the most exalted Wisdom's kind rule. To be sure, I cannot flatter myself that I shall ever be able to divest myself entirely of whatever foolishness occasionally troubles me or makes me unhappy down here. In fact, I have the feeling that even in the beyond I shall occasionally have to suffer so that others may become happier, and shall frequently do something unwise simply because it seems wise to me.

Moreover, I realize that I shall never become entirely one with the source of all perfection; shall never be able to enjoy completely untroubled the pure pleasure of comprehending the whole truth. But I shall come ever closer to my goal. I shall become increasingly more aware that I cannot ever suffer for others without becoming a better and, in an inward sense, a more perfect person. Mine will be an ever deeper realization that all my wisdom is but foolishness if it desires anything other than what an all-wise Providence has arranged for me. And I shall become increasingly aware that like all others of my kind I have been singled out and destined by our Creator to be righteous and happy in that righteousness; to search for truth; to love beauty and do the best I can—which means to worship Him and to do good.

REWARD AND PUNISHMENT
[*From Mendelssohn's comments on his correspondence with Thomas Abbt*]

Fall 1781

. . . After much contemplation its seems clear to me that in this world things are not quite as poorly organized, good fortune and misfortune not quite as badly distributed, reward and punishment not quite as arbitrarily dealt out as some people assert with much lament and complaining, or as they would have us believe in order to make our life-to-come appear more enticing.

All my reflections, however, can shed true light on the questions under discussion only if life here is not the absolute end for us; if, that is, our soul will permanently endure. Only then will the inner dignity and sense of perfection our soul acquires here (while we pursue the good) represent a really lasting value for us. Only then will the suffering of the righteous turn out to be a true gain, and every struggle a true victory of the virtuous against fate. Even if the good man were to be defeated temporarily, he could be sure of his final triumph. For his very effort gives his spirit an inner dignity and sublime beauty well worth his noble sweat. Based on this premise, genuine good will can never be entirely frustrated in achieving its end, for it is also an end in itself.

If, however, our life down here did represent all that was apportioned us by the hand of Providence, and our entire existence filled only that dimension of space and time which can be measured, then our [religio-philosophical] system of hope and expectation, worthiness and unworthiness, would be most narrowly circumscribed indeed. In that case, we could survey, from its beginning to its absolute end, the entire inner sequence of cause and effect in the realm of morality, and judge both virtue with its inner and outer rewards and vice with all its consequences. In that case, too, the righteous man who is defeated in his earthly struggles—frequently having wagered his entire existence, his very being, while thus engaged—would be truly lost, and lost forever.

If our life really came to an end with our body's death, the vice-ridden individual (trying to gain his ignoble ends and achieve what he, with his perverted sense of values, considers happiness) would die without having seen the errors of his ways, without having learned anything. In that case, Providence would indeed be unjust, and actually more so to the cheated oppressor than to the oppressed; more unjust to the persecutor who, setting his foot on the neck of the innocent, believes himself supremely happy than to the persecuted who breathes his last breath after having remained loyal to truth and justice throughout his suffering. In that case, good

165

and evil, reward and punishment, would indeed have been distributed most unevenly.

We expect in our future life not a righting of wrongs suffered here, so as to satisfy a certain kind of vindictiveness, as Mr. Abbt calls it. We expect that justice which will enhance our soul's perfection, a perfection the soul really does acquire through its virtue and righteousness, its struggles and suffering [on earth]. As a true, an inner reward for our good and kind deeds we expect that spiritual substantiality, continuity, and endurance without which virtue's suffering would be true suffering, evil's triumph true triumph, and much of what appears to be moral disarray on this earth a lasting disarray indeed. . . .

He who anxiously inquires about virtue's reward has never genuinely loved virtue as such. He who expects benefit from every benevolent act does not yet understand true happiness. He has not yet reached that level of morality at which one becomes aware that virtue carries its own inherent reward; that exercising one's moral faculties means true spiritual happiness; and that the struggle, self-conquest, and self-sacrifice frequently needed for acts of benevolence cannot receive a better reward than another opportunity to triumph once again in a similar struggle.

Those who feel that things are badly arranged in this life and in disarray [with regard to divine justice] do not realize that along with the kind of [mechanistic] order they would like to see in this world would go the disappearance of all moral values, all virtue and righteousness. In a world where everything would be meticulously arranged according to their notions of [divine] justice, all virtue would be rewarded, and every act that is morally good would have to result in some corresponding material good. Virtue would never suffer, vice never triumph. But in such a world there would be no opportunity to show pity, patience, generosity, or steadfastness, or to engage in the protection and delivery of the virtuous, or in a fight to the death for friends or country. And whatever virtue might still be pursued would be neither noble nor lovable; nor would vice be ignoble and repulsive. For the former would have become profitable, the latter harmful, and anything one might say about virtue would appear as no more than part of the [divine] economy. . . .

166

THE THREAD OF LIFE IS NEVER BROKEN

[*To Thomas Abbt. Having elaborated his frequently expressed view that man's purpose and destiny on earth is the fullest development of his physical and intellectual potential, hence the attainment of that greatest possible perfection Mendelssohn equates with happiness, he continues as follows.*]

Berlin, Fall 1781

. . . But what becomes of these fully developed human faculties in the life to come? Here, I think we can and must be satisfied with a general answer: the thread [of life] is never broken. We shall continue and fully accomplish there what we had already started and only interrupted here. But if one wishes to know exactly in what shape or in which region we shall live there—whether with an ethereal body or with some of our present senses and limbs— reason asks us humbly to withdraw and fall silent. We cannot even know with any degree of certainty what the next day will hold in store for us. How, then, can we dare to foretell or even merely assume anything that might occur in infinity itself, and after so complete a transformation of our entire being?

Nor can we gain any surer knowledge of all of this through revelation. For revelation would speak to us in a language we cannot understand, and presuppose a knowledge of fundamental concepts we simply do not possess. We may, in our next life, experience the disclosure of new senses; or senses similar to our present ones may be more perfectly developed so as to raise us to a higher level of awareness and lucidity. New sources of enjoyment may open up for us, or we may find a greater latitude or wider scope for different kinds of spiritual activities and exertions. Still, here on earth we cannot really depict any of this. Anything we may have been told about it is a knowledge merely of words and shadow-images, somewhat analogous to what the deaf man gets to know about the pleasures of music or the blind about the beauty of paintings. . . .

PROGRESS OF MANKIND VERSUS
INDIVIDUAL PROGRESS
[*To August von Hennings* [1]]

June 25, 1782

. . . In your last letter, you voice regret that mankind's progress is so negligible. You say humanity climbs up a few steps at certain times, only to sink that much the lower at the next moment. You therefore feel mankind is subject to a perpetually circular motion, so that at long last it merely arrives at the point from which it had started. And all this leads you to the conclusion that man cannot be meant to achieve perfection.

My counterargument runs as follows:[2] true, nature does not intend the perfection of mankind; its goal is the perfection of man, of the individual. Every single human being is meant to develop his talents and abilities, hence become increasingly perfect. And precisely because each individual ought to strive for perfection, mankind as a whole must repeat that cycle about which we complain so much. Mankind as such is, however, not a being with a life of its own. It is, rather, an entity comprised of a succession of human beings. One might compare it to a river whose waters do not keep their separate identity for even one moment, though they bestow a nameable identity on the stream.

In principle, the succession of human beings, mankind, is also capable of making progress; but this is not the kind of progress the individual can make. If mankind were to progress continuously and corporately, new arrivals on earth would find no opportunity to make use of their own faculties, to develop their highest potential. Yet this would appear to be nature's true purpose.

Our existence down here resembles a station by a post route. If those coming behind us are to be carried over the same road, the carriage horses must return to their starting point. The postilion,

1. See page 64.
2. See also pages 200–201.

to be sure, must make the same trip over and over again. But he represents merely the means by which successively arriving travelers are enabled to continue on their way.

Assuming, for a moment, we were to improve our capabilities to such a degree that the craftsman would need neither mind nor skill to create his product; that we had cleansed our religious notions of every prejudice; had reached a point in commerce where the products of any one country would be available in all other countries at all times; had freed all governments of tyranny, all courts of chicanery, all custom-sheds of harassment, all literary reviews of provocative statements: what, then, would be left for our children to do?

Should they continue to press forward? The road surely leads into infinity. Yet they arrive in this world as we once arrived. They have the same talents, the same faculties, hence must either find for themselves the same inducements we found, or else let their potential go to waste. Not having started where we did, they cannot continue from where we stopped. They bring with them an impulse that will be frustrated unless it meets some resistance. Where shall they practice their intellectual gifts when all their needs can be satisfied without any effort of their own? How shall they pursue their love of freedom when they have never experienced tyranny; their love of truth when all insights are handed to them predigested, as it were, and without any effort on their part? It is obvious that mankind must here or there regress if the individual is to make progress.

Precisely because the development of the individual represents man's natural destiny, mankind at large cannot always remain in the state it has reached by its own effort. . . . To enjoy certain things without having labored for them, to gratify certain needs without effort spells death to any human ambition. And here you have a compelling argument against all Epicureans: human happiness lies more in man's struggling and striving than in the consumption of the fruits of his labor. . . .

HEART AND MIND

[An Outline for Considering the Question: Has Man a Natural Inclination Toward Vice? From "Minor Writings in Philosophy and Aesthetics."]

The term "intelligence" is too broad. There are many kinds of intelligence, with different individuals possessing one or the other, just as there are many kinds of imagination which differ from poet to painter, from sculptor to architect. The kindhearted nitwit must have certain insights lacking in the most cunning scoundrel. The former is aware that man cannot be happy unless he makes someone else happy. He may not know how to go about promoting the happiness of others and may, in fact, choose a most unsuitable means toward this end. Nevertheless, he senses that one cannot enjoy oneself while others suffer but feels that one's joy increases as one brings happiness to others. . . .

Give to a composer the poet's imagination, and he will remain a mediocre musician unless he also possesses the kind of imagination appropriate to his own subject matter and art form. The term "imagination" is too general to be applicable to the specific needs of different artists. And the same holds true for all cognitive knowledge.

In common usage, we distinguish between heart and mind, kindness and cleverness. Yet philosophical terminology, though surely manifesting a keener intellectual acumen than does our daily usage of language, seldom demonstrates a sounder common sense. What daily usage keeps apart, philosophical terminology should not bring together. Even granting that the determinist is right, and cognitive knowledge is all that counts in the end, there is not just one kind or manner of cognition. Any moral act must comprise both—knowledge of its final purpose or end and knowledge of the means to achieve that end. The former is determined by man's benevolence or, if he is not intellectually but merely emotionally aware of his motives, his so-called "kind heart." The latter—knowledge of the means—is referred to as intelligence. Both together represent wisdom. In the wise man, benevolence and intelligence are combined. He is determined to generate as much happiness as possible, and knows by what means to accomplish this end.

I should, however, be careful not to deny all virtue to the kindhearted but slow-witted man. He may admittedly cause some harm despite his best intentions. Yet he is more truly virtuous and has more moral merit than the shrewdest villain. Permit me to pursue this thought, though it has no immediate connection with the problem under discussion.

The goal of all our desires is our own happiness. We achieve this state partly directly (by our efforts to increase our own physical and intellectual perfection), partly indirectly (by promoting the happiness of others and therefore also achieving our own). We are both ends and means; or we are merely ends while the means is a being other than ourselves, a being whose happiness we have at heart. The former effort is motivated by love of self;[1] the latter, by love of others. Without love of self, though, there can be no love of others, hence no implicit goal. And without love of others we cannot satisfy our love of self; love of self, as we have said, implicitly requires objects outside of ourselves.

With regard to love of self, then, intelligence and wisdom must coincide, and there is no distinction between the dim- and the sharp-witted. For all of us have (as indeed we must have) the good will to promote happiness. But we are prone to error when it comes to choosing the best means toward this end. How does this happen? I think in the following way:

Owing mainly to a certain error in judgment, we sin against our love of self or disregard our duties against ourselves. Whatever is palpably present to our senses exerts the strongest influence upon us. The sensualist sacrifices to this palpability whatever the future may hold for him—something he will surely regret once that future arrives and the present has receded into the past. Similarly, anything pertaining to the senses is given preference over the merely spiritual, for the impact of the sensuous is strong as long

1. This term [German: *Selbstliebe*] should not be read in its negative connotation of egocentricity. In Mendelssohn's usage, it means an awareness of, and subsequently a respect for, one's uniqueness as a person.

171

as one's physical needs remain unsatisfied. Against one's better judgment, one gives in to animal needs, thereby neglecting one's spiritual perfection.

Ignoble minds are prone to such misjudgments. Their imagination would have them believe that their needs are greater and their [moral] abilities less than they really are. Every [spiritual] expenditure therefore makes them fear some future want. This may be due to a certain lack of intelligence. But it is surely only a certain kind of intelligence that these miserable wretches lack.

The virtues of self-love consist largely in the ability to depreciate (as prescribed by reason) the significance of the tangible and physical and to appreciate the significance of the intangible and spiritual. Exercising this ability will help us disregard the lure of the physical, so that reason will not be frustrated in its attempt to establish a balance between what is and what is not evident to our senses, between the physical and the metaphysical. Control of our emotions and the ability rationally to check their influence upon ourselves is called stoicism. And we call enthusiasm the capacity to be equally sensitive to that which is intangible and that which is tangible, to the immaterial as much as the material. Man's love of self ought to be accompanied by a measure of enthusiasm so as to provide some checks and balances for his stoicism.

Man's social virtues are grounded in a similar ability to set the cold intellect of the stoic philosopher aflame with the fire of the enthusiast, so that he may compare and bring into proper balance the far and the near, the more remote and the immediate [concerns of man].

The lowest rung of man's social virtues is occupied by his love for his progeny or his own kind—those he considers his extended self. With this love goes a readiness to sacrifice, on occasion, even his self-interest. To a certain degree, animals also possess this innate love (a phenomenon to which we must give this designation until we shall have learned to understand it better). The meanest and most witless human being, too, is capable of this love, a love that actually often gives rise to the greatest crimes.

In cases of a collision of interests, it is a low, criminal reaction to set one's limited ego above all else, putting the demands of a

172

crass egotism above one's love of family. The same holds true when we permit the love for our family to take precedence over justice, or over our love for our country. And that love can, in turn, become a vice if it usurps the place a universalist humanitarianism should occupy in our hearts. It is only rarely that crimes are committed for the sole satisfaction of selfish needs or physical drives. Largely it is man's love of his own kin that outshouts the voice of general humanity, turning him into a swindler, thief, or robber. At times, his misdirected ambition speaks more loudly than the voice of his country, or of humanity at large. At other times, it is his love of country that causes man to disregard all demands of justice and humanitarian love. Here, we have once more a kind of misjudgment that might be called lack of intelligence if it were not so frequently coupled with much cleverness, with a certain type of mental acumen. Here, too, the remedy is [a correct mixture of] stoicism and enthusiasm.

By stoicism I mean an ability to control oneself under all circumstances: de-emphasizing the significance of immediate concerns, we permit them to influence us no more than is compatible with reason and truth. And by enthusiasm I mean the ability to emphasize the more remote concerns of our moral life; to listen to the government's voice and its laws as did Socrates,[2] though his love of life, the entreaties of his friends, and the tears of those he loved might easily have interfered with his judgment. . . .

For these reasons, the wise man will always be just and on occasion even unbendingly severe where the average kind man would possibly show pity and the worthless man might be swayed easily. The sage does not love merely what he sees, nor is he moved merely by what is palpably present to him. His love encompasses his most remote descendants as well as those he cradles in his arms; the most distant fellow citizens as well as those who are nearest to him; men in the outmost regions of space and time as well as his neighbors and acquaintances. He looks at the world

2. The Greek philosopher who, as reported in Plato's *Phaedo* (and Mendelssohn's paraphrase of this work in the following pages), accepted the death verdict of the Athenian court, subsequently drinking the poison provided by that court rather than flee the city as his friends had suggested.

with spiritual eyes, and in wise moderation apportions to society and its conditions as much of his interest and as great a share of his love as is their just due within the harmony of the whole.

In a word: the ability to control his emotions by reasoned judgments and, in turn, to make tangible what otherwise might remain mere rational conceptualization—this, I think, is the great secret anyone wishing to attain the heights of heroic virtue ought to possess.

SIN AND DAMNATION
[*To Brother Maurus Winkopp* [1]]

March 24, 1780

I am much obliged to you for your letter of the first of this month and should like to thank you for the extraordinary pleasure it gave me. If the working out and subsequent sharing of useful insights can be said to be a matter of merit, the awakening of a spirit like yours must be called the sweetest reward one could possibly reap. I have already several times had the good fortune of finding in the most hidden nooks and corners—some of them actually inaccessible to me—minds that are in perfect harmony with my own. For example, I felt as if I had unexpectedly come upon a brother in the La Trappe Monastery, a brother I had long thought dead. . . .

I grant that the effects of sin are everlasting, as are the effects of all causes. But while it is true that causal relationships are inescapable in the realm of nature, this is not true in the realm of human volition. Here, the consequences of man's acts are not inevitable. Sin need not necessarily lead to eternal damnation, as is being asserted, for it may yet be outweighed by the good in man's soul.

This, then, constitutes my hope: my sins will not cause me eternal suffering, though their effects will endure forever, leaving behind recognizable traces. But at some time to come, my evil

1. See page 98.

inclinations may be outweighed by the good. Then, a sense of the good will prevail in my soul, and I, along with you and all our brethren, our fellow human beings, shall partake of eternal bliss. . . .

ON DIVINE JUSTICE
[From "The Soul," an essay originally written in Hebrew, published after Mendelssohn's death, in 1787, and soon thereafter translated into German]

In my view, all punishment is intended to benefit and educate the sinner. What I mean is this: man's inability to distinguish between good and evil leads him into sin. But once the interrelationship between sin and punishment becomes clear to him, man will realize that by choosing evil he has rejected the good. This is the purpose of punishment. True, inflicting certain penalties on an offender can occasionally also serve as a means to educate others —to warn them, that is, not to commit similar sinful acts. Both intents, however, are equally justified, for one act of Providence usually serves a thousand different purposes.

But since a human judge is incapable of accomplishing two objectives at once, he must punish the miscreant in order that others may learn to obey and fear [the law]. God, that just Judge, however, will not bend the right of the individual to the good of society, as a human ruler might have to do. All God's ways are just, and all His acts with regard to every single individual beyond reproach. He never punishes a sinner unless it is both for his own good and for that of the community. If the sinner would only realize the consequences of this punishment—that is, the true happiness it will eventually bring him—he might actually implore God, the all-just Judge, to discipline him. For punishment heals the sickness of the soul, binding up its wounds. Without it, the soul cannot be restored except in a miraculous, supranatural way.

Thus viewed, the meting out of justice represents not an evil but exclusively a good—for the world, the individual, and the

175

community. The sinner who endures God's chastisement should therefore cease his grumbling. For far from constituting a reprisal, punishment, as we said before, is the sinner's medicine and cure.

You may object: "But why was Reuben destined to sin—and subsequently suffer for his own good—while Simeon was never meant to sin at all? Does God—He who is above all imperfection —thereby not act unjustly? Why are not all men destined to be perfectly righteous so that there would be no need to punish sinners?" . . .

By the same token, you may ask: "Why is there a hierarchy [of moral awareness] among us creatures?" But once you inquire why all men are not perfectly righteous, you may as well step down a rung to ask why rocks are not animate beings, or else step up a rung and inquire why men are not angels.

I do not think we need belabor this point. These questions simply make no sense, and their answer is known even to a beginner: the world cannot possibly exist wtihout a hierarchical order [of its creatures].

PART FIVE

On the Immortality of the Soul

Editor's Note

Throughout his writings, Mendelssohn returns again and again to the question of the soul's immortality. As a pious Jew, he takes it for granted that man has a soul and that this soul was created by God. And as an eclectic philosopher he defines that soul variously as the animating principle of human life; as an active force inspiring man to rise from an animal to a truly human level; or as a nonmaterial, simple substance related in its essence to that Prime Simple Substance which is God. Minimally, the soul is described as the ability to think, will, and feel. But, regardless of how it is defined, does the soul perish along with its body or does it survive—and if so, how?

Far from claiming originality as an "epoch-making" thinker, Mendelssohn derives his views of life and death from widely divergent thought-systems, readily admitting that he seeks no new paths by which to arrive at some insight or truth when there are already well-traversed and perfectly serviceable old ones. Eclecticism is no derogatory concept for him. He gratefully accepts illumination from any accessible source of light. His convictions are rooted as much in Judaism (as he interprets it) as in the philosophies of Plato or Leibniz. And to convey these convictions to his readers, he prefers "to use an anachronism rather than omit any convincing arguments" for "proving" the immortality of the soul.

The arguments Mendelssohn uses range from the belief in an all-good God whose very nature makes it inconceivable that He should totally destroy any living thing or substance, through the assertion that death represents merely a transition from one state of life to another, to the contention that the soul must enter into an after-life—if only to fulfill its destiny, the "end-purpose of all creation": to strive incessantly for greater perfection; to progress ceaselessly toward an ever more profound moral and spiritual awareness; and, imitating God, gradually to approach divine perfection.

The way to such perfection, however, starts here on earth. Living is but a preparation for dying, dying but a transformation into more "enchanted" living. To realize these truths is to possess wisdom, a wisdom that, transcending boundaries of time and space, "knows only a universal fatherland, a universal religion."

HE WHO CREATED THE SOUL
WILL NOT DESTROY IT
[The following paragraphs were taken from the essay "The Soul."]

The Supreme Being never destroys; all the Eternal's acts are good in themselves—and if they occasionally seem evil to us, this is (as is well known) due merely to our own nearsightedness.

Even acts that appear to be evil to our limited vision are in reality good when viewed within the totality of creation. If we were to know all things as does the Most High, we would praise Him for occurrences that now seem evil to us. For they only appear to be evil . . . as Maimonides pointed out in his *Guide for the Perplexed*.

Destruction of a thing, however, is clearly a real (not just a seeming) evil, and all acts generating evil are evil in themselves. Hence the Lord can never wish to destroy a creature completely. This goes to show that man's soul does not die a natural death along with his body; it is not ever arbitrarily destroyed but is, on the contrary, indestructible. And this is what I wished to demonstrate.

PHAEDON—A PRELIMINARY OUTLINE

[*This is a first draft, worked out in 1762, of those proofs for the immortality of the soul Mendelssohn intended to use in his* Phaedon (*which was published in 1767*). *The propositions comprising the proofs reflect the thought of both Plato and Leibniz.*]

First proof for the immortality of the soul:

1) All natural things are subject to perpetual change.
2) This sequence of changes cannot ever come to a standstill, unless all forces of nature were suddenly to become inoperative.
3) Instead, there is a constant alternation between those opposite modes of existence of which any given thing is capable.
4) This alternating change does not take place suddenly, as by a leap,[1] but by a gradual transition from one opposite state to another. This transitional state, whether designated by a particular name or not, is always extant [though not always perceptible].
5) Death and life are opposite states of the same thing.
6) The transition from life to death represents the waning of [vital] forces, [that is, the process of] dying.
7) Death does not mean total annihilation, for no force in nature would suffice to destroy a thing completely. And as no conversion from being to nonbeing is possible, such destruction would necessitate a real [though impossible] break [between being and nonbeing].

---

1. See *Phaedon*, p. 191.

8) Consequently, the souls of the departed are still extant.

9) Hence, they are still subject to change. If death were a uniform, immutable state, all of nature would finally have to become uniform and immutable, for every living thing must die. Given this premise, nothing that is dead can ever return to life.

10) Thus, death represents a transition to another state [of being].

11) Unless nature were to change its very character, this [death] is a transition to life.

12) Changes within nature occur in a circuitous rather than in a straight line.

Second proof:

The soul is never merely passive; it is a constantly active force.

1) The soul harbors many dim notions of which it is not [fully] conscious. For, inasmuch as certain pertinent questions will draw much mathematical information from any person with at least a rudimentary notion of the concept "extension," it follows that this concept must comprise within itself all other mathematical theorems. As those questions are put to him, man's soul simply becomes more keenly aware of this or that theorem [which it had "known" all along].[2]

2) Our phantasmata show that some concepts—often, as it were, lying dormant in our soul—will come alive when associated with other, somewhat similar notions.

Hence it is most likely that concepts are not created by external effects at all. Instead, they are products of thought-associations, elicited from the soul on those occasions when it remembers certain related, already known theories. Our awareness of some previously accumulated knowledge may thus be the sole criterion by which to distinguish between remembering and learning, an awareness characteristic of the former but lacking in the latter process.

As we acquire some new knowledge, form abstract concepts

2. Point one is reminiscent of Plato's dialogue *Meno* and its theory of knowledge as such, and particularly of mathematical knowledge.

or remember previously learned subject matter, our soul does not remain passive. . . . It is an ever-active force that was already operative before it was joined to a particular body.

FROM THE PREFACE TO *PHAEDON*

Following Plato's example, I let Socrates explain to his disciples, during the last hours of his life, why he believed in the immortality of the soul. The dialogue the Greek author called *Phaedo* contains many an extraordinarily beautiful passage that merits being utilized for the propagation of the doctrine of immortality.

I have taken over the dialogue's form, organization, and rhetorical devices, seeking merely to reformulate the metaphysical proofs in keeping with contemporary tastes. In the first part I could keep fairly close to my prototype. Some of its arguments, it seemed to me, needed only negligible changes while others had to be reworked so that their reasoning would have that compelling logic the modern reader misses in the Platonic dialogues. The long and violently emphatic declamation against the human body and its needs (which Plato seems to have written more in the spirit of Pythagoras than that of his teacher) had to be much tempered to reflect our own clearer insights into the worth of this divine creation. Even so, it will still sound strange to many a contemporary reader. I must confess that I retained that particular passage solely because of Plato's winning eloquence.

Later on, however, I felt compelled to depart completely from Plato. His proofs for the immateriality of the soul seem, at least to us [moderns], so superficial and capricious they hardly merit serious refutation. Whether this reaction of ours is due to the fact that we have a better grasp of philosophical problems or merely a poorer command of the ancients' philosophical language I cannot judge. In the second part, I chose a proof for the soul's immateriality originally offered by Plato's disciples and later accepted by several more recent philosophers. It seemed to me not only convincing but also most convenient to have this proof demonstrated in accordance with the Socratic method.

In the third part I had to resort completely to the more recent thinkers, letting Socrates speak almost like an eighteenth-century philosopher. I preferred to use an anachronism rather than omit any convincing arguments.

In this way, the present blend of translation and original composition came into being. Others may decide whether I merely restate what has already been said quite often, or whether I also have something new to offer. It is as difficult to say something entirely new about a subject already treated by so many eminent minds as it is ridiculous to pretend one has done so.

Had I decided to quote authors, the names of Plotinus, Descartes, Leibniz, Wolff, Baumgarten, Reimarus [1] and others would frequently appear. In that case, the reader would probably have had a clearer notion of my own contribution [to this work]. The mere lover of philosophy, however, does not care whether he owes a certain logical proof to this or that writer. And the scholar surely knows how to distinguish between mine and thine in such important matters. . . .

[In the Postscripts to both the second and third editions of his Phaedon, *Mendelssohn states frankly and modestly]:*

I have never fancied myself as an epoch-making philosopher who would become renowned by creating a system of his own. Where I find a well-traversed path, I see no need to seek a new one. If my predecessors have [already satisfactorily] defined the meaning of a term, why should I deviate from it? If they have brought to light some truth, why should I pretend to be unaware of it?

1. Plotinus (205–270 C.E.), neo-Platonic Greek philosopher; René Descartes (1596–1650), rationalist French philosopher, mathematician, and scientist; Gottfried Wilhelm Leibniz (1646–1716), monadologist German philosopher, physicist, and mathematician; Christian Wolff (1679–1754), rationalist German philosopher and mathematician; Alexander Gottlieb Baumgarten (1714–1762), Wolff's disciple; Hermann Samuel Reimarus (1694–1768), German deist philosopher and psychologist.

TO CERTAIN "LOVERS OF TRUTH":
A REPLY TO THEIR CRITICISM OF *PHAEDON*

. . . When I had to grapple with the problem of immortality, I found it difficult to decide what, in this context, was mere surmise, what convincing argument. And I asked myself on what grounds a Socrates of our time might proceed to prove the soul's immortality to both himself and his friends. As one believing in the validity of reason, he would surely appreciate and accept any rational argument put forward by other philosophers, regardless of their national origin or religious commitment.

We can agree with someone on specific truths derived from our common ability to reason, and yet feel unable to believe those truths he accepts on faith alone. Moreover, those lovers of truth who so highly recommend brotherly tolerance in political matters would do well to practice the same tolerance among themselves.

Religious matters should be left to the individual conscience. We should not judge [by our own standards] that which gives another a sense of inner security and peace. If we genuinely love our fellow man, we must not argue with him in areas where his heart speaks louder than his mind. We can only trust that all-merciful God will consider our beliefs as justified as they appear to our own conscience.

Rational insights, however, we wish not merely to share in a spirit of brotherliness, we wish to enjoy them—all of us together, as we enjoy the light of the sun. If its brilliance illuminated you, my brother, before it touched me: do be happy! But do not feel either pride or the uncharitable urge to block out my share of that light.

Was the man who brought this or that truth to light your countryman or coreligionist? How nice! It is certainly pleasant to be so closely related to mankind's benefactors. That does not mean, however, that their insight is not something from which all of us should benefit. Greek philosophy profited barbarians too. In fact, it helped to liberate you, too, from barbarianism—a state you have only recently outgrown.

Wisdom knows only a universal fatherland, a universal religion. Even where it tolerates divisions, it disapproves of the hostility and divisiveness you have made the basis of your political institutions.

This, I think, is the way a man such as Socrates would speak in our own day. And seen from this perspective, the mantle of a more recent philosophy which I have draped around his shoulders should not appear quite so unsuitable after all.

PHAEDON, OR ON THE IMMORTALITY OF THE SOUL

[After an almost literal translation (into German) of the beginning of Plato's Phaedo, *Mendelssohn departs from the classic text, presenting his own latter-day version of that famous dialogue. In the following excerpts,* Phaedo *reports to his eager listeners how Socrates discussed the nature, functions, and immortality of the soul (in addition to related topics) with his disciples and friends a few hours before his death. For greater reading facility, the discussants' names are in most instances omitted, and the arguments somewhat condensed.]*

"Is the term 'highest perfection' a mere conceptualization, or does it stand for a real Being that exists independently of ourselves?" Socrates asked.

"It stands indeed for a real, unlimited Being, existing independently of ourselves."

"And supreme goodness and wisdom? Do these exist in reality?"

"By Jove, they most certainly do. They are attributes inseparable from the most perfect Being, without which that Being could not exist."

"But who taught us to be aware of [the existence of] this Being that we have never seen with our eyes? We have neither heard nor touched it, nor have any of our physical senses ever transmitted

186

to us a concept of wisdom, goodness, perfection, beauty, or intellect. And yet we know that these things do exist independently of ourselves, having the highest degree of reality. Can anyone here explain to us how we developed these concepts?"

"Could it have been with the help of Jupiter's voice?"

"Listen, my friends," said Socrates. "If we were to hear the lovely sound of a flute in this room, wouldn't we run to find the flutist who so delighted our ears? By the same token, we would wish to know the master who created a painting we are contemplating. How, then, is it possible that we should not inquire about the painter who created within us the most perfect picture ever seen by the eyes of gods or men, an image of the highest perfection, goodness, wisdom and beauty?" . . .

"Abstract concepts are transmitted to the soul [1] not by external sense impressions but by internal observations of its own activity. In this way, the sould becomes conscious of its own essential nature and attributes. . . . As our soul reflects upon its own nature, which represents a mixture of positive and negative elements, it begins to sense the nature of other nonphysical entities, their strength and weakness, perfection and imperfection. And it comprehends such notions as intellect, wisdom, motivation and intent, beauty, justice and a thousand other abstract concepts about which we should be left profoundly ignorant were we to depend on our physical senses alone." . . .

"To be sure, the soul cannot form a true image of a Being higher than itself, nor even of one possessing greater capabilities. Yet it can conceive of the possibility that something exists which has more substance and is less deficient, something, in short, more perfect than the soul itself.

"To put it differently: the soul cannot see more than a glimmer of the most supreme Being or highest perfection, for it cannot fully comprehend that Being's true nature. But contemplating that which is true, good, and perfect in its own nature, and separating this from the deficient and unessential elements with which it is intermingled, the soul can conceive of a Being that is pure essence, pure truth, pure goodness and perfection." . . .

1. In his Postscript to the second edition of *Phaedon,* Mendelssohn explains: "I call 'soul' the ability to think and to will."

"You see, my friends, how far the lover of wisdom must remove himself from the impressions and concerns of his senses if he is to grasp the nature of that entity whose comprehension constitutes true happiness—the supreme and most perfect Being. As his thoughts take flight, he must close his eyes and ears; he must, as far as possible, forget his body with its pains and pleasures so that, in solitude, he may concentrate completely on the powers within his soul and their inherent efficacy. On this flight, man's body is not merely a useless but actually a burdensome companion." . . .

"Our one and only desire, the true philosopher holds, is to know the truth. But as long as we are burdened by our own bodies here on earth, as long as our soul is afflicted with this earthly plague, we cannot hope to see this desire fulfilled. We are supposed to search for truth. But, alas, our body permits us little leisure for this important pursuit. Today its care demands all our attention. Tomorrow it is beset by illnesses that upset us. And at other times, different matters—love, anxiety, drives, desires, whims, and follies —distract us incessantly. Our senses lure us enticingly from vanity to vanity, condemning to futility our search for wisdom.

"What engenders war, rebellion, strife, and disunity among men? What else but the body and its insatiable appetites? Greed is the mother of all unrest, and our soul would not covet such peculiar possessions if it did not have to satisfy its body's rapaciousness. Thus we are kept busy most of the time, with rarely enough leisure to pursue the study of philosophy. And if, at last, one does succeed in finding an unoccupied hour in which one might expect to get hold of the truth, that disturber of our happiness, the body, interferes once again, and instead of truth offers us its shadowy images.

"Our senses dangle before us unwelcome figments of their imagination, filling our soul with confusion, darkness, insolence, and irrational stirrings. How can it think deeply and gain an insight into truth in such a general upheaval? Impossible! We simply have to wait for those blissful moments when stillness without and tranquillity within create for us the happy opportunity to forget our body completely and let our mind's eye look for truth. It is then that we fully understand why we cannot until after our death reach the goal of our wishes—wisdom. There simply is no hope of attaining it while we are alive.

"As long as it inhabits the body, the soul, we must assume, cannot discern truth. Given this assumption, I can see only two possibilities: either we shall never know truth, or we shall know it only after death. Having left the body, the soul will in all probability be less impeded in its progress toward wisdom than before. If, therefore, we wish to prepare ourselves for the bliss of possessing true knowledge, we must not yield to our body more than is absolutely necessary. We must curb its desires and lusts and practice as often as possible our capacity for thinking until it pleases the supreme Being to set us free. Then, liberated from life's follies, we may hope to behold the source of all truth, the supreme, most perfect Being, contemplating it with senses that are pure and holy. And our happiness may possibly even be enhanced by being shared with others. One who is not yet holy, however, is not permitted to touch such holiness." . . .

"The separation of body and soul is called death; is that right?" asked Socrates.

"Right."

"Doesn't it follow, then, that genuine lovers of wisdom must bend every effort to come closer to [an understanding of] death—to learn, that is, how to die?"

"It would seem so."

"Would it, then, not be highly irrational, indeed downright ridiculous, if a man, having spent his entire life learning how to die, were sad at the approach of death?"

"That is beyond argument."

"Actually, then, death can never hold any terror for the genuine philosopher but must always be welcome to him."

[*Socrates, Cebes, and Simmias carry on their dialogue.*]

"Life and death are opposite states, right?"

"Right."

"And dying is the transition from life to death?"

"True."

"This great transformation presumably affects the soul as well as the body, since they were both so intimately connected in this life."

"That stands to reason."

"Observation can teach us what happens to the body after this significant event [death], for whatever has extension remains present to our senses. But the whereabouts and the state of the soul after this life can only be matters of intellectual speculation, since with the body's death, the soul has lost the means to make its presence physically felt." . . .

"As the body decomposes, nothing is lost. Its disintegrating components continue to exist. They bring about and suffer changes, undergoing new compositions and decompositions until, through an endless change of transformations, they change into elements of another natural compound. Some parts turn into dust, others into moisture; this evaporates into air, that becomes part of a plant and later of a living animal—to be transposed, in turn, into food for a worm. Is all of this not borne out by experience?"

"It is indeed."

"Thus, my friends, we see that death and life are physiologically not as separated as they appear to our senses. They are but links in a chain of ceaseless transformations, closely interconnected by gradual transitions. There is no exact moment of which we could definitely say, "Now the animal dies," just as little as one can say definitely, "Now it falls sick," or "Now it becomes well again." Naturally, these changes appear distinct to us who do not notice them before a certain time has elapsed. Suffice it to say, though: we realize that in reality life and death are not separated from each other.

"To illustrate this assertion, let me give you a telling example: our eyes, their vision limited to a certain geographical area, make a very clear distinction between morning, noon, evening, and night. To us, these points in time seem separate and set apart one from the other. But anyone able to observe the entire globe at once would be clearly aware that changes from day to night go on continuously, so that every moment actually comprises within itself morning and evening, noon and midnight.

190

"In the same way, the days of the week, seen as a whole, are indistinguishable. For whatever is continuous and contiguous can be separated into distinct, discrete parts only in our imagination or because of our delusory sense impressions. Our mind can well discern, though, that we must not stop where there is no real division. Is that clear, my friends?"

"Perfectly clear."

"By saying that the soul dies," Socrates continued, "we posit one of two possibilities: either all its powers and faculties, its ability to act and react, come to a sudden end so that it disappears, as it were, abruptly. Or the soul, like the body, undergoes gradual changes and innumerable transformations that go on in a steady progression. And somewhere in this progression a point arrives where it is no longer a human soul but something else, much in the way in which the body, having undergone innumerable changes, ceases to be a human body and turns into dust, air, plant, or even part of an animal. Or can you think of a third possibility, a still different way in which the soul can die?"

"No," Cebes replied. "A sudden or gradual death seem to exhaust all possibilities." . . .

"Then let us examine both. The first possibility is: the soul perishes suddenly, disappearing abruptly. Such a death would seem to be possible. But can nature really bring it about?"

"It cannot, or at least not if what we said before is true—namely our assertion that nature never destroys anything completely."

"And weren't we right in our assertion?"

"Between being and not-being there yawns a terrible abyss, and it is not in the (constantly if only gradually changing) nature of things to leap across this chasm." [2]

"Quite right. But is it conceivable that the soul could be destroyed by a supranatural power, a deity?"

"Oh, my dear friend," Socrates called out, "how fortunate, how safe we are if all we have to fear is the hand of that One and Only who is able to perform supranatural acts! [3] What has troubled us so far is the question whether it is not our soul's nature to be

2. See "Outline," point four, page 181.
3. It is interesting to note how Mendelssohn switches here from quasi-Greek to Jewish terminology.

mortal, and we have been trying to prove this fear unjustified. Is it possible that God, that all-good Creator and Sustainer of all, could destroy the soul by a supranatural act? No, Cebes. We should be more justified in fearing that the sun might turn into ice than that the very epitome of goodness would perform so arch-evil an act as the soul's destruction."

"It did not occur to me," said Cebes, "that my question is almost a blasphemy."

"Then we need no longer be frightened," Socrates went on, "by one of the two possible ways in which the soul can die: sudden destruction; for such destruction is impossible in nature." . . .

"We therefore have to examine only one other question: whether the soul's innate powers might not disappear in the same gradual manner in which the parts of a body's machinery disintegrate. Let us, then, follow body and soul, those faithful companions who supposedly share even death, on their journey and see what finally happens to them.—As long as the body is sound, with all movements of its machinery serving to maintain the whole, and as long as the implements of feeling and emotion are intact, the soul is in full possession of all its powers—feeling, thinking, loving, detesting, comprehending, and willing. Right?"

"Without doubt."

"But now the body sickens. An obvious imbalance in the machine's movements becomes manifest. Many parts are no longer working in harmony to maintain the whole. Instead, they seem to be at cross-purposes. And the soul?

"Experience shows us that it grows gradually weaker. Its emotions become confused, its thinking incoherent, and it frequently acts against its own interest. Eventually, the body dies. That is, its customary motions no longer seem to aim at the maintenance and continued existence of the whole organism. The soul may still experience some weak stirrings, creating certain dim notions. But this would represent the limit of its remaining power.

"Presently, physical decomposition sets in. The different elements constituting one single machine, which until now have served one common purpose, begin to assume wholly different functions, turning into the varied parts of entirely different machines. And the soul? Where are we to leave the soul? Its machine

192

is decaying. Its remaining parts, no longer really its own, have ceased to represent an entity capable of being ensouled. With its limbs, senses, and other implements or transmitters of feeling and emotion gone, does the soul lie completely waste? Has whatever it once felt, imagined, desired, or detested—have all its inclinations and passions disappeared without the slightest trace?"

"Impossible," Cebes said. "For what would that mean if not complete destruction? Yet we have seen that nature cannot completely destroy."

"What then are we to think, my friend?" asked Socrates. "The soul cannot perish in all eternity. For the final step, no matter how long delayed, would still be a leap from being to nothingness, and such a leap is out of character with the nature of either a simple substance or that of a compound. Hence, the soul must endure, or exist, eternally. But if it exists, it must act as well as be acted upon. And if it acts and is acted upon, it must form concepts, since feeling, thinking, and willing constitute the soul's proper activities. Concepts, however, always start with sensory impressions; but where are these to originate in the absence of physical implements, of sense organs?"

"Nothing seems more logical than the sequence of these deductions," said Cebes, "and yet the result is an obvious paradox."

"Only one of the following alternatives can be true," Socrates continued. "Either the soul must be destroyed, or it must continue to entertain certain notions even after its body's decay. One feels inclined to doubt both these alternatives; yet must not one of them be true?

"We stated that our spirit cannot be destroyed by nature.[4] Consequently, the soul's possible destruction offers no way out of our predicament, and we must turn back: the soul cannot perish. It must endure after the body's death, must act, react, and form concepts. But here we encounter the difficulty that it seems impossible for our spirit to form concepts in the absence of sensory impressions. Who, however, can assure us that this is really im-

4. Here, the argument shifts from divine power to the power of nature; moreover, Mendelssohn begins to use the terms "spirit" and "soul" interchangeably. This may be due to the influence of Leibniz (see page 184), who equated "soul" with sentient life and "rational soul" with mind or spirit.

possible? Is it not merely our experience that would tell us so, simply because we have here, in this life, never been able to think without sensory impressions?"

"Nothing else."

"But are we then justified in extending our experience beyond the limits of this life, denying any possibility that nature might let the soul continue to think, even without its well-organized body? What do you say, Simmias? Shouldn't we find it ridiculous if a man who never left the walls of Athens were to deduce from this limited experience that no form of government other than a democracy is possible?"

"Nothing would make less sense."

"Or, if a child in its mother's womb were able to reason, could it be persuaded that it might enjoy the invigorating light of the sun once it were separated from its matrix? Wouldn't its present condition cause it to consider such a thing impossible?"

"In all probability."

"And are we, dim-witted as we are, any more rational when we, incarcerated in this life, let our experiences be the sole judge of what nature might or might not be able to do after death? A single glance into the inexhaustible resources of nature would convince us of the unreasonableness of such a position. How poor, how weak would nature be if its power did not extend beyond our own experiences!" . . .

"One thing is sure, my friends: our spirit triumphs over death and decay. Leaving the corpse behind to fulfill the Supreme Being's purpose in a thousand different forms here on earth, our soul—obeying natural though supraterrestrial laws—rises above the dust and, reflecting on the power of the infinite, continues its contemplation of the Creator's works.

"But must not our soul, alive and able to conceptualize even after the body's death, continue to strive for [eternal] happiness, as it used to do in this life?"

"Probably," said Simmias. "But I cannot be sure, and should like to hear your own reasons for this assumption."

"Here are my reasons," Socrates replied. "If the soul is able to think, it must form a variety of concepts. Some of those it will consider attractive, others repulsive. In short, the soul must have

194

a will [that is, the ability to discriminate, accepting or rejecting concepts "at will"]. But if it has a will, can this be directed toward anything but the highest degree of well-being, eternal bliss?"

This seemed self-evident to all present.

"But what constitutes the well-being of a spirit that no longer has to consider its body's needs?" Socrates went on. "Food and drink, love and physical pleasures have ceased to gratify it. Anything that delighted man's senses, palate, eyes, and ears in this life no longer commands the soul's attention. It may be left with hardly more than a faint and probably rueful memory of the pleasures it enjoyed in its body's company. Does it seem likely that it would still long for those past joys?"

"That seems as unlikely as the possibility of a man born deaf expressing a desire to listen to beautiful music," was Simmias's reply.

"Or do you think the soul might wish for wealth?"

"Certainly not; for it can in all likelihood no longer enjoy personal possessions or goods of any kind. And even ambition—a drive hardly reflecting physical needs, hence conceivably able to survive the body—cannot be of any use to a departed spirit that has left behind not only its body but along with it such follies as the striving for worldly honor, power, and wealth, or the privileges that go with a noble birth.

"Thus, all that remains to distinguish one spirit from another, or raise it above others, is wisdom, love of virtue, and an understanding of the meaning of truth. The soul may, however, continue to enjoy the spiritual joys it derived on earth from such immaterial things as beauty, order, harmony, or perfection. For the emotions all these evoke are integral to the soul's very nature and can therefore never leave it. He who has taken care of his soul on earth by pursuing wisdom and cultivating both virtue and a sense of true beauty has surely every hope of proceeding on the same path after death. Step by step, he will draw nearer to the sublime Being, the source of all wisdom and epitome of all perfection, and to its pre-eminent manifestation, beauty itself.

"Do you, my friends, remember those enchanted moments when your soul, beguiled by some spiritual beauty, forgot the body with its needs and completely gave itself over to that heavenly emotion? Only some divine presence can create such supreme delights in us. In fact, any experience of spiritual beauty affords us a glimpse of the deity's nature. For whatever beauty, order, or perfection we see here is merely a faint image of that absolute beauty, order, or perfection [to be encountered after death].

"If it be true, then, that after this life our ambition knows no other goal but to attain wisdom and virtue, and our desires are directed only toward spiritual beauty, order, and perfection, our continuing existence will consist in constant contemplation of the deity; and that heavenly delight will be our rich, our eternal reward for all our noble endeavors here on earth.

"What are all our troubles compared to such an eternity? Of what account are poverty, revilement, or even the most ignominious death if they serve to prepare us for such bliss? No, my friends, as long as we can be sure of having led a righteous life, we cannot possibly feel sad to begin our journey to so blissful a state. Only the man who offended gods and men during his life by wallowing in animal pleasures, offering human sacrifices to the Moloch "honor," or taking a vicious delight in the suffering of others, only such a man must tremble on the threshold of death."

[*Having stated his own convictions, Socrates invites his listeners to express theirs, to ask questions or raise objections. Responding to this invitation, Simmias admits that he has certain doubts concerning some methodological details of Socrates' discourse. He does, however, accept wholeheartedly the central doctrine of the soul's immortality; for if he did not, all his previous beliefs would be shattered.*]

"If the soul were mortal, man's reason would be but a dream, sent by some deity to delude him. Virtue would lose that radiance which makes it appear divine. The beautiful and the sublime—in the moral as well as the physical realm—would no longer serve as image of divine perfection. Man's lot would be the same as any animal's: to forage for food and to die. A few days after our death, it would no longer matter whether we had been a credit or discredit to our fellow creatures, nor whether we had contributed to their weal or woe. If our spirit could indeed perish, our wisest [religious] legislators, the very founders of our society, would have deceived us if not themselves. Robbed of his hope for immortality, man would be the most miserable creature on earth, his misery compounded by the fact that his ability to think about his condition awakens in him the fear of death and a sense of despair. I do not know how those in fear of the soul's eventual destruction can ever overcome their anxiety. The bitter thought of death must gall their every pleasure. They cannot enjoy the satisfactions of friendship or of the mind's search for truth; they cannot take any delight in beauty or perfection, nor can they worship their Creator [5] without being plunged into despair by the terrible thought, haunting them like some specter, of their soul's perishability.

"My own conception of the deity, of man's virtue and worth and his relationship to God does not permit me to doubt his destiny. Hope for a life to come resolves all my scruples. Vindicating the nature of the deity [whose goodness would have to be questioned were one to assume that the soul can be destroyed], this hope restores nobility to virtue, radiance to beauty, charm to every pleasure; it sweetens all misery as it gives a new perspective even to the troubles that beset us in this life."

[*The discussion, its arguments based largely on Leibniz's monadology,[6] now turns to questions concerning the state in which the soul might survive the body. Will it be akin to sleep? To a deep swoon? To what degree will the soul retain consciousness and perceptivity? All discussants are agreed that the soul could not partake of what is referred to as "eternal bliss" un-*

5. See page 191; in this and the following paragraph, Mendelssohn once again employs Judeo-Christian rather than Platonic terminology.
6. Leibniz (see page 184) taught that the world is an aggregate of simple material as well as immaterial substances (somewhat like atoms) called monads. These monadic units possess consciousness to a varying degree. They were created by God, the uncreated "Prime Monad," possessor of the fullest possible consciousness. The soul, highest in the hierarchy of created monads, is also highly conscious. As a simple substance (not, like the body, a composite of diverse elements) it is irreducible: it can be neither subdivided nor dissolved into perishable elements. Consequently, it survives the body intact: it is immortal.

less its spiritual and moral awareness were to remain intact and transcend anything of which even the keenest mind and wisest heart are capable on earth. Since this seems to be a self-evident truth, the conversation now veers around to observations about the nature of truth. It is not truth that is uncertain, elusive, or fickle, but man's mind that cannot easily cope with the eternal verities, hence tends to give up in disgust or despair its weak attempts at comprehension. Socrates, however, admonishes his listeners to spare no effort in their search for truth, even though it might be almost impossible logically to prove the validity of certain insights. But he feels that even a logically unprovable truth is very likely to be "true" if it brings spiritual comfort to man and leads to the moral advance of mankind.]

"Searching for truth," Socrates said in conclusion, "we mortals flounder around on the seas of [irrational and erroneous] beliefs until reason and cogitation shed their light upon our sails, announcing to us a happy landfall. Reason and cogitation then steer us away from the sense impressions of the physical world, guiding our spirit back to its home, the realm of thinking beings. Created and finite, those beings [and their nature] can be conceived of and clearly comprehended by others like them, by ourselves. After that, however, reason and cogitation raise our mind to that elemental source of all thinking and all that can be thought, that all-comprehending yet incomprehensible Being of which we know at least that much (and this is some consolation): everything that is good, beautiful, and perfect in both the physical and intellectual world derives its being from and is sustained by this omnipotent Being. If only we are profoundly convinced of and moved by this truth, and possessed by it in our innermost heart, we need not know any more in order to feel reassured in this life and eternally happy in the life-to-come."

[*In the world as we know it, a world characterized by an overall harmony and perfect balance of its constituent parts, only the human mind can gain an insight into truth. Yet there is a*

purposeful interconnection between the different strata com-
prising the universe. These strata range from inanimate to
animate nature, from thinking man to a possible if not prob-
able realm of some higher intelligences. Each class in the
hierarchy of beings fulfills the purpose its creator intended.
The debate on these and related topics goes on between
Socrates and his visitors.]

"Would you say that all created beings capable of thinking and willing resemble each other?"

"I would indeed."

"Now, some admittedly have a keener mind than others, hence truer insights, more perfect understanding, or broader comprehension. Would you agree, however, that there are no sharp demarcation lines dividing them into distinct classes but that, instead, all of them constitute one kind of intelligent being, though they operate on gradually ascending levels of consciousness?"

"Yes, I would."

"Moreover: if there are minds [*Geister*] superior to our own, created intelligences imperceptibly susperseding each other in degrees of perfection and thus approaching ever more closely the Infinite Spirit—are they not all members of one species, though their number be great?"

"They certainly are."

"And as they differ only in degree but not in principle from each other, so their final purpose, too, must be similar in principle. What we are discussing here, my friends, therefore concerns not mankind alone but the entire realm of thinking beings. For all finite beings are endowed with certain gifts they can develop and perfect. Man's innate mental faculties unfold with amazing speed, forming his common sense, intelligence, reason, imagination, a sense of the good and the beautiful, generosity, love of his fellow man, social attitudes, and whatever other virtues you care to name, virtues no mortal has yet been able *not* to acquire.

"True, we call some people stupid, foolish, insensitive, or cruel. Comparatively speaking, these designations may occasionally be justified. Yet never did there live a simpleton who did not show some signs of intelligence, or a tyrant in whose bosom did not

199

glimmer some spark of humanitarianism! All of us [have the ability to] acquire the same virtues; the difference between us is only one of degree, of more or less. Not even the most godless individual can succeed in counteracting entirely the purpose for which he was created. The very obstinacy with which he refuses to follow the right path may reflect an innate and originally good drive which he is simply not putting to the right use. The abuse of his native gifts causes man's failings, his miserable performance. Properly used, though, these gifts can bring him closer to the real goal of his existence—even against his will. There is no man, my friends, who has not benefited from his contact with his fellow men, who has not left this world more perfect than he entered it.

"And this holds true for the totality of thinking beings. As long as, self-aware, they can feel, conceptualize, will, desire, or detest, they continue to develop their innate gifts. The longer they use those gifts, the keener and more effective their faculties become. The intelligent beings themselves increase their capacity to find happiness in the contemplation of true beauty and perfection." . . .

"All thinking beings, from the most ignorant man to the most perfect of all created spirits, are destined to work on perfecting themselves and others. Their destiny is commensurate with both God's wisdom and their own abilities. Man's path has been mapped out for him, and not even his most perverted will can cause him to leave it completely. No living and thinking being can fail to practice and develop his cognitive and volitional faculties, hence come closer to perfection—though some with firm and others with faltering steps.

"When will their goal be reached? Never so completely, apparently, as to block their road to further progress.[7] It is the nature of all created intelligences to keep reaching for a perfection beyond their level of current attainment. The higher they climb, the more still unseen distances open up before them, urging them on. The goal of their striving is continuous progress (analogous to the nature of time itself).

"Imitating God, man can gradually approach His perfection;

7. See page 168 ff. for Mendelssohn's view on the moral progress of the individual and mankind.

this approximation constitutes spiritual happiness. But the road to this goal is without end and cannot be completely traversed in all eternity. Throughout his life, man's striving is therefore without limit. All human desire, lofty or base, points to infinity. Our desire for knowledge is insatiable as is our ambition. Even our greed for money keeps nagging and disturbing us, though we can never satisfy it. Our sense of beauty seeks infinity; and whereas the sublime may well intrigue us merely because it is unfathomable, our lusty appetites turn to revulsion as soon as we reach satiation.

"Wherever we encounter barriers we cannot surmount, our imagination feels fettered, and the very heavens seem to close in on us. What we really like is to give free reign to our imagination, letting it push the borders of space into infinity. This limitless striving, setting itself ever more distant goals, is commensurate with the nature and destiny of spiritual beings [*Geister*]. And the wondrous works of the Eternal provide this striving with enough substance and sustenance for all eternity. The more deeply we penetrate into the mysteries of these works, the more vistas open up before our greedy eyes. The more we discover, the more we find to explore. The more we imbibe, the more inexhaustible appears the source.

"We therefore have every reason to assume that this striving for perfection, this growing in inner excellence, constitutes the destiny of rational beings, hence also the end-purpose of all creation. We may safely say that this cosmic structure, great beyond measure, was created so that rational beings, progressing step by step in moral and spiritual awareness, may gradually become more perfect, finding their happiness in their inner growth.

"It is inconceivable that the ultimate Being should have devised a cosmic plan that would allow the progression of those who strive for perfection to come to a halt; or, worse still, that they should suddenly be pushed back into the abyss, losing the fruits of their labor. . . . Is it commensurate with divine wisdom to bring forth a world, and put into it spirits capable of attaining happiness by contemplating its miracles, only to rob these spirits—a mere moment, yet for all eternity—of their ability to contemplate and be happy?

"Is it commensurate with divine wisdom to let a constantly appearing and disappearing, shadowy phantom of happiness be the end-purpose of its wondrous creations? No, my friends: it is not for nothing that Providence has instilled in us a desire for eternal bliss. This desire can and will be satisfied. The goal of creation will endure as long as creation itself, and those who admire divine perfection will last as long as the work in which this perfection becomes manifest. As we serve the Ruler of the world by developing our abilities here on earth, so we shall continue to practice virtue and pursue wisdom in the life-to-come, under His guidance. Carrying out the divine intent, we shall incessantly strive for greater perfection, taking our place in the chain stretching from us into infinity." . . .

"To deny the soul's immortality," Socrates added, "means, among other things, also to deny God's Providence. On the premise that man's life is narrowly circumscribed by birth and death, people feel they can gain a total view of this life by following its course with their own eyes. This, they assume, gives them all the knowledge they need to judge the ways of Providence, if indeed there be a Providence.

"Now, their observations reveal that much happens in this world which apparently is incongruent with our concept of God's attributes. Certain events would seem to be incompatible with His goodness, others with His justice. Occasionally one is tempted to believe man's fate is determined by a causative power delighting in evil. In that mood, one seems to make a strange discovery: the physical aspect of man's life shows nothing but order, beauty, and harmony—visible proof of divine wisdom and goodness, of an all-wise plan, of a perfect correspondence between means and ends. Yet in man's societal and ethical life—or at least in as much of it as is disclosed to our view—the traces of these divine attributes are all but invisible. The triumph of vice, perpetration of evil deeds by crowned heads, persecution of innocence and oppression of virtue are no rare occurrences. The innocent and righteous suffer no less than the evildoers. Mutiny succeeds quite as often as does the wisest act of legislation, and an unjust war quite as well as the attempt to eradicate a monster. The same holds true for all endeavors seeking mankind's advance. Good fortune or misfortune happen to good and evil men alike, without notable distinction.

202

They appear (at least to the sophists of whom we are speaking) to be distributed without regard for virtue and merit. If some wise, kind, and just Being were benevolently concerned with the fate of man, should not the moral universe give some evidence of the same wise order we so much admire in the physical world?" . . .

"In my view, the moral universe denies its Creator's perfection just as little as the physical one does. Just as in the physical world the disorder of its parts—that is, thunderstorms, cloudbursts, earthquakes, floods, or pestilence—dissolves into the harmony of the immeasurably great whole, so do the fleeting distempers of the moral world and their effects on man's life serve merely as a transition to eternal harmony. Thus, momentary suffering leads to never-ending bliss, and passing afflictions to enduring well-being.

"To gain a proper perspective of the life of even one single individual, we would have to see it in its eternal dimension. Only then would we be able to judge the ways of Providence. But then, my dear friends, we would assuredly feel neither resentful nor dissatisfied, nor would we wish to complain. Instead, we would adore and worship the Ruler of the world, admiring His wisdom and goodness.

"For all the reasons we have enumerated, we may be absolutely sure that there is a life-to-come, and our hearts and minds may be at peace."

[*The question where, and in exactly what manner, the departed spirits (alias souls) will continue their existence can, however, not be answered with certainty. Poets and storytellers may give free reign to their imagination in these matters. Socrates can do no more than share his own convictions with his friends. But before getting ready to drink the poison brought to him by a messenger of the Athenian court that had found him guilty of the crime of sedition, he makes this concluding statement:*]

"As for me, I am satisfied in my conviction that I shall forever be under God's care; that His holy and just Providence will protect and guide me in the next life as it did in this; and that the beauty and moral excellence my spirit will soon behold constitute my true happiness. This moral excellence manifests itself in a sense of moderation, righteousness, and freedom. Love, benevolence, recognition of God's will, and the endeavor to carry out His intent give evidence of it, as does our submission to His holy will. All these await me in my future life, toward which I shall now hurry. More I need not know in order to start out, cheerful and confident, on the road that will take me there." . . .

SOURCES FOR MENDELSSOHN TEXTS

GS   *Moses Mendelssohns gesammelte Schriften,* ed. G. B. Mendelssohn, 7 vols., Leipzig, 1843–1844

GSJA *Moses Mendelssohn: Gesammelte Schriften,* Jubiläums Ausgabe (Jubilee edition), Berlin, 1930

SW   *Moses Mendelssohns sämmtliche Werke* (in one volume), Vienna, 1838

MK   M. Kayserling, *Moses Mendelssohn: Sein Leben und Wirken,* Leipzig, 1862; 2nd ed., Leipzig, 1888

SOURCES FOR INDIVIDUAL PASSAGES

Part One: Personal Reflections
Autobiographical Data—GS V, p. 525
The Daily Grind—GS V, p. 149; p. 171
Intellectual Pastimes—GS V, p. 52
Engaged to Be Married—MK, 2nd ed., p. 122
On Wealth, Friendship, and Sociability—GSJA XI, pp. 232, 235, 247
On Wigs—GSJA VII, p. 261
The Right of Domicile—GSJA XI, p. 310
In Praise of Marriage—GSJA V, p. 671 ff.
Lack of Formal Education—SW, p. 916
No Intellectual Companionship—SW, p. 917
Equanimity in the Face of Criticism—MK, 1st ed., p. 521
A Father's Concern—GS V, pp. 670–672
Friendship with Lessing—GS V, p. 580; GS VI, p. 127
Counseling in Matters of Faith—GS V, p. 495; p. 647

Majesty versus Excellency—GS V, p. 679
Epigrams—SW, pp. 1004–1006

Part Two: His People's Defender and Mentor
Intercession on Behalf of Swiss Jews—GS III, p. 106
Petition to Stay the Deportation of Jews from Dresden—GS V, p. 544
Reluctance to Participate in Civic Affairs and Political Projects—"Briefe
    Moses Mendelssohn an Isaak Iselin," *Baseler Jahrbuch* 1923, p. 6 f.;
    SW, p. 682; GS V, p. 493
Not Even a Single Step—GS III, pp. 366 ff.
A Model Society in Germany?—GS V, pp. 626–627
Suitability of Jews for Military Service—GS III, p. 667
No Cultural Improvement for the Jew—GS III, p. 182
Producers and Consumers—SW p. 688 ff.
Are Any Members of Society Expendable?—SW, p. 687
An Outcry against Defamation—*Lessings Werke,* ed. Petersen und Ohls-
    hausen, (Berlin: Bong & Co.), vol. VII, p. 41
Philanthropy: An Extraordinary Thing?—GS III, p. 416 f.
Wisdom's Highest Goal—GS V, p. 544
Restrictions and Frustrations—GS V, p. 566
A Plea for Intramural Tolerance—SW, p. 697
On Taking an Oath—GS VI, p. 405
On Burials—MK, 1st ed., p. 557 ff.
Translating the Psalms—GS VI, p. 128
Against Bastardization of Languages—GSJA VII, p. 279

Part Three: A Seeker of Truth
Revealed Religion versus Revealed Legislation—GS III, p. 311
Revelation, Salvation, Redemption—GSJA VII, p. 73 ff.
Judaism and Christianity—GS III, p. 128 ff.
On Jesus—GSJA VII, pp. 361–63
On Faith and Reason and the Abrogation of Mosaic Law—MK, 1st ed.,
    p. 495; GSJA VII, pp. 90–98
Original Sin—GSJA VII, p. 96
On Ceremonial Law—GSJA VII, pp. 97–98
On the Messiah—GSJA VII, p. 363
On Miracles—GSJA VII, p. 43 ff.; p. 89
Making One's Own Religious Decisions—SW, p. 525
Rejection of Conversion—GSJA VII, p. 8 ff.; p. 41 ff.; pp. 103–105
Against a False Union of Faiths—GS III, p. 361 ff.
Against Christian Missionary Zeal—GSJA VII, pp. 360–61
Religious Tolerance—GS V, p. 495; p. 597
The Common Bond of the Jews—GS V, p. 669 ff.
The *Aleinu*—SW, pp. 950–53

FURTHER READING

Altmann, Alexander. *Moses Mendelssohn: A Biographical Study.* University, Ala.: University of Alabama Press, 1973.

Barzilay, I. E. "Moses Mendelssohn." *Jewish Quarterly Review* LII (52), 1961, pp. 69–93; 175–86.

Jerusalem and Other Jewish Writings by Moses Mendelssohn, trans. and ed. Alfred Jospe. New York: Schocken Books, 1969.

Jospe, Alfred. "Moses Mendelssohn." *Great Jewish Personalities in Modern Times,* ed. Simon Noveck. Washington: B'nai B'rith, 1960, pp. 11–36.

Meyer, Michael. "Moses Mendelssohn: The Virtuous Jew," and "An Ephemeral Solution." *The Origins of the Modern Jew.* Detroit: Wayne State University Press, 1967, pp. 11–56.

Patterson, David. "Moses Mendelssohn's Concept of Tolerance." *Between East and West,* ed. Alexander Altmann. London: East and West Library, 1956, pp. 149–63.

Rothman, Walter. "Mendelssohn's Character and Philosophy of Religion." *CCAR Yearbook* XXXIX. Cincinnati: Central Conference of American Rabbis, 1929, pp. 305–350.

Walter, Hermann. *Moses Mendelssohn: Critic and Philosopher.* New York: Bloch Publishing Co., 1930.

Index

Abbt, Thomas, 20, 22, 23, 62, 63, 156, 159, 160, 162, 163, 164, 167
Abudraham, Rabbi David, 151
Aleinu, 12
  and Christianity, 150-51
  origin of, 149-50
Alim Literufah (Healing Leaves), 15
Alsace, 12
Americans, 73
Animals, importance of, 160-61
Anti-Semitism, 88-89
  criticism of, 93-94
  in Dresden, 80-81
  restrictions from, 98-99
  in Switzerland, 79-80
Ashkenazi, Solomon, 5

Basedow, Johann Bernard, 95
Becker, Sophie, 50, 70
Being, and soul, 186-87
Berlin, and Jews, 6
Berlin Academy of Music, 7
Best, Paulus, 69
Biur, 15, 16
Body, and soul, 188-90, 192-96
Bonnet, Charles, 132
Buber, Martin, 41
Burial, and Judaism, 102-104

Campe, Joachim Heinrich, 95
Ceremony
  bond of, 147
  See also Ritual
Christ, Jesus, 120
  divinity of, 123
Christianity
  contrasted with Judaism, 111

  See also New Testament
Church-state relationship, Mendelssohn on, 27-29, 33
Civil liberties, 82
  importance of, 141
Companionship, 63
Conscience, 69
Consumer, nature of, 90-92
Conversion, rejection of, 132-39
Cranz, August Friedrich, on Mendelssohn, 24-26
Criticism, reaction to, 64
Customs
  and Judaism, 148
  See also Ceremony; Ritual
Das Forschen nach Licht und Recht, 24-26
Daughter, death of, 159
Dawidowicz, Lucy, 7
Death
  fear of, 196-97
  and soul, 189-97
  See also Immortality; Life after death
Doctrine, and Judaism, 148, 149
Dresden, expulsion from, 80-81

Earth Is the Lord's, The (Heschel), 7
Eclecticism, and soul, 179
Emden, Jacob, 37
English, characterized, 55
Enlightenment
  and Jews, 10-11
  tenets of, 9
Epigrams, 73-74
Evil, punishment for, 202-203
Excellency, versus majesty, 72-73

209